The Rich Detective

H. R. F. KEATING

**MACMILLAN
LONDON**

First published 1993 by Macmillan London Limited
a division of Pan Macmillan Publishers Limited
Cavaye Place London SW10 9PG
and Basingstoke

Associated companies throughout the world

ISBN 0–333–58520–8

9 8 7 6 5 4 3 2 1

A CIP catalogue record for this book is available from
the British Library

Phototypeset by Intype, London
Printed and bound in Great Britain by
Mackays of Chatham PLC, Chatham, Kent

The Rich Detective

Riches beyond the dreams of avarice are the last thing on Detective Inspector William Sylvester's mind when he returns to England after a holiday in Spain. The lottery ticket he bought so casually on holiday lies crumpled and forgotten in his wallet . . .

Sylvester is immediately ordered to tackle a highly delicate enquiry: for an anonymous letter, containing allegations of murder, has been received by the Chief Constable and identifies a wealthy antiques dealer as the perpetrator of a ruthless scam against defenceless old ladies. Sylvester is soon on his way to the opulent home of Charles Roanoke – and what he witnesses there convinces him that the allegations against Roanoke should be taken very seriously indeed.

But as Sylvester attempts to gather firm proof of Roanoke's guilt he finds that the doors are closing to protect a powerful and influential man. Then, building up to a show-down with his superiors, the detective is contacted by a journalist with the news that he has won a million pounds in the Spanish national lottery. Suddenly master of his own destiny, Sylvester resigns from the force. But in his single-minded determination to pursue Roanoke until justice is done Sylvester finds that unlimited wealth brings weightier dilemmas than he could ever have thought of . . . and can sometimes exact a terrible price.

1

Bill Sylvester, Detective Inspector William Sylvester, came to a halt just outside the gleaming white-painted farm gate of the newish sprawling Tudor-style house. Need my warrant card. Could be a sodding difficult customer, our Mr Charles Roanoke.

He plunged one hand after another into his jacket pockets.

First day back on the job after three weeks in sunny Spain. Leaving the flat in a tear. Jamming on the clothes he had worn the day before. And now this. Tricky a case as they come. Trust bloody Sugden to lumber me with it. Plus bloody Detective Sergeant Cross. Mikey the fly, worker of the system, expenses expert.

So where's that warrant card?

He took a jumbled fistful out of his right-hand pocket.

Remains of airline ticket, passport for God's sake, letter from Mother, unopened, boarding card from the plane, second lottery ticket Pepita sweet-talked me into between last kisses, and yes, got it.

'All right, my son. Let's go.'

And at that moment there came a shot. A clear hard puff of sound in the unstirring sun-etched autumn air.

'By Christ, we've got him,' Mikey shouted, tugging the gate wide and setting off at a run towards the long concrete garage on the far side of the house.

'Stop. Leave this to me.'

But he went across the orangey-rich gravel of the sweeping drive at speed, past the parked askew tomato-red Bentley, on to the garage side-door. Snatch at the handle.

The stinging smell of cordite hit his nostrils the moment that – check of abrupt caution – he stepped in.

Charles Roanoke, tall, shoulders broad in a suit of fine black-

and-white check, waistcoat burgeoning, ruddy of face, blood-bursting, was standing at the far end of the wide building, a shot-gun under his arm.

Striding past the Range Rover just inside, for an instant his eye was caught by a wine-filled goblet on the workbench beside Roanoke. A small ruby glow in the cool greyish light from the roof windows.

But no corpse to be seen. Not the least sign.

And at once he realised he had not actually expected one. Roanoke might be a murderer, even a multiple murderer, but shooting was not his method. Not if what he had been told about him was true.

'Mr Roanoke?'

He drew in a long breath and contrived a careful politeness.

The big man had turned towards the two of them. In the dif-fused light hard to see the expression on his face.

'Yes?'

But now wariness, something not quite suspicion, plain at least in his voice.

'Detective Inspector Sylvester, South Mercia Police.' He flipped open the warrant card. 'And this is Detective Sergeant Cross.'

'Oh, yes?' Tiny pause. 'And what can I do for you?'

'You can tell us first off why you were using that gun,' Mikey Cross slammed in.

Inwardly Sylvester cursed. What point in warning a slob like that to keep his mouth shut?

A wide, white-teethed grin split Roanoke's large red face.

'I was committing a murder, Sergeant,' he said. 'On this rather nice seventeenth-century flour chest.'

He glanced at a square piece of oaken furniture, its legs in the air, on the concrete floor a few feet in front of him.

'Distressing,' Sylvester said.

He left a beat.

'Isn't *distressing* the more usual term for taking a shot-gun to produce a few artificial wormholes?'

'Among other things it is, Inspector.'

Roanoke's turn to pause now.

'Television has a lot to answer for.'

He grinned again, teeth flashing in the cool grey light. A pillar of self-confidence.

'But I'm forgetting my manners. Gentlemen, will you take a glass of wine?'

Without waiting for an answer he turned, reached up to a shelf next to a big old red-painted fire-extinguisher, took down two more large goblets.

'No, thank you.'

'Yes, lovely.'

The two of them spoke together.

Sylvester suppressed his fury. Mikey could wait.

Splashily Roanoke poured into both glasses. Mikey reached forward, took the fuller one and with a brief 'Cheers' tossed back almost all its contents.

'Damn it, Sergeant,' Roanoke said. 'That's not horse-piss you're drinking. Savour it, man, savour it.'

Check to notions acquired in his brief researches. Not a crass money-grabber? Someone with genuine feelings for the finer things? So no greed-ridden murderer? And, true enough, there was damn little evidence in that letter to the Chief Constable.

Dear Sir,
   I feel it is my duty to bring to your attention certain facts about one Mr Charles Roanoke, dealer in antiques, resident in the South Mercia Police area. Over the past few years he has been the recipient of large bequests made by aged persons from whom he had purchased furniture before their retirement to live in nursing homes or similar establishments. Mr Roanoke had the habit of regularly visiting his wealthy clients, and in a number of cases wills were altered in his favour. Shortly afterwards the persons in question unexpectedly died. I do not wish to name names since I lack the resources of the police to make my information absolutely fool-proof. But you can take it from me that this is the truth.
   I am your obedient servant,
   Pro Bono Publico.

The typewritten sheet – mass-produced paper – memorized more or less word for word.

Bloody Detective Chief Superintendent Sugden plainly hoping, fingers crossed, all the potential complications will turn out to be a mare's nest. But hanging on to the letter till Bill Sylvester steps

7

into his office, all chipper from three weeks in Spain, to be stuck with a case, whichever way it goes, that can only be a sodding headache.

Still, the Big White Chief himself must think it well possible something will emerge. That Roanoke has actually persuaded these old people, whoever they are, to make him bequests. That he even advanced the moment for the money to fall into his lap.

What would he have used? Poison, almost for a cert.

But either way, sooner or later Mr Pro Bono will have to be found. If only to be given a good talking-to. At least the fellow's letter provides a clue. Of sorts. That old-fashioned Latin.

Meanwhile a few discreet questions to Mr Charles Roanoke, dealer in antiques, resident in the South Mercia Police area. If Mikey Cross can be kept from gobbling up the first hint of anything suspicious, running amuck with it.

'Mr Roanoke, it's a minor matter. I dare say just some simple misunderstanding. But it's been reported to us that your – your standard of living, shall we say – is much higher than your business activities would seem to warrant. I've been asked to have a word.'

'Have you, Inspector?'

'You understand, sir, how these things happen. Probably some business rival, a matter of spite. But we have to follow up.'

Roanoke drank from his goblet, and smiled.

'Simple,' he said. 'I do spend a lot, I agree. It's because I happen very much to like the good things of life. As you might have discovered, Inspector, if, like your sergeant here, you had consented to drink my Latricieres-Chambertin.'

'Shall we say "Not on duty", sir?'

'Very prim. But I suppose our police force has to have its share of killjoys.'

'That's as may be, sir. But you were accounting for the apparent discrepancy between your business activities and, for instance, this house, the Bentley, the Range Rover there, even the wine, which Sergeant Cross certainly appreciated.'

'Was I accounting in detail for all that, Inspector? And do I really have to? Can any envious Tom, Dick, or Harry set the police on to a fellow citizen who happens to have an income above the average?'

'Rather far above the average, sir, if I may suggest it. Not everybody in South Mercia could build a house like this.'

8

'More fools they, Inspector.'

'I dare say, sir. But that would seem to leave us just where we were.'

'And where were we?'

The insolent contempt in the cool blue eyes unmistakable.

'We were enquiring about the difference between the extent of your business dealings and your private outlay, sir. I'm sure there's a simple explanation.'

Again he used the minute pause.

'One that wouldn't involve examining your books.'

'Oh, I assure you, Inspector, you will find nothing out of order there.'

'I'm happy to believe it, sir. But, as you must know, in your line of business there's plenty of opportunity to keep transactions out of the books.'

'What is this, Inspector? Are you now accusing me, with no evidence whatsoever, of fraud? Because if you are, I promise you your Chief Constable will get to hear of it.'

That old one.

'Wouldn't it be easier, sir, if you were just to answer my question?'

The steady glare in the blue eyes challenged.

And faltering, just.

'Well, I still can't see that it's any business of yours. But, if you must know, a few years ago I inherited a certain amount of money.'

Mikey Cross stirring from where he had put himself just to the rear.

Jump in, quick.

'There we are then, sir. All cleared up. Painless procedure.'

Yes. Faintest slackening of tension in that dark-complexioned face. Trust it passes Mikey by.

'Well, I think we can bid you good day then.'

Turn as if to go.

Mikey already almost through the door.

And, at it himself, swing back round.

'Oh, perhaps you should give me the exact figures. For my report, you understand.'

9

2

Sylvester saw Charles Roanoke's whole well-fleshed body tauten.

'I must have the details, you know,' he said.

'Very well.'

Forced tightness in Roanoke's voice.

'I was left a considerable sum, about sixty thousand pounds, some six years ago by a Mrs Bathurst. She was a lady, without any family, whom I had befriended, and she chose to leave her money to me rather than to some ridiculous little charity she had once been interested in.'

'I see. I understand you built this house about six years ago. Was that with the sixty thousand?'

For a moment he looked as if he'd like to hurl his full weight on to this intruder. Flatten him out of existence.

'Yes? Sir?'

'If you must know I did, yes, build the house with what Margaret Bathurst left me. Work of that sort was very much less expensive then than it is today.'

'Yes, sir. I know that.'

He waited for something more.

Nothing came.

'So we still have to account for your present standard of living.'

'Really, Inspector, I don't see —'

'I explained, sir. We have to check these things out. I must have the details. Even if I have to find them out some other way.'

'Grubbing about like a— Like a filthy dung-beetle.'

'You can put it that way, if you like, sir. Police work often is filthy enough. But is what I shall find – and I will find it, you know – really so filthy? So filthy that you can't simply tell me about it here and now?'

Momentary fiercely compressed frown on the florid face.

'No, of course there's nothing filthy, as you put it, about the matter. It's simply that one does not like one's personal circumstances to be pried into by every Jack-in-office who chances to come along.'

'I quite understand, sir.'

Again he waited.

'I have, as it happens, been left other sums under somewhat similar circumstances. You know how it is, Inspector.' Back to politeness now. 'Old people on their own are often very lonely, even when they have families. It's something I feel keenly about, meeting as many of them as I do in the course of my professional activities. Widows, women who have never married, widowers indeed, who can no longer look after themselves and have to move into some retirement place, or a nursing home. And they need to get rid of much of their furniture, or all of it. It's often first-class stuff. So I get to meet a good many of them. And— Well, I don't want to boast particularly, but after our business dealings are completed I often make a point of paying them friendly visits. If we hit it off together. And once or twice people have shown their appreciation by leaving me something in their will.'

'Very commendable, sir. And how many such bequests have there been? Exactly?'

Another tightening of the facial muscles. Then a hint of something else. Touch of bravado.

'There have been, yes, just two others. A Mrs Forth, who left me as a matter of fact only three thousand or so, and a Miss Pettiman, Miss Elspeth Pettiman, who made me a somewhat larger bequest.'

'How much?'

Mikey Cross. He'd just been aware of him sauntering back in. Now, hands in pockets, he shot out his question.

Roanoke fighting for an instant to control himself. Then a broad grin.

'How much? Quite a lot, Sergeant. A quarter of a million, more or less.'

'Lucky old you.'

'I think that'll be all we need from Mr Roanoke, Sergeant.'

Let the anger rip a bit.

Turn back to Roanoke.

'Except perhaps the addresses, sir. If you can remember them.'

Give him a flick of irony. Sting him just a little. Should be enough.

'Oh, I can remember, Inspector. Quite easily. You see, all three ladies had retired to the same place. It's called Astwood Manor, a nice old house where they can keep some of their furniture in their own rooms.'

'Thank you, sir. I think that's all, and I trust we shan't have to trouble you again.'

'All right old bugger, if you want my opinion,' Mikey Cross said, swinging to the heavy white farm gate. 'Nice and ready with the drink, even if he did bite my head off about it. And you can't blame him for smarming up his old pussies. Not if they're going to go leaving him a quarter of a million.'

'They didn't all leave him that, Sergeant. Nor is it all that much by today's standards. It wouldn't bring him in much more than eight or nine thousand a year after tax. And that for someone like him would be peanuts.'

Afterwards he asked himself whether it was Mikey's easy championing of the man that had made him decide, in little more than an uprush of instinct, that the writer of the letter to the Big White Chief had got it right.

Till Mikey had offered his comment he had been prepared to believe that Roanoke, unpleasant though he found him, was guilty of nothing worse than 'smarming up his old pussies'. But then he was suddenly sure Roanoke had, somehow or another, made ruthlessly certain the pussies never changed their wills once drawn up in his favour. Or it may have been, he reasoned, nothing to do with Mikey's careless assessment. Simply that, as soon as he had had time to sort out his impressions, he had seen Roanoke for what he was. A murderer.

But whichever way it had happened, he knew that, long way to go though there must be, he had a major enquiry on his hands.

And in his hands, as far as he could, he was determined to keep it.

He shouldn't, he reckoned, have all that much difficulty. Sugden was one for whatever was least hassle and hope to make Assistant Chief in time to collect the pension. People like him made the force as ineffectual as it often was. If only the average citizen knew . . .

No, he could face Suggers with too much evidence, provable or not, for him to be able to slide out of authorizing further enquiries. And those would be almost certainly left to him. Probably in the hope he would come a cropper. The trouble, more likely, would be that Suggers would cling to just reporting there was nothing to Pro Bono Publico's letter.

So find Pro Bono. How? Through one of those pussies of Mikey's, of course. Dead pussies. Greedily murdered pussies, perhaps. But not, with any luck, unremembered.

Astwood Manor Home for the Retired. Sylvester, Mikey Cross disposed of with a flea in his ear, read the board beside the entrance gates. Discreet gold lettering on a black background, with underneath in smaller letters *Visitors Welcome At All Times.*

Nice old house, too, calm in the tranquil evening sunlight. Must cost a packet to run, though. Long sweeping lawns, beautifully mown. Well-filled flowerbeds. And a hell of a heating bill. Let alone the upkeep. Freshly painted window frames. Big tiled roof. Everything hunky-dory. No wonder Miss Pettiman had a quarter of a million to leave to Roanoke. Fees would have to be huge. But then, if you've got it, what better to do with it in your last days than get yourself as much comfort as you can?

Good luck to her. Good luck to them all.

Only Miss Pettiman and Mrs Bathurst and the one who'd turned out not to have so much after all, Mrs – um – Forth, had they had good luck in the end? After they'd succumbed to Roanoke's charms?

He left the car on the verge opposite and walked up the drive – not a weed in it – rang at the front-door bell. Waited.

The door was opened by a young black girl wearing a pink smock-like garment he guessed was more or less a uniform. Wide smile.

'Can I help you? You come to see one of the residents? I don't remember seeing you before.'

She bubbled.

Not the best sort to have in a goodies-crammed place. Too ready to chat about the workings. Gift to any enterprising tea-leaf.

But better things to do than worry about Astwood Manor's security.

'I'd like to see the proprietor if he or she's available. I am a police officer.'

13

Face lighting up in a mischievous grin.

'What she done then, Mrs Milton?' Hasty correction. 'No. Only fooling. She wouldn't do nothing she didn't ought. Promise.'

He prevented himself grinning back.

'Just a matter of business. If Mrs Milton could see me for a few minutes.'

'Come in. I'll find out.'

She put him to wait in a small room, prettily furnished, just inside the hall. Chintz covers on the chairs. Chintz curtains to match. Fresh paper-fan in the empty fireplace, but the gentle heat from a radiator. Bowl of big bronze incurved chrysanthemums on the coffee table. Neat pile of brochures beside it.

He flipped through one. Impressions confirmed. Anyone coming here has to be pretty well padded. Happy hunting ground for Charles Roanoke all right.

But keep him out of the picture when this Mrs Milton turns up. Nothing hard to go on so far, and the fellow mustn't get any sort of warning. Must be snug enough as it is, if Pro Bono had to content himself with 'lacking the resources to make my information absolutely fool-proof'. As much as to say: no more than an educated guess. No point in giving our Mr Roanoke chance to cover up even better.

The door opened.

Mrs Milton went with the decor. Late middle age, carrying herself well. Bit too well. Bit remembering to do it. Or, yes, corset. Good one, too. Don't see many of them nowadays. Very afternoony dress over it. Some sort of brownish flowery material. Silk? Flicks of lace here and there. Chatelaine, that's the word. What she's aiming at.

He introduced himself.

'It's about a former resident here, a minor enquiry. A Mrs Bathurst.'

'Yes?'

Caution in every inch of the corseted body. Lot to lose, this lady.

'It's just that I'm anxious to find out about a charity Mrs Bathurst used to support. One I understand she was at one time intending to make a considerable beneficiary under her will.'

'Oh, but, no, Inspector Sylvester. I cannot— That is we, my husband, Major Milton and I, cannot betray the confidence of one of our resident guests.'

14

'But, madam, Mrs Bathurst has been dead for a number of years.'

'No, Inspector. Whether a guest enjoying the dignity and calm of Astwood Manor is deceased or not makes no difference. It is essential that any lady or gentleman coming to reside under our roof, with full facilities for care, should believe that – that any little eccentricities, as my husband the Major calls them, shall not be broadcast to the world.'

Broadcast, for God's sake.

Restrain yourself.

'I absolutely understand that, madam. But I'm only asking one quite simple thing. Just if you can recall the name of the charity Mrs Bathurst was interested in.'

'No, Inspector, I am afraid I cannot help you. What any of our resident guests tell us is sacrosanct. That is the word my husband, whose advice on such matters I entirely rely upon, invariably uses.'

He kept on at her. But he knew he would get nowhere.

Too devoted to the role a house like this lets her play. Her chance to fart-arse about like a lady of the manor. Anything that even remotely threatens that going to be hugger-muggered away. Every time.

Too bad.

But still need to know which 'ridiculous little charity', Roanoke's words, Mrs Bathurst had been going to leave her sixty thousand to. Almost bound to be some small-time local affair. And no one more frustrated at the loss of all that money than whoever runs it. Who'll be, too, more than likely, the sort of poncy git who'd sign an anonymous letter Pro Bono Publico. And who'll know, with luck, more about Roanoke than he dared put in that letter.

At last he gave up, managed to thank Mrs Milton, more or less, left.

But, getting into the car, an idea struck him. He glanced at his watch. Not far off six. He sat where he was.

Patience soon rewarded. Ten minutes later, teetering down the wide drive on heels much too high, came the little black girl who had let him in. Pink smock gone, short shiny blue mac tightly wrapped round her, bright-red white-spotted scarf on her head.

He swung open his passenger door.

'Going into town? Want a lift?'

She came tittupping over. Not a moment's hesitation.

'Not like the fuzz, come all over polite.'

But she settled her pretty little rear on the seat beside him as if he was a boyfriend who waited for her every evening.

'Well,' he said, manoeuvring out into the road, 'to be frank, it's not just politeness.'

'Tell me something new. Old Prune-face didn't come out with whatever you wanted to know. She don't never tell no one nothing. Sacrosanct, she says. Sacrosanct. So you thought you'd get it out o' me.'

He laughed.

'And will I?'

'It's anything I know, why not?'

'Well, bit of a long shot, but how long have you worked back there?'

'Seems like for ever. Five years. No, six. Six, going on seven.'

'Right. So d'you remember a lady called Mrs Bathurst?'

'Nah. Can't say I do. Get so many of 'em. Come one day all up and doing, then 'fore very long off they go. Feet first. Poor old souls.'

'Um. Does her being interested in some charity, some local charity, bit of a piffling affair, ring a bell?'

Prompt collapse into giggles.

'What's so funny?'

'Dawder,' she gasped out.

'Come on, pull yourself together, for God's sake. What's got into you?'

She managed to stop.

'No, was when you said piffling charity. Knew who you meant straight away then. Old Mrs Bathurst and her Dawder.'

'Dawder? There can't be a charity called that. What you on about?'

'Well all right, ain't actually called Dawder. Can't remember what it was really. Dringfield and Westmarch Dogs something or other. But she always said Dawder. Old Ma Bathurst. Saved her fifty-pees for it. Put 'em in a little box on her dressing table. *That's one for Dawder.* Can hear her saying it now. Course she lost interest in it after he come.'

'He? Who? Who d'you mean?'

'Creep that come to polish her few bits o' private furniture.

16

Said me and the others wouldn't do it proper. Used to come every week, and in the end the old girl went and left him every penny she got. Remember that now.'

Christ, I'm there. Or some of the way. What a turn-up for the books. Any luck be a couple of witnesses, say he exercised undue influence. Still got to find what he used, of course, the final touch. Used and got away with. But I'll have the bastard yet.

'Good girl. Just what I wanted to know. What's your name then?'

'Name? 'Ere, what you after? I don't want nothing to do with you pigs. Not more than save meself a wait for the bus.'

'OK, OK. Calm down.'

But by the time he had driven her to the end of her street – forbidden to go any further, mustn't risk being seen with a copper – he had got out of her what he might need if he ever came to have a case to bring to court, address and name. Which was Green, Princess Green.

'Well, you're my princess, darling, I'll tell you that.'

3

The Dringfield and Westmarch Dogs Refuge – no difficulty finding it in the phone book – was a solitary house far out beyond the once isolated, now suburban, village of Dringfield. Even in the bright September sunshine it looked plainly dreary. Walls of pebbledash, faded into a nothing yellow. Gate to the neglected garden hanging askew and unpainted. Path to the front door, once inappropriately tiled, now weedy and pock-holed. Behind, from two long corrugated-iron huts inside a wire enclosure, five or six dogs whined dispiritedly.

Sylvester, with at his heels a mutinous-looking Mikey the fly, sulking after his dressing-down the day before, negotiated the sagging gate and went up to the door. He put a thumb on the fat white button of the tarnished brass bell.

Nothing happened.

He clenched his fist and hammered. Repeated it. Then at last footsteps inside.

The man who opened the door was perhaps fifty, though still fixed in some earlier persona. Baggy grey trousers. Tweed jacket with leather pads at the elbows. Soft woollen tie in a shade between faded brown and yellow. Round spectacles on a pale, pinched face. Sticking-out ears.

'Sorry,' he said. 'Actually, I was in the lav. I'm on my own here, and it's sometimes a bit awkward.'

My man, by God. Pound to a penny.

Warrant card out, better stowed than the day before. 'I would like to speak to someone in authority.'

Look of hangdog guilt coming at once came on to that pale face. Oh, yes, Pro Bono Publico all right.

'Well, yes, I suppose that's me then. My name's Maffin, Peter Maffin. I'm actually Secretary of the Refuge.'

'Then if we may have a word?'

'Oh, yes. Yes, of course. Er – Come in. Yes.'

Led them into what, if this had been a house in a street in the town, would have been the front parlour. Now an office. Shabby. Trestle table by way of a desk. Shelves in unpainted plywood, piled with browning papers and pamphlets. Clumsy old manual typewriter on a side table which, from the tiled surround at its back, must have once been a washstand. No shade on the single fly-spotted bulb hanging from the centre of the ceiling.

'Well.' Peter Maffin swallowed. 'What can I do for you, Inspector?'

Sylvester did not answer.

Instead he went over to the big old typewriter, picked up a sheet of paper lying beside it, rolled it in, and, as rapidly as the grimy works allowed, tapped out *The quick brown fox jumped over the lazy dog*.

He took from his inner pocket a photocopy of Pro Bono Publico's letter. Typeface at least clearly the same.

He thrust the photocopy out towards Maffin.

'You wrote this. Why?'

Maffin, blinking hard behind his round spectacles, barely glanced at the sheet.

'No,' he got out with a gulp.

'Don't be silly, sir. Anyone can see that it was typed on this machine here. In your office.'

'I don't see that that's necessarily so. You scarcely looked at whatever it was you typed out.'

Give him a good heavy theatrical sigh.

'Shall I make a more detailed comparison then?'

'If you like. But, no. No, I don't see why you should come barging in here and use my typewriter just like that.'

'So you admit it is your typewriter?'

'No. No, it's not mine. Not strictly speaking. It belongs to the Refuge.'

'I dare say. But nevertheless it is a typewriter in your office. Or are you going to tell me this office isn't yours but it, too, belongs to the Refuge?'

Maffin thrust back his narrow shoulders and glared.

'Certainly not. I wouldn't demean myself.'

'So you agree now that this letter was written on that typewriter? By you.'

'No. No.'

Maffin shook his head from side to side, not so much a cornered animal as a cornered schoolboy.

Try the deeply pained expression.

'Look, sir, I know you wrote this. You know you wrote it. Why not admit it? And then we can get down to discussing the contents.'

But the cornered creature had spotted a tunnel of escape.

'I don't agree that that letter was typed on my machine. You can't be certain of that without a full expert examination.'

Quite right, my little friend. Bully for you. All the same you're my boy, and you're going to admit it.

'Very well. Shall we talk about something else? About the late Mrs Margaret Bathurst, for instance.'

A single quick blink behind the glasses.

'Or are you going to deny having known Mrs Bathurst?'

'Certainly not. Mrs Bathurst was a good friend of the Refuge for many, many years.'

'But not at the end of her life?'

'I don't know what you mean.'

'I think you do, sir. I believe you expected the Refuge to be left a considerable sum under Mrs Bathurst's will, and that you were disappointed.'

'Mrs Bathurst had every right to leave her money to whomsoever she wished.'

'No doubt. But she had been going to leave it to this Refuge of yours, and then in her last months alive she changed her mind. She left what you were going to get to the gentleman mentioned in this letter. This anonymous letter signed Pro Bono Publico. Where were you educated, Mr Maffin?'

'I – I don't see what that's got to do with anything.'

But now Mikey Cross emerged from his sulk.

'Just answer the question,' he butted in, bored contempt slurping out of his voice.

A look of fear, nothing less, flittered across Maffin's pinched face.

OK, take advantage. The sympathetic smile.

'Not really a very alarming question, sir, and relevant I assure you.'

Maffin visibly melting.

'I was at the Grammar School here, as a matter of fact. When it was a grammar school.'

'Ah, yes. Pity they all went. I had the same sort of education myself.'

Maffin easing down step by step. In a minute we'll be having a cosy chat about teaching standards. Only we won't.

'And the particular thing we learnt in those days was Latin. Yes?'

'Well, yes. Yes, I learnt Latin.'

'I'm sure you did, Pro Bono Publico.'

Maffin's fighting spirit, such as it was, evaporated.

'Oh, for God's sake,' he shouted, 'why not admit it? Yes. Yes, Inspector, I wrote that letter.'

'Yes. Well, now shall we talk a little about what you claimed in it? My Chief Constable was considerably impressed.'

Maffin brightened.

'I just felt it was my duty. Someone had to draw attention to the matter. But, well, I didn't see why I should get further involved than was necessary. So— So I used a pseudonym. I mean, once the business had been drawn to police attention, it was up to them.'

'Very understandable. But, tell me, just what was it you were drawing attention to?'

'Well . . . Well, to that man.'

'To Mr Roanoke, the antiques dealer?'

'Yes. Yes, him.'

Maffin tried to stop himself saying more. But, forcing its way up like a fat gas bubble in a mud-spring, the outburst came.

'He's a murderer. A vile murderer. He murdered Mrs Bathurst. And— And before that he— He seduced her. No. No, that's not what I meant. Not— Not that. It was her mind he seduced. The Refuge meant everything to her. She gave us almost all our funds. She used to come out here every week. Until her health began to fail. That was when she sold her house and went to Astwood Manor. And she sold her furniture, nearly all her furniture. So, that— That man was able to follow her there. He said her things needed special care. It was his excuse. And he poisoned her mind. At first it was only her mind. But in the end, when she'd changed her will in his favour, he poisoned her himself. He poisoned her, Inspector.'

'But nothing at the time indicated the death was anything other than from natural causes.'

He had called up the files. No inquest had been held. Doubtless Mrs Bathurst had been under medical supervision at the time of her death, and there had been no grounds for thinking it was other than in the course of whatever illness she had. Or from mere old age.

'Yes, I know. I know that, Inspector. That's why I said in my letter that I hadn't got positive proof.'

'Yes, you had very little of that. Sir. But what you did have, let me suggest, was a certain amount of spite.'

'Spite? What spite? Why should I have felt any spite?'

'Oh, come, Mr Maffin, there you were, counting on getting one day a very considerable sum of money for this Refuge, of which you are in sole charge. Then you hear that you haven't got a penny. Don't tell me you viewed that with total cheerfulness.'

'But— But— But, Inspector, that money was never coming to me, to myself. No one ever suggested it should. It was to be for the use of the Refuge. We could expand our work, and there are repairs. A great deal of renovation is needed.'

'I can see that, sir. But let me suggest to you again that the spending of all that money would be entirely in your hands. You would be, in all but the most literal truth, a rich man.'

'No. No. There are the trustees. The money would be in their hands. Entirely.'

'And they wouldn't accept your recommendations for its use? Is that really so? Come, you'd virtually have a free hand. To spend all that money.'

Maffin blinked and blinked behind his spectacles.

'Well, I suppose they would agree to my recommendations. In most cases. I am happy to say they have always placed the fullest trust in me.'

'I'm sure they have. So that leaves us with you yourself to all intents and purposes expecting to receive a very large legacy. And when you did not, what did you do, Mr Maffin? I suggest that out of sheer spite – yes, spite – you eventually wrote this letter to my Chief Constable.'

'No.'

Maffin swallowed.

22

'I've got proof of what I said. I mean, not proof that would stand up in a court of law. But I didn't write that letter without good reason.'

'Oh, yes?'

Again Maffin swallowed. His Adam's apple working up and down in his skinny neck.

'It's like this,' he said. 'When Mrs Bathurst first went to Astwood Manor I used to visit her. It was rather an arduous journey, on my bicycle, but she was such a good friend of the Refuge that I didn't mind. And so, you know, I was aware that she was not seriously ill. She was in poor health, of course, and she was elderly. But she could well have lived years longer.'

'Hardly grounds for accusing Mr Roanoke of murdering the lady. Because that's what you have done, however obliquely.'

'No. No, there's more than that. You see, by the time Margaret Bathurst died I had become quite a regular visitor at Astwood Manor. I knew all the staff. And— And I was quite a favourite with one of them in particular, Nurse— Well, I think I had better not give you her name.'

Time for the uncompromising police-officer look.

'I think you had, Mr Maffin.'

Swallow. Swallow.

'Very well, if I must. A Nurse Dexter, Mrs Mary Dexter. She's a widow. Well, I continued to see her, at intervals, after Margaret Bathurst passed away. We— We met in the town sometimes. And later she mentioned that another resident, Mrs Julia Forth, whom I had known slightly, had died a little unexpectedly, just as Margaret Bathurst had done, and she said something about— About Mrs Forth leaving Mr Roanoke a rather fine bureau he had been caring for at the manor. I didn't really think much about it at the time.'

'Yes, sir?'

'Well, and then my friend, Mrs Dexter that is, happened to mention a third unexpected death, unexpected except that anyone as elderly as the residents at Astwood Manor may be expected to pass on sooner or later. This was a Miss Pettiman, Miss Elspeth Pettiman. And later I remembered having read in the local paper that she had left something over a quarter of a million pounds. It didn't say it was to any charity, or anything, but I asked Mrs Dexter the next time I saw her – we attended a concert together at the Assembly Rooms – whether that man had also been one of Miss Pettiman's visitors.'

'That man? Mr Roanoke?'

'Yes. Yes, him. And when she told me he had been, a frequent visitor even, I— Well, I took action. I went to London. To the Wills Office, where you can look up anybody's will for a small charge, you know.'

'Yes, Mr Maffin, I know.'

'Well, in the end I found it. Her will. And she had left everything to him. Everything.'

'And that's all? That's the full extent of your evidence? Your suspicions?'

'Well, yes. Yes, I suppose so. But it's enough, isn't it? Enough to warrant further enquiries?'

'It may be, Mr Maffin. It may be.'

4

Detective Chief Superintendent Sugden, square deep-pink bald head, broad nose supporting large rimless glasses, weighty frame secure in leather-backed swivel chair. Every scrap of paperwork on the desk in front of him long ago dealt with.

'Well, Bill' – geniality just about achieved – 'nothing to that Roanoke business, I suppose. I've met the chap as a matter of fact. Rotary and so forth. Seems decent enough. Doing well, I believe.'

'Yes, sir, he is doing well.'

Leave just a pause. Naughty, but too tempting to resist.

'If only by dint of collecting fat bequests from old pussies.'

'Left money, eh? Well, no harm in that. Doesn't make him what that crank who wrote to the CC made out.'

He reached towards the green private-line telephone at the corner of the big desk, almost patted it, withdrew.

'No, sir, no harm in that. Not necessarily. But there is one awkward little fact. Or even three.'

Geniality vanished from the large face.

'Inspector, I don't want to hear a lot of socialistic backbiting about the fellow. I'm not unaware of the sort of opinions you hold, you know.'

'I keep my politics to myself, sir. In so far as I have any.'

'You know what I mean, Inspector. You're a tight-fisted bastard, that's what it amounts to. Nobody sees you out with the boys when a big case has been cracked. Or, when there's a stag night it's always Sylvester who volunteers to stay on duty.'

One Hamlet-type palpable hit. Don't underestimate Suggers. Didn't get where he is without plenty of pig-shrewdness.

'It's my way, sir. I don't think I'm any the worse a copper for it.'

A long silent glare.

'Well, what is this fact of yours then? These three facts. Or four, was it?'

'Just three, sir. The facts that, in three cases where Mr Roanoke was left money, he had made a point of visiting the ladies in one particular expensive retirement home. In order, so he claimed, to look after their remaining bits of furniture. And – this was something Pro Bono Publico didn't rise to making clear in his letter – each of their deaths was to some extent unexpected.'

'For God's sake, Inspector, if people are old they're going to die sooner or later, aren't they? What can be unexpected about it? You don't think I'm going to send a report upstairs with evidence of that sort?'

'No, sir. But I don't think, with respect, it's something that can be ignored. For one thing, the unexpectedness can almost certainly be vouched for by the nurse who looked after the ladies.'

'Who said I was going to ignore anything? Don't jump to conclusions, Sylvester. You're all too apt to do that.'

'Yes, sir.'

'So what do you propose to do about these not very well-established facts of yours? Are you going to get me any supporting evidence? Or, better, something that knocks all this into a cocked hat.'

Home and dry. But bury deep the smile of triumph.

'There's several lines of enquiry I'd like to take up, sir. I've identified the sender of the letter of course, and I don't think there's any need for further action there. And he doesn't know, for certain, anything more than he's already said.'

'Well, that's something. Put it in your report.'

'Yes, sir. Then I propose to see the nurse and find out exactly why she thought those deaths came sooner than they might have done.'

'I take it, though, death certificates were duly issued in all three cases. No doubt for the good and sufficient reason that there was nothing suspicious in any of them.'

'Quite so, sir. But I think each case should at least be looked into again. A few discreet enquiries. The CC would want to know, sir.'

'Yes, yes. And what else? Or is that all you propose to do?'

'No, sir. It occurred to me there might be other cases our

26

informant knew nothing about. What I'd like, sir, is to use as many of the Aides as can be spared to go to every high-class retirement or nursing home in the neighbourhood. See if they can suss out anything.'

Sugden grunted.

'Plenty of enquiries for them to cut their teeth on without that, Inspector. Time is money, you know. There's such a thing as the Police Authority budget. We haven't got unlimited funds to throw around.'

'No, sir. I understand, sir.'

And who's going to make sure his accounts don't cause any ructions? Bloody cheek to accuse me of not lashing out on anything. Suggers wouldn't do it with cash he has to account for, however good the reason.

'Well, take two Aides, if you must. For two days. Not more. And you'd better use the women.'

Chauvinist pig.

Louring glare through the big square spectacles.

'No, Inspector. Not for the reason you think. But because a woman's more likely to get you your information. What's called the sympathetic touch.'

Another point to you, Mr Sugden. Sir.

'Yes, sir. Thank you, sir. Not much use going round the shops for the source of whatever poison was employed, but—'

'If poison was employed at all, Inspector. If, if, if.'

'Yes, sir. If. But it might be worth checking on Mr Roanoke's business activities. Income and expenditure, that sort of thing. I thought I'd take care of that myself, sir.'

'Oh, you did, did you? And I suppose it never occurred to you that I might have other work for you? The area crime rate is nothing to write home about, you know.'

'Yes, sir. Any further enquiries would, of course, be subject to whatever else you might want me for, sir.'

Another grunt.

'Oh, very well then. But don't make a pig's breakfast of it. Conscientiousness is all very well, Inspector, but it can be taken too far. And I've noted that about you before this.'

'Yes, sir. Thank you, sir.'

Sylvester was careful not to interview Peter Maffin's Nurse Dexter at Astwood Manor, happy hunting ground for Charles Roanoke. Even the remotest chance of another meeting with him best avoided.

Until there were things to say.

So he arranged to see the nurse at her flat in the town. As he stepped into its sitting room he did automatically what he had long ago taught himself. To stop and take a long, steady survey.

The room small but nicely got up, and in apple-pie order. Subdued floral wallpaper. Reproduction of Van Gogh's *Sunflowers* over the fireplace. Flame-effect gas fire below, issuing gentle warmth this beginning-to-be-chilly September evening. Row of china ornaments on the mantelpiece, Staffordshire shepherdess, probably worth a bob or two, two dogs with spotted coats, pretty little vase, empty. All sparkling. Thick plum-coloured velvet curtains drawn over the window. Wall-to-wall carpet in the same shade. Comfortable armchairs either side of the fire. Coffee table beside one with two good-quality women's magazines. Dark-wood sideboard opposite the window, with telephone and, tucked away, a radio in a wooden cabinet. Neatly piled phone directories and magazines on the shelf below. Standard lamp with fringed parchment shade beside one chair. Small bookcase behind the other. Not easy to see the titles. Whole effect: very snug.

He even allowed himself a moment of amusement in trying to spot any traces Peter Maffin might have left behind. To no avail.

Nurse Dexter was short and solid with a round, practical-looking face centring on a sturdy button of a nose. Not difficult to imagine her at work, bustling purposefully, standing no nonsense.

All right, Peter Maffin had said nothing about the 'unexpected' deaths making her suspect cases of murder. But there wouldn't be much that got past her. At a guess, she knows Maffin well enough not to put ideas into his head. Which hadn't prevented them arriving there of their own accord. And with precious little evidence.

So, care needed.

He thanked her for letting him come to see her, refused coffee, took the armchair she offered, the one he imagined her comfortably seated in watching TV. No, this was one of the rare sitting rooms with no set goggling blankly down. Then make it listening to the cosiness of Radio Four and reading one of her magazines.

'This is a strictly confidential enquiry, Nurse, and I must ask you not to talk about it to anyone.'

Round face showing neither avid interest nor any anxiety.

'Recently, the Chief Constable of South Mercia received a letter, an anonymous letter, insinuating the deaths of certain ladies at Astwood Manor Home for the Retired were not as straightforward as had been assumed.'

He waited.

Thoughts gone back at once to circumstances she'd tried to blot from her consciousness?

Face looking a trifle anxious. As well it might with her position at the Home. But no obvious sign of a bad conscience. Of suspicions wrongly stifled. Fingers of the stubby hands, with the well-trimmed square-cut nails resting on her knees, not tightening by as much as a millimetre.

'You will understand that enquiries have to be made into any such allegations.'

'Yes, of course. And am I right in thinking these certain ladies had been under my personal care?'

'I presume they must have been. You are a full-time nurse at the manor?'

'Yes. Yes, I am. But I hope there was no suggestion that I benefited from money they left. I make a point, when any of my elderly patients start talking of their wills, to say quite firmly that I do not wish to benefit. I have enough for my comfort, thank goodness, I tell them, and any intrusion of money matters all too often creates unpleasantness.'

Patently forthright. Almost certainly telling the exact truth.

'No, there is no question of that at all.'

'Then are you— Did this anonymous letter, rather, claim that the deaths were due to some sort of negligence? Negligence on my part?'

'No, no. Your name was not even mentioned.'

'I see.'

Smallest of flickers in the dark-brown eyes. Sudden realization what her friend Peter Maffin must have done?

'Might I know the names of these ladies, Inspector?' No trace of a tremor in her voice. 'I don't see how I can be any help to you unless I do.'

'Yes, of course. Enquiries have revealed they are a Mrs Bathurst, a Mrs Forth, and a Miss Pettiman.'

29

'Yes, I see.'

She fell silent, looking down at her two well-rounded knees.

Now she knows for certain who wrote to the CC. Her Peter Maffin in for a sharp dressing-down.

'Well, Inspector, I will not conceal from you that each of those ladies did die a little unexpectedly. But, you know, however well in themselves a person of their considerable age might seem to be – they were all in their eighties – the body can give up at any moment. Very often it's impossible to say what begins it, but the decline can be very rapid.'

'And you think that this is all that happened? In three cases one after another?'

'One after another, you say. But, as I recollect, there was something like three years between each of those deaths. You could hardly call that one after the other.'

'No, I see that. But was there any similarity in the manner of those deaths, unexpected as you agree they were? Can you remember?'

Looking straight ahead, brown eyes sharply alert.

'Yes, I can as a matter of fact. And the symptoms, yes, did have a certain similarity. They began with nausea, though there was nothing in that. Digestive upsets are common enough at that age, whatever care is taken over diet. And I can assure you, Inspector, that the standard of hygiene at Astwood Manor is extremely high. We are regularly inspected, you know.'

'Yes, yes. But the accusations in the letter to the Chief Constable were not of negligence.'

'No, I gathered that.'

Again she sat pondering. This time he intervened.

'You were saying the last hours, or days was it, of these ladies began with digestive upsets. Or what appeared to be digestive upsets. But there were further symptoms, graver ones?'

'Well, yes. And, yes again, as far as I can remember without the records, they were much the same in all three cases. Complaints of a feeling of vertigo, and eventually some convulsions before the final moments.'

He pulled out his notebook and scribbled.

'What you're saying, Inspector,' her voice came to him as he wrote, 'is poison. Isn't it? Otherwise you would hardly be asking the questions you have.'

Sharp enough.

He held his face blank.

'But, Inspector, what you must understand is that symptoms of that sort are by no means a certain indication of poisoning. I've been in private nursing for more than thirty years, and have had more than a little experience of cases of this kind. Almost every one of which, I may say, turned out to be nothing but someone's over-heated imagination. So let me add this. All the residents at Astwood Manor have, for the past ten years or more, been under the care of our medical officer, Dr Hardew. Which means they are seen by him regularly, and, if any of them shows any sign of illness, he is invariably called at once.'

She leant forward, a little pugnaciously.

'Now I dare say you've got it into your head that Dr Hardew is some old dodderer who'd sign a death certificate any time he was asked. But there you're wrong. He's hardly fifty, and although he practises as a GP he has made a speciality of geriatric work. You're not going to tell me that any of my patients have been murdered under that man's nose.'

Sylvester came away with doubts running this way and that in his mind. If Nurse Dexter was right about her Dr Hardew – have to see the man for myself – it was hard to see Peter Maffin's suspicions as anything other than what she had suggested. Product of an over-heated imagination.

Yet there was his own feeling about Roanoke. Leaving the fellow's garage, with shadowy in the background the pieces of fine furniture that provided his luxury life style, he'd found himself convinced – Just in opposition to Mikey Cross? Or by something in Roanoke's attitude somewhere? – that he'd been challenging a murderer.

Was I? All right, the fellow's unpleasant. Aggressive, contemptuous, too damn pleased with himself and his money. OK, so that makes him someone who'd smarm his way to nice fat inheritances. But it by no means necessarily makes him a poisoner.

But I'm still convinced. Something more than having too much money is wrong with Charles Roanoke. Never mind there's precious little in the way of evidence. Never mind Nurse Dexter's well-qualified and alert doctor.

He looked at his watch. Getting on for ten. Too late now to arrange to see this Doc Hardew.

But not too late – he thought abruptly – to drown the doubts.

31

Not in drink. He had always been careful not to succumb to that temptation, the average detective's way of thrusting aside the rolling burden of vice and stupidity. No, but almost certainly Jude would still be at her working flat. She aimed to be there for the odd late punter till ten every weekday. And she wouldn't mind staying on a bit. So . . .

5

Detective Chief Superintendent Sugden thwarted Sylvester in getting his interview with Dr Hardew. Almost as soon as he had got in to check the night messages, he was summoned. He cursed. He knew he would be given only the minimum time to pursue Roanoke. But he had not expected Suggers to stop him this soon. Or could he really be needed for something else?

He was needed, he found. But how much?

There had been, Sugden said with heavy portentousness, a robbery at the home of the Lord Lieutenant of the county. A necklace from Garrards, gold, in the form of lover's knots, the gift of the Lord Lieutenant to his spouse on their thirtieth wedding anniversary. The theft had been discovered only late the night before. A headquarters officer must, of course, take charge.

'Very good, sir. I'll get out there pronto.'

'I should hope so, Inspector. And you'd better take DS Cross with you. You'll need somebody with his head screwed on.'

Or somebody delighting in being your pet spy.

But nothing else to do but to set off at once. Bar stretching that 'pronto' to cover a quick briefing to the two probationary women detective constables allocated for enquiries at retirement homes. June Smithson, Maggie Adams.

June a high-flier, would-be intellectual, parader of Open University textbooks, though not above using her good looks to help her on her way. Once he had peered over her shoulder to see what she was reading – a habit never conquered since college days – and found it was Maynard Keynes' *Economic Possibilities for Our Grandchildren*, vaguely remembered as a classic. She had glanced up at him, touch of impudence, and quoted: 'There is no country and no people that can look forward to the age of leisure and abundance without dread.'

33

'What d'you think? You in the grip of dread, sir?'

He had cottoned on then. Every female newcomer to the CID challenged to 'pull Bill Sylvester'. Something asked for by a resolute avoidance of in-house entanglements.

'Depends if we have reached the age of – what was it? – leisure and abundance, Constable. You may think so. I have my doubts.'

End of battle, if not of war.

Maggie Adams, he guessed, not even egged on to campaign. Nice enough, but in no way sexy and not even all that bright. Podgy, rather whey-faced, inclined – he saw now – to spots. But alert, ready. In her eyes a steady look of determination.

Could be, in fact, someone in my own mould. Making the police her career because she's dedicated, for whatever reason, to beating crime.

'Any whiff of any deaths, even as long ago as seven or eight years past, that were unexpected. Not easy to define. But a chance to exercise a bit of judgement.'

And off to the countryside home of the Lord Lieutenant, with Mikey Cross spouting just the sort of envious sentiment Suggers had attributed to himself.

The business even more complex and tedious than expected. The Lord Lieutenant, though affecting a modestly democratic way of life, had more than a few subordinates, if only a handful of them strictly servants. But almost thirty people had had access to the bedroom where that very expensive present had been left for anyone to see and snatch.

So interviews, even shared with Mikey, had taken all of two days. Then much checking of records, locally and with London, to see if the Lord Lieutenant had contrived to employ anyone with a criminal past. Next, hours checking and cross-checking movements. From which it emerged a young daily worker in the kitchen, who should not have set foot elsewhere, had not been in her place all the time. Some sharp interrogation and, yes, wide-eyed with wonder at the stately, time-hardened opulence all around, she had crept off to explore, and in the big unoccupied bedroom fallen prey to temptation.

Lover's knots pure gold necklace uselessly hidden behind a loose brick in her parents' cottage.

Even when the poor girl had been charged still a fat sheaf of paperwork to produce. Meticulously, in view of Detective Chief Superintendent Sugden's personal interest. So no opportunity to make an appointment with Dr Hardew. And no time till well after the two Aides' spell assisting him was over even to have a word.

But, when at last he managed that at least, neither had anything to tell. They provided lists of places visited. June Smithson, perhaps with closer collaboration in mind, pointedly mentioning a few they had not had time to get to. Nowhere had there been any deaths giving rise to the faintest suspicion.

Part of him wanted to go over the whole list again. But that he knew was impractical. Suggers evidently convinced there was no longer any need to do anything about Peter Maffin's letter. Beyond letting some days go by to make it seem full enquiries had been made.

So he was assumed to be available for other duties. And Suggers never one not to take advantage of his willingness to work while others played.

In the end he snatched time one evening to go out to Dr Hardew. Seeing with his own eyes the man who signed those death certificates even more of a compulsion now than when he had come away from Nurse Dexter.

Despite the time that had passed since that collision with Roanoke – Spanish holiday seeming weeks away – his conviction that the man was a great deal worse than a charmer who had won himself a couple of hefty legacies was yet stronger. There had been something, a hint of cockiness at some stage in that encounter in the big garage with its looming pieces of well-polished high-priced furniture, that had been not quite right. No more than that. But the impression, though he could not pin down what had given it to him, refused to go away. Roanoke was a murderer. A poisoner. He believed that. And, though there was nothing so far that could be called evidence, he was not going to let him get away with it.

A pleasant house not far from Astwood Manor. At the foot of its short drive Sylvester came to a halt. He took in a reasonably well-kept garden, a double garage with doors open to reveal a big Citroën and a battered Morris estate, a glimpse at the back of a small orchard, trees heavy with fruit ready for picking. The house itself. Three bedrooms probably. Brick built, creeper covered, woodwork in an unobtrusive green. Trace of smoke drifting from the chimney-stack, probably from a log fire. And, tacked on at the side, a newish extension housing the surgery.

Very agreeable, if something of a drain to keep up. But with

Astwood Manor residents bound to be private patients that wouldn't be exactly a burden.

He rang at the front-door bell. Dr Hardew himself answered.

Tall, lean of body and lean faced, hair only just greying. Suit of country tweeds, quiet tie, pair of spectacles just visible in the top pocket. Air of assurance.

'Inspector Sylvester. Right on time. Do come in. I thought we might go into the surgery, save bothering my wife with business.'

He led the way through the hall – two large bookcases, three or four oil paintings, of nothing much, big bowl of yellow chrysanthemums, smell of furniture or floor polish – and into the surgery through a door that still looked as if it was newly there.

But if the house was conventionally comfortable the surgery was something else. It gleamed with modernity. Glass-topped desk with a computer unit to one side and a crane-like, frosted black metal reading-lamp on the other. Tubular steel chairs behind and in front. Aseptic shelves filled with clean-backed, formidable-looking medical books. Large metal filing cabinets. And along the whole of the inner wall an array of apparatus to grace a TV science-fiction show, VDU screens, grey-painted metal boxes spattered with dials and glinting with tiny red lights, fat corkscrew-curled cables linking one to another, a little white plaque warning in incised red letters of high voltage.

'Sit down, Inspector, sit down.'

Rather more of a command than he liked.

He took the chair in front of the big desk. And made a performance of pulling out his notebook.

'Yes, Inspector?'

'The late Miss Pettiman. I imagine you've looked up your records?'

By way of answer the computer flicked into life. A few keys tapped.

'Here we are.'

'Right. No point in beating about the bush. For reasons I am not at liberty to go into I have grounds to suspect that Miss Pettiman's death was possibly not from natural causes. Is there anything in your recollection or your records that, on second thoughts, might leave room for those suspicions to be correct?'

For answer Dr Hardew extended the long, scrupulously kept fingers of his right hand towards the computer screen.

36

'I pride myself, Inspector, on the thoroughness of my care. Particularly my care for such patients as Miss Pettiman.'

Because they pay. Pay for all that stuff banked along the wall there. Your pride and joy.

But no point in saying it. The fellow making himself clear enough.

'I'm sure you are extremely thorough, Doctor, but . . . ?'

'But there is nothing, absolutely nothing, here in my most careful record of Miss Pettiman's health over her last years that gives me the slightest reason to regret having signed the death certificate.'

No more than he had expected after what Nurse Dexter had said. And yet . . .

Plough on.

'There are a couple of other cases. Also patients at Astwood Manor. A Mrs Julia Forth and a Mrs Margaret Bathurst.'

'Very well.'

A spate of tap-tapping on the computer keyboard. Prolonged study of whatever had come up on the screen. More tapping, and more reading. Finally a cool gaze across the big glass-topped desk.

'No, Inspector. I am bound to say there is not one scintilla of evidence in my notes of anything in any way untoward in the deaths either of Mrs Bathurst six years ago or of Mrs Forth this year. Absolutely nothing.'

With a snap Sylvester closed his notebook. In it no more than a scrawl or two made to keep up the pressure.

But a well-manicured hand put out to check his departure.

'Let me say this before you go. I am well aware that when a doctor has signed a death certificate and there are subsequent questions, he will be expected to fight every inch of the way to defend his judgement. So I would like to assure you that in this case, in all three of these cases, there is not anything that I feel I have to justify in any way.'

Eyes flicking to the formidable array of electronic apparatus.

'Those ladies received the very best of medical care. Their deaths, when they came, may have been a little unexpected, but each was altogether in the natural course of things. At that age the terminal process could have set in at any time. And that is what happened. Neither more nor less.'

Momentary pause. Then something extra. Added with emphasis.

'Nor, I may say, were what I might call the external circumstances such as to give rise to any suspicions. Not even from the mere presence of a visitor immediately before the onset of the final phase.'

His tentacles quivered at this, even though what had been said ought finally to have quenched that feeling about Roanoke.

'You can assure me of that, Doctor? That none of those ladies had any visitors immediately before their deaths? Your records are as detailed as that?'

'As I said, I pride myself on the complete thoroughness with which I treat patients of this sort. The presence of visitors at a critical point in any illness is a factor that ought to be taken into account. I take it into account. All nurses at Astwood Manor have instructions to make a note of any visitor, and of the length of their stay. Even, I may add, of what reception the patient gave them. So I can assure you that in none of the three cases you have drawn my attention to was there a visitor to the patient in their last hours.'

He smiled then. An arrived-at smile.

'A sad thing, of course, the lonely end. A very sad thing. But it happens all too often with the very elderly, when there are no close relatives remaining.'

A signing-off. The polite generality.

He pushed himself to his feet.

6

Could he trust himself? Despite every check he believed Charles Roanoke, issuer of floridly confident charm – damn it, with a smile and half a dozen words he won over Mikey Cross – was capable of speeding the legacies he had needed by administering poison.

But how?

What poison had he used? How had he deceived someone as obviously alert as Dr Hardew, backed as he was with all that mass of electronic apparatus? Or even commonsensical and experienced Nurse Dexter?

All very well to work on a hunch, that often unanalysable awareness of minute signs a witness gives that something is not as it is being shown to be. Yet hunches can come unstuck.

And hardly a minute to hammer out a way ahead. Detective Chief Superintendent Sugden seemed to be taking a particular delight in loading him with work. Not that he objected. Police work was what he had rejected a career in industry for. And he had never regretted it.

But worse came.

Drawing him aside in the CID room, Sugden bestowed a casual word.

'Been meaning to see you, Bill. I've had a chat with the CC about that business.'

A pause.

Buggered if you're going to get a quick 'Yes, sir' to show I know what 'that business' is.

A slight tightening of the lips in the deep-pink, well-fleshed face.

'That stupid letter the CC was sent. Well, we've looked at it all again in the light of what you found about that chap, whatever

39

his name was, Maffin. And we're agreed the fellow's almost certainly some sort of nutter.'

He prickled.

'Is the Chief Constable saying, sir, no enquiries are to be pursued?'

'No, no. Of course not. Just that he— That we both doubt there's really anything much in it. But, no, there's no question of forgetting all about it. I mean, those Aides I let you have, did they get anywhere, going round nursing homes and so forth?'

Point to Suggers. Who probably already knows the answer, some devious way.

'No, sir. I'm afraid they didn't. But it was pretty much a long shot in any case.'

'Well, keep up the good work, Bill. Keep up the good work.'

Clear signal. No actual opportunity to do that.

So he made time to talk to the informants he had in the world of antiques. To find out whatever he could about the man still vivid in his mind's eye from their one meeting. He even wondered, once or twice, whether his best hope might be to contrive a second meeting 'accidentally'. See if he felt the same about him face to face once more. Or, just possibly, out at that fat-cat house there would come back to him whatever had, just for an instant, rung a bell of falsity.

But too much of a risk. If the fellow had poisoned three times and got away with it, finding himself confronting again the officer who had made those initial probings could well alert him. Into taking extra precautions.

If he had any precautions to take. If he was that triple murderer.

He did discover that Roanoke was spending hard. Talk about a new boat, a £30,000 job. Jokes about appalling complications run into having an indoor pool installed. The luxuries, presumably, out of Miss Pettiman's quarter of a million.

But, so gossip went, his business was not doing as well as it might.

'Good lord,' one of his rivals said, dipping into the faintly sparkling odiferousness of the large vodka tonic he had bought him, 'other day the fellow purchased the entire contents of Broughtley Abbey. Stuff been hanging about for three years or more. Some good pieces, of course. But a hell of a lot of things no one wants nowadays.'

40

Another swirl and swallow at the V and T.

'God knows where he gets the cash from to lay it out like that.'

God knows. And so do I.

But this was all he learnt. Other cases made their demands. Forged twenty-pound notes circulating, and someone in the Regional Crime Squad with a tip they were being counterfeited here. If he snuffled round sussing out where exactly that was, wouldn't he be doing more for what he saw himself as being in the world for than by brooding, pointlessly, about Charles Roanoke?

Or, wider view, shouldn't he really take a hard look at himself? Not let crime, of whatever sort, dominate his entire life? Crime wasn't all there was. Other people, most other people, gave themselves time off. For enjoyment. And half an hour every now and again with Jude could hardly be seen as all the pleasure he was entitled to. Weeks now since his self-enforced spell in the Spanish sunshine and the embraces of— What was her name? Yup, Pepita.

Then – it was a Thursday, a day he had got through without a single far-away period picturing the florid face, the chill eyes, the confident well-fleshed body of Charles Roanoke – there came what looked like a break-through.

Out of the blue, in the form of little, podgy Probationary Woman Detective Constable Adams, whey-faced as ever but at least – he registered – at present without any spots.

'Inspector, can I have a word?'

What's this? Nothing, far as I know, for her to have a word about. Can't be she's been sent in to 'pull Bill Sylvester'. Poor kid.

So what she said was a complete surprise.

'It's about those enquiries we made for you, June Smithson and me, last month.'

'Oh, yes?'

'You'll think it's silly of me, sir, but I've been worrying about them.'

You and who else?

'No, I don't suppose I'll think it silly of you. And if I do, I'll try not to show it.'

'Yes, sir. Well, it's just this. You remember we made out a list, June and I, out of the Yellow Pages, of all the likely places, and divided them up between us. Only we left to last anywhere on

41

the very edge of the area. There were a hell of a lot of places to go to, sir.'

'I was only allocated two days of your precious time.'

'Yes, sir. Well, you see, there were three places we never got around to. And I kept worrying about them somehow. And so— Well, yesterday was my free day, and I hadn't anything much else to do. So I thought I'd just go out to those places. And— Well, sir, I think I struck lucky.'

Good for you. I may have been right about you. Bit obsessed. Like yours truly. Not one for making yourself enjoy yourself in your time off, falling back on the work.

Which, damn it, is worth doing.

'So, just what did you find?'

She brought it all out in a rush, and only a little muddled. At a retirement home at Oxleigh on the far side of the county from Astwood Manor, a place called the Old School, the housekeeper had actually burst into tears at her tentative enquiry about unexpected deaths. There had been a Miss Gallitly, 'actually a sister of that big millionaire, Gresham Gallitly, the take-over expert they're always writing about in the papers, sir'. Everyone at the home had been sure she would be with them for many years to come. But she had suddenly developed an illness and then had died, rather unpleasantly.

Already, at the scent of big-money Gresham Gallitly's name, his interest had shot up. Now it took another leap.

'Unpleasantly? What do you mean by unpleasantly? Did this housekeeper of yours actually use the word? Give any details?'

A blush.

'I – I don't know, sir. I mean, that was the impression I got. But I can't remember what she actually said. I didn't know you'd want anything verbatim, sir.'

'No. Well, not your fault. I dare say I'll go along there myself in any case. Well done. Good piece of work.'

'Thank you, sir.'

He took an hour away from an enquiry the RCS had asked to be made about the notes forgeries to go out to Oxleigh. The Home was a smaller place than Astwood Manor, but no less well kept up. A large flint-built Victorian building at the edge of the village, the former school sold when money-to-spare weekenders had ousted the farmworkers whose children had gone there for a hundred years and more. Its two stone doorways still inscribed *Boys* and *Girls*. Two pretty gardens dotted with benches in place of knees-grazing playgrounds.

Calling to mind the name of the housekeeper who had been so distressed at Miss Gallitly's death, he tugged at the ancient bell-pull.

Mrs Horrocks was in, the maid who answered said. She would fetch her.

Wobbly with fat. Round, pinkish face fleetingly crossed by unexplained worries. Old-fashioned wrap-around flowered dress. Inclined to peck like a mindless hen at anything that came her way. A flower tweaked in a vase. A dirt-mark on a door rubbed at, without success.

She led him into her sitting room.

'Oh, dear, not very tidy, I'm afraid. I wasn't expecting— But then I couldn't have . . .'

Dart at a cushion in the lop-sided basket armchair. A little shake. Cushion in any case too thin to plump out. Swift trip over to the big old mahogany chest of drawers cramming one wall. Flick at a streak of dust on one of its fat lower knobs.

'Do sit down, Inspector. It is Inspector, isn't it, or do I have to say Detective Inspector?'

Without producing an answer to the only half-asked question, he pulled forward the single other chair besides Mrs Horrocks's side-leaning basket affair, a dining chair put out to grass.

Mrs Horrocks, bleating vague apologies, plumped down her wobbly weight. Wafted herself up again immediately.

'But you're just the man.'

She made a swaying rush to the chest of drawers, tugged open one of its top drawers, dived in with both hands, emerged clutching a big green plastic magazines-binder.

'Now, it's this. You can tell me if it's really legal. It doesn't seem somehow right.'

'I'm afraid, madam, I—'

She rushed on.

'No. You see, I saw this advertisement in the paper. The paper I sometimes borrow, you know. And I thought it all sounded so wonderful. And— And I sent away for it. But then— Well, it's really too awful.'

43

He sighed.

'I'm afraid I'm not quite following. What is it that you sent away for?'

'Oh. No. No. Well, you see it's this. *One Thousand Houseplants and How to Love them*. And, you see—'

She stopped and heaved a breath.

'You see, Inspector, Detective Inspector, what I hadn't realized was that you only get ten plants in each issue. And— And I've said I'll subscribe to them all. But I can't possibly afford that. It's going to come to two hundred and fifty pounds. And I'm not really interested in house plants, you see, only . . . Well, it seemed such a bargain.'

Jesus. How some people manage to bugger up their lives. Not a bean to her name, it's plain enough. And she ups and buys something she can't possibly afford, and isn't even really interested in.

'Yes. Well, I suggest you just write to the people and tell them you don't want any further issues. I think you'll find they won't trouble you any more.'

'Oh, will they let me off, really? Oh, isn't that good of you? I mean, I shouldn't have asked really, should I? Not to a whole Inspector, Detective Inspector. I mean, I did think of asking that nice Mr Roanoke for his advice.'

Roanoke. Roanoke, by God.

Pay dirt.

But Mrs Horrocks plopping and burbling on.

'I mean, he knows so much about the world, doesn't he? Furniture and all that. Antiques. The way some old things are so valuable. Thousands and thousands of pounds. And others not. Not at all.'

She darted a glance at her big battered chest of drawers, as if wishing it somehow could have been one of the thousand-pound things. And heaved a great plump sigh.

'But how awful of me. Perhaps you don't know Mr Roanoke. He's—'

'Oh, yes, I know Mr Roanoke. Quite well, as a matter of fact.'

'Oh, you do, do you? I'm so glad. Then you must know how kind he is. How kind he was to poor Miss Gallitly. Coming all the way out here. Only of course he does have that nice big car. Such a cheerful shade of red.'

'Yes, that was kind of him. And he came out frequently, you said? What was that for? To have tea with her?'

'No, no. No, he came to look after her furniture. She brought several very nice pieces with her when she came, you know. And Mr Roanoke said they needed special care. So he would come and give them a good polish.'

'And be rewarded with tea? Did they have it in Miss Gallitly's room?'

'No, I told you. He just came to do the polishing. So tactful, I always thought. He always arrived when lunch was well and truly over, and he never stayed more than an hour.'

So no slipping something into the old dear's teacup while the charm was being laid on. But . . .

'And Miss Gallitly did so look forward to their little chats. That's what she called them. Little chats. You could hear them talking as you went by. I mean, one wasn't eavesdropping, but her door does give on to the big passage, and one has to go up and down, you know. And then Mr Roanoke always was careful to leave the door ajar. The smell of the polish, you know. Verbena. Very nice, but, well, rather strong.'

No hole-and-corner stuff behind closed doors then. So how . . . ?

'I take it residents keep their own things in their own rooms, besides whatever furniture they have. Tea services, things of that sort?'

'Oh, yes, yes. The management always make a point of saying that. In the advertisement, you know. Full privacy. Own furniture and china, if desired.'

Aha.

'So even if Miss Gallitly didn't entertain Mr Roanoke to tea, she would have her own things, sugar basin, milk jug, silver teapot, I dare say. Pretty box for biscuits?'

'Well, yes.'

Mrs Horrocks seemed to have accepted the turn his questions had taken, as he had counted on. But he still had, it seemed, said something that mildly scandalized her.

'But you mustn't think Miss Gallitly's tea service had to be stuffed into some cupboard in her room. Oh, no. We manage better than that. Any resident who has their own private things of that kind has them kept in a specially safe cupboard out in the kitchen.'

Thank you very much. One way and another you're in a fair way to giving Charles Roanoke a bloody hard and fast alibi.

He tried another tack.

'And Miss Gallitly died very suddenly, you said?'

'Did I? Did I? Well, I suppose I must have done . . .'

She swayed up from her creaky old chair and made a dart at the chest of drawers. The runner across its top adjusted by half an inch. And then put back again.

She flumped back into the chair.

'Poor Miss Gallitly. Yes, it was sudden. It seemed very sudden to us. One day she was just as she always was, not absolutely well, you know, but able to get about. And cheerful. She was always cheerful. And then she had that little gastric attack. Well, more nausea really. And, quite suddenly, she seemed to get much worse. And then—'

'Yes?'

'Well, then I'm afraid— Well, convulsions. And next thing she had gone.'

'Very sad. And, I suppose, there wasn't time to get the doctor?'

'Oh, yes, yes. No, the management is very particular about that. I have strict instructions. The least sign of any illness and Dr Matheson is to be called at once.'

'So he saw Miss Gallitly? Quite early on?'

'Yes, yes. As soon as she complained of the— The nausea.'

Still not very helpful. Have to see this Doc Matheson.

'Tell me, Mrs Horrocks, how long ago was it that Miss Gallitly died?'

'Oh, Detective Inspector, it's hardly three months now. It was the first of September, I remember distinctly. You see, I thought somehow she wouldn't live till the new month. But she did. Just. By an hour.'

He had not realized it was as short a time ago. Maggie Adams had mentioned no date.

And then, in a moment, he saw what it had been at that interview with Roanoke that had given him the tiny jar he had felt. It was when he had asked if the three legacies he had admitted to had been all he had had. He had answered that they were. But there had been something very slightly wrong in the way he had replied. An unexpected touch of bravado.

Now it was clear why. Because the fellow had been telling a lie

46

by giving him the merely factual truth, and had not quite been able to suppress the pleasure he was feeling over the trick. At the time of that interview he had not actually benefited from Miss Gallitly's death. Her will could hardly have been proved so early. So what he had said had been the truth. But not the full truth. He had been about to benefit, as he would very well have known. Because he had murdered Miss Gallitly for her money only three weeks, or to be exact twenty-two days, earlier.

7

Looking back on what Mrs Horrocks had said as he drove away from the Old School, Sylvester felt the urgency of the hunt fast running in him. He had caught out Roanoke over saying at their interview that he had received only three legacies. But there was something more. Something yet more significant had come to light.

It had not been apparent to him while he had been coping with Mrs Horrocks's attempts to make clear her thoughts, such as they were. But, as soon as he had begun to go over in his mind the various things she had succeeded in telling him, he had seen it. The fact of the matter was that all the circumstances which had, it seemed, contributed piece by piece to an alibi for Roanoke ought to be seen in a different light. The very opposite light.

Roanoke – he felt surer and surer of this the more he thought of it – as soon as he had fixed on Miss Gallitly as another victim had taken every precaution not to do anything that might look suspicious. It had all been there. He had deliberately not come to visit at lunch or at tea-time, when in theory at least he would have had the opportunity to administer poison. He had stayed with her, too, for the shortest reasonable time. And, perhaps more of a give-away than anything, he had always made a point of leaving the door of her room open, on the pretext of the furniture polish he used being highly scented.

Yes, now his case against the man had some substance to it.

All right, he was far away from having proof. Certainly nothing he could see the Crown Prosecution boyos being happy about. He had hardly enough to go with to DCS Sugden. But that, surely, could be remedied. There was more to be learnt about Miss Gallitly and her relations with Roanoke.

For one thing he needed to know all about her will. When had she changed it in Roanoke's favour? Because no doubt she must have done. Roanoke had admitted that three other old ladies had done that. All but boasted of it.

And how much had she left him?

The facts could be easily enough obtained at the Wills Office in London, if at the cost of some hours of grubbing work. Then the doctor who had been with Miss Gallitly in her final illness must be talked to, even though like Dr Hardew at Astwood Manor he must have signed a death certificate. Finally, it might be worth attempting to find out, from other residents at the Old School, what if anything Miss Gallitly had said about a bequest to Roanoke. Whatever could be brought to light on those lines might be useful when it came to preparing evidence for the trial.

And, by God, that trial, sooner or later, would come.

He had to wait until he next had a free day to make his investigations at the Wills Office. To be given official time for that would mean going to Sugden with what he had at present. And that, for all that it said plainly to him that Roanoke had made away with Miss Gallitly, was by no means factual. Suggers would not authorize any expenditure until faced with no alternative.

All he managed in the mean time was to go out one evening to see Miss Gallitly's Dr Matheson. He found him to be every bit as conscientious as Dr Hardew, if without the latter's penchant for equipping himself with all the latest in medical electronics. And, not much to his surprise, like Dr Hardew he had had no doubts at all about the death of such an elderly and infirm patient.

So when, the following Wednesday, his free day was about to come he decided to make sure he would not find it cancelled, unless suddenly a raid on the banknote forgers came up. Casually he told Mikey Cross, a crony of Sugden's despite their difference in rank, that he wanted to go to London to get a new suit. It was, he calculated, the sort of expedition acquisitive Mikey would see as not to be given up without a fight. And Suggers was not one to involve himself in a battle he could avoid.

'We going to see the last of that leather jacket of yours then?' He had smiled.

'Can't make any promises, Mikey. But, yeah, I think the time's come to lash out a bit.'

'Some pretty impressive bird to pull. Can't be anything else.'

'Well, no harm in having a really good suit ready and waiting.'

'This can't be the Bill Sylvester I know.'

In London he had better luck than he had expected. And worse. Frances Mary Gallitly, of the Old School Residential Home, Oxleigh, South Mercia, he discovered within an hour of entering the Wills Office, had by her testament dated only seven weeks before her death left the sum of ten thousand pounds 'to my dear brother, Gresham Gallitly, of Flat 14, Flamborough Court, Portland Street, London W1, and of Gallitly House, Whitecross Street, in the City of London, and the sum of five hundred pounds to Mrs Elsie Horrocks, of the Old School Residential Home, for each year that I shall have resided at the said Home, in gratitude for her faithful and kind offices' – so maybe she'll get to love her thousand houseplants yet – and 'the residue absolutely to my most dear friend, Charles Maurice Roanoke, of the Farm House, Willmingham, in the county of South Mercia, in recognition of his very great kindness.'

Good luck in the swiftness with which he had located this document. Bad luck in the terms in which Frances Mary Gallitly had had it drawn up. Because there was no indication of just what sum that residue might amount to. No doubt, though, Charles Maurice Roanoke had gained a pretty good idea before he had made sure Miss Gallitly could not change her old lady's mind. He would not have risked his crime otherwise, nor taken the precautions he had.

But the rest of the day lay in front of him. In London where, in the City, stood Gallitly House.

Pausing on the pavement outside the place before going in, he thought that 'stood' was a pretty good word for Gallitly House. It was a huge new tower with the air – no doubt intentional – of being planted immovably just where it was, of owning its freehold down to the very centre of the earth. Its façade of greeny glass rose up and up, floor after floor, po-faced, stating prestige, stating money.

He went in.

To discover that all those floors were not necessary for Gresham Gallitly, take-over monarch, to conduct his operations. All but the top of the tower, in fact, was leased to other businesses, ones that needed executives by the dozen senior and junior, as well as computer operators, secretaries, even cleaning women.

Gresham Gallitly seemed to need little more than the very top floor, most of which was taken up by an enormous foyer. There at a huge desk, bare all but for a single unobtrusive white telephone, sat a receptionist – long nails immaculately red-polished – looking distantly at two deep soft-leather sofas and a single low table with on it a display of flowers no less huge than the rest of the room.

He gave her his name and rank and said he wanted to see Mr Gallitly 'on a personal matter'.

He was sent to sit on one of the sofas, his choice. Both so far from the receptionist's desk that her murmur into her telephone was altogether inaudible.

Long wait.

Purr of phone.

'Mr Gallitly is engaged all today. But if you could let him know the nature of your business . . . ?'

He heaved himself out of his sofa's softness, went across to the desk, pulled his wallet from his back pocket, flipped out a card from the wad of papers inside it, took a silvery ballpoint from beside the telephone and wrote on the back. *In connection with the death of your late sister.*

The receptionist took the card and went through an inner door – tight sheath of a black dress, thoroughbred haunches, hair styled to freezing point – and was away for less than two minutes.

'Mr Gallitly says that if you can wait till he is due to go to lunch he should be able to talk in the car.'

'When will that be, then?'

'Mr Gallitly leaves for lunch today at twelve forty.'

He looked at his watch.

'OK. I'll come back then. Wait for him down below, shall I?'

'Mr Gallitly leaves by his private entrance at the side of the building.'

'I'll be there.'

But, as he turned to go, there came a sharp little rebuke.

'Inspector, I believe you've dropped a piece of paper.'

He looked back.

Damn it, something must have fluttered from his wallet when he had pulled out his card.

He stooped, conscious of the receptionist's steady stare, and picked it up. Spanish lottery ticket. Why on earth had he kept that?

He looked for a waste-paper basket. The huge room did not seem to run to such an object. He stuffed the slip away.

He ought, he thought as the steel-sided lift dropped him down to ground level, to have endured the receptionist's distant stare for the hour or so he would have had to wait. As it was, he would have to kill time wandering about the City. Damned if he was going to sit somewhere and drink an unwanted cup of coffee, unwanted and no doubt ridiculously expensive. He had spent too many hours in cafés as a detective constable on obbo to have any relish for that.

Passing the window of an outfitter's shop he saw a sports jacket with a £225 label on it with some trousers a snip at £99. So that was what his imaginary new good suit would cost. That or more. Well, sod it. Never mind what Mikey Cross says, the old leather jacket's still in good enough nick.

It occurred to him then that if he could find a public library it might do no harm to find out what he could about take-overs expert Gresham Gallitly before he met him. Almost all he knew of the man was seeing his name in occasional headlines.

He began glancing down side-turnings as he walked.

But he was out of luck, or almost so. He did find a library – it was just down a turning from the corner where a garish temporary shop was selling out-of-fashion clothing, *Italian Trousers £10 and £25* – but he had so little time left by then that all he could do was to get hold of the business section of the week before's *Sunday Times* and read the one piece they had on Gallitly. A quick skim that added little to what he vaguely knew.

> . . . the hot breath of the predator . . . a profit on the 24 hours of dealing of around £4m . . . asset-stripper . . . a powerful and seldom predictable force . . . the mere sound of his name sent the shares sharply up . . . aggressively parsimonious . . .

Aggressively parsimonious. So I've something in common with the great man, then. If Suggers's opinion of me is worth anything.

He got back to the side entrance to Gallitly House with not much more than a minute to spare. The take-over giant's car was there waiting. Stretch limo. On a double yellow line. Chauffeur in grey uniform doing the impassive at the wheel.

The unobtrusive side door of the building was opened. For a moment a blue-uniformed commissionaire held it wide. Then Gresham Gallitly stepped out. Sylvester had little time to observe him. Tall, lean, bare-headed, narrow lightly tanned face unmovingly set. Short top-coat in a beige colour that had probably cost as much as one of his junior staff's monthly salary. Trousers, of a dark blue suit with a narrow white stripe, visible below.

Sylvester took a step forward.

Gresham Gallitly glanced towards him.

'Inspector Sylvester?'

'Yes, sir. Good morning. It's good of you to find time to see me.'

'Yes. Step in, Inspector. We should be on our way.'

He slid into the back of the great long car. Strong waft of leathery smell from the wide pale grey seat. Infinite amount of room for the legs. Chauffeur distant behind the thick glass partition. Discreet telephone hanging just below.

Gresham Gallitly had hardly settled himself when the car rolled, almost silently, forward.

'Well, Inspector, there's some difficulty over my sister's will?'

'I must ask you not to pass on what I have to say to anyone else, sir.'

He had been going to continue, but somehow Gresham Gallitly took the exchange back to himself.

'I am hardly likely to do that, Inspector.'

Put in my place.

'No, sir. But I am bound to give that warning. The fact is that my Chief Constable received a communication recently making certain allegations we are bound to look into. And your late sister's name has arisen during the enquiries.'

'Very well. What can I tell you? I really had very few dealings with my sister, you know. She was considerably older than myself.'

He turned his carved-wood face towards Sylvester, and a twitch of a smile appeared on it.

'I was in fact twenty years her junior,' he said. 'I am what they call the runt of the litter.'

He turned back.

Well, well. *The predator . . . the mere sound of his name . . . the asset-stripper*. Things fall into place. What this fellow always wanted, despite this bloody great car and that bloody great office and the fancy top-coat, was not money but power. The money used to attain power. And power he had got.

But on with the job, Sylvester.

'You are aware, sir, I take it, that your sister left the bulk of her fortune to a certain Mr Charles Roanoke?'

Another frosted twitch of a smile on the oak-carved face. But this time no turning of the head.

'There, Inspector, you are under a misapprehension. My poor sister in fact left the bulk of her fortune, as you put it, to myself. Quite unnecessarily, I may add. You see, she never had any idea of the state of her finances. One perhaps should not have expected her to have done. But the fact of the matter, as I understand it from her solicitor, is that her estate will hardly cover half the sum she believed herself to be leaving to me. There will be no residue.'

For an instant, as his thoughts swung and circled at this revelation, he wondered how amid the whirling reversal poor Mrs Horrocks's love for a thousand houseplants would survive. But no question of asking the statue by his side anything about that.

And in any case the statue evidently had been thinking as rapidly as himself.

'Inspector, am I to gather from what you have said that it is believed my sister was murdered?'

Blunt enough.

'I am afraid, sir, that in the present state of our enquiries I am unable to answer that.'

For a moment then it looked as if the accumulated power was about to be used to demand the answer.

He braced himself for battle.

But the moment passed.

'Yes, I see your difficulty, Inspector.'

Half a minute more for thought.

'However, let me say this. Since it is clear that no one will in fact benefit from my sister's death, I would be happier if my name did not arise in any investigations you pursue. I hope we understand each other?'

That could be answered only in silence.

Oh, yes, I understand you all right. But if it should happen that the best or only charge we can pin on Mr Charles Roanoke is the murder of your namesake, Mr Gallitly, then, money-powered as you are, you're going to find out there are some things no one can make a take-over bid for. And one of them, thank God, is the South Mercia Police.

8

Time to show Suggers a bit of backbone, Sylvester decided next morning, kicking the door of his cramped little office shut behind him. Damn it, if as had been hinted to him he was barred from further promotion on account of 'arrogance' – or, not taking superiors' words for gospel – then he might as well take advantage.

And give Suggers something to think about.

He hauled up his typewriter and then fished out several sheets of fresh carbon-paper. First, get all he had learnt down in order. Next, by mistake on purpose, give Suggers the carbon copy looking almost, but not quite, as fresh as top sheets. Suggers after all was a detective, however much of a creeper too. He wouldn't miss the fact that there was more than one copy of the report in existence.

So end of dodging, Detective Chief Superintendent, sir.

It was before he had got to the end of the first page of his typing that he made his discovery. And sat for a moment glaring at the machine in front of him and cursing himself for not, days and days ago, seeing what he just had.

He had been about to list the names of the first three old ladies who had left Roanoke legacies, two very large, one small, and was intending to put them in the order in which the deaths had occurred. But then he had realized he was simultaneously holding in his mind two different chronologies. He checked his notebook. Yes, Roanoke in that interview in the grey light of his huge garage had said he had first received £60,000 from Mrs Bathurst, then some £3,000 from a Mrs Forth and finally the fat sum of a quarter of a million from Miss Pettiman. But Dr Hardew, tapping out on his computer – he riffled forward to the page in his notebook where he had made what he had thought of as mere jottings – had stated clearly that Mrs Forth had died 'this year'.

So this – it had been obscurely bothering him – was why Roanoke had needed to set to work on Gresham Gallitly's apparently rich sister so soon, it seemed, after acquiring a new quarter of a million. That third legacy had been the unexpectedly small sum of only £3,000. And Roanoke at their interview, conscious of just having added Miss Gallitly to his tally of victims, had tried to disguise that need of his for more money by switching the order of the bequests.

At once his anger with himself at having fallen for the trick evaporated.

Bloody Charles Roanoke had been, hadn't he, just a little too clever. He ought to have known that sooner or later this piece of misdirection would be revealed for what it was. And then the question would be asked: why had he told his lie? Answer: because he had committed a murder. And three others before it.

So on with the typing. With a yet stronger case to put in front of Detective Chief Superintendent Sugden's squirmy eyes.

Something more, too.

Roanoke had now for a second time miscalculated his prospects from a seemingly wealthy old lady. Mrs Forth not so long ago had palmed him off with the proceeds of a piece of good furniture. Miss Gallitly, in all good faith, in her will still to be proven had left him precisely nothing. Would he soon be looking for yet another victim? Was he so cocky that he would try his trick a fifth time?

Detective Chief Superintendent Sugden did not think so. He thought, or affected to think, precious little of the whole of Sylvester's chain of logic.

'Thin, Inspector. Thin as poor man's piss. Not one solid fact to bring in as evidence. Not a document. Not a fingerprint. Not even a single sworn statement. And, above all, not the least bloody indication of how Mr Roanoke can have poisoned even one of his supposed victims.'

'He's clever, sir, I'm not denying that.'

'Yes, so clever he can poison four people one after the other when they're all under constant medical supervision, and no one a whit the wiser. You're going to have to do a hell of a lot of work, Sylvester, before you convince me he's a wrong 'un. Let alone a jury.'

Sylvester thrust a foot in the tiny door-gap he saw.

'But you agree, sir, that more work ought to be done?'

Sugden's jowly pink face on the far side of the big desk took on an expression of double lugubriousness.

'I know there's nothing to put before a jury yet, sir,' Sylvester added quickly. 'But you can't deny that Roanoke's been lying. Lying through his teeth. And there can only be one reason for that.'

'No, there can't, Inspector. Mr Roanoke may have a dozen good reasons for not telling the exact truth.'

'Yes, sir. But shouldn't we probe those reasons? Find out what precisely they are?'

Find out they don't exist. Sir. Sir. Sir.

A heavy sigh floated over the well-cleared surface of the desk.

'All right, Sylvester. But be warned. If you land me with a perfectly innocent respectable citizen complaining of police harassment, you'll find yourself looking at every offence from top to bottom in Police (Discipline) Regulations.'

'Yes, sir.'

But he had got what he had wanted. And in the next few days he made all the use he could of the time he had manoeuvred Sugden into granting him, perhaps all the more easily for the hunt for the counterfeiters having apparently shifted to Birmingham. He read up as much as he could on poisons. Suggers had put an unerring fat finger on the weakness of his case there. Unless eventually he could show what poison it was that had ended the lives of those four old ladies, and how it had been given to them, he would hardly see Roanoke in the dock.

Because, despite Sugden's objections, his belief in Roanoke's guilt had not been lessened in the smallest degree. Suggers, faced ultimately with all the Press hoo-hah and relatives' objections that inevitably arose when there was any possibility of an exhumation, was naturally determined to see Roanoke as someone pure as a new-washed lamb. But that Roanoke was not. He was not.

Yet no amount of research in Taylor and in Glaister did any good. There were poisons, too many of them, that produced convulsions and nausea, much as Nurse Dexter and Mrs Horrocks at the Old School had described. But none of them, it seemed, could be administered other than directly. Nor could they be used without it being evident to any trained medical eye that they had been. But nevertheless this was what must have happened four times in succession if his suspicions of Charles Roanoke were correct.

More actively, he needed to find out who Roanoke might now have in his sights. Get some firm indication of that, and Suggers would damn well have to allocate as many bods as necessary to keep the fellow under the closest observation. And then . . .

Yet, even in the business of tracing Roanoke's immediate activities, difficulties loomed. At all costs he must not be alerted. He had, after all, recently bought a £30,000 boat. A sudden dash across the Channel or over to Ireland, and he might well evade arrest for ever.

So no question of keeping an eye on the man himself, much as he would like to. He couldn't guarantee to do it without being seen, sooner or later. There were plenty of coppers in the CID room capable of following a suspect, of course. But none of them really to be trusted to persevere in noting every little detail. They would tail Roanoke all right, put down in their notebooks where he went, how long he stayed there, whom he had met if only by description. Each entry would be meticulously timed. No skin off any bugger's nose looking at their watch. But they would not have the determination finally to pin the man down, to seize on every little thing about him and at last fasten him to the ground like giant Gulliver pinioned by a thousand Lilliputian ropes.

Eventually he fixed on using little pale-faced Maggie Adams, just made up to full Woman Detective Constable. To her, with some reluctance, he confided most of his suspicions. The fewer people who knew that Roanoke was in all probability a four-times murderer the better. Nowhere like a CID room for gossip. And gossip apt to leak.

'What I want you to do is get out to that house of his in a motor. Different one each day, if you can. I want to know where he goes, who he sees if you can get near enough without letting him catch on. Anything and everything you can pick up. Take a couple of different headscarves, couple of different jackets. All right?'

She looked at him – there were a pair of sharply red spots on her left cheek just beside the nose – with a touch of irritation.

'I was already doing that sort of thing when I was a kid of twelve. Sir.'

He hovered for a moment between ferocity and acknowledgement. Finally settled.

'All right, put me in my place.' Pause. 'But not too often, yes?'

'Very good, sir.'

'And keep me in touch. All the time. Right?'

'Yes, guv.'

So the first occasion when she radioed in to say Suspect had left home driving a red Bentley, number CMR 1, he got out to the big mock farmhouse himself as fast as he could. No search warrant, of course. But a fellow could call, couldn't he? And would have to look about if there was no answer when he rang at the bell. Might even peer into that big garage. Or look in at a back window just in case his ring at the bell hadn't been heard. Bells did fail to work sometimes. And if he found a door open and the premises apparently deserted, it would be his duty as a police officer . . .

But he was unlucky.

A perfunctory tug at the black iron bell-pull beside the wide oak front door. No point in making too much noise. But from inside there came a prolonged clanging. Then, worse, the big door swung back.

A girl was standing there, still clutching the inner handle. In her twenties. Lush figure clingingly covered in a white towelling robe. Plenty of make-up. Full head of goldeny hair, wet at the ends. Feet bare, and wet footprints on the wide polished floorboards behind her.

'Ooh-er,' she said. ''Scuse me. Was just coming from the pool.'

Sylvester sighed inwardly. He had hoped for no one, but a tart like this he could well do without.

However . . . Might be some mileage to be had.

'Mr Roanoke?' he asked. 'Is he by any chance at home?'

'Ooh, no. He had to go out. To a sale, he said. Be gone all day. I've been having a swim.'

'So I see.'

'Yes, Charlie took me out to dinner last night, and— And, well, you know how it is.'

'Yes. You don't happen to know where this sale is that he's gone to?'

If little Maggie lost him, be as well to have some back-up.

'No. No, 'fraid I don't.'

'He didn't happen to say if he was calling anywhere on his way to this sale, did he? Or on the way back?'

'No. No, he never said anything about that. We didn't, as they say, exchange many words this morning. You know how it is.'

'Yes.'

'Yes. Well, as a matter of fact we only met for the first time yesterday, so we didn't have much to chat about. If you get my meaning.'

She gave him a full-out smile, leant towards him.

'I'm with the Lloyd Webber at the Alhambra, actually. You seen it?'

'No. No, I don't get much time for that sort of thing.'

'Oh. Well, pity. Can't tell you anything more about Charlie, though. Sorry and all that.'

She had continued to look at him with unconcealed appraisal.

'I say, you wouldn't like to come in for a swim, would you? Have to be in the noddy, actually. Charlie doesn't seem to go in for swimsuits. But, if you don't mind, I'm sure I don't.'

'No. I must be getting back, thanks all the same.'

Then, turning away, he made one last attempt to rescue something from the ruins.

'Oh, yes. Charlie was telling me he was having trouble over his new pool. That all safely dealt with?'

'Well, it was OK just now. Though the people have left their board there. So I s'pose they may be coming back to do something more. You sure you won't come in?'

'No. Really I just called by on the off chance.'

A thought.

'But tell me the name of that firm doing the pool. Thinking of having one put in myself.'

In my grotty flat.

'Yeah, that's easy. Rice and Co. Like in Andrew and Tim. Get it?'

'Yes. I get it. Well, goodbye. And thank you.'

'You quite sure . . .'

He turned quickly away and strode towards the wide white farm gate.

*

A few cunning questions at Rice and Co. half an hour later. From which it became plain Charles Roanoke had not paid his bill. Little enough to add to his file. Yet a comfort to have it confirmed the man, for all those outward signs of affluence, was strapped for cash. Hungry for a new victim.

For the next three days, however, there were no signs Roanoke was doing anything about acquiring a new source of wealth. He left his house only twice. On the Sunday he stayed put, in the company of Miss Susie Frank, from the Alhambra Theatre, according to Maggie Adams. She had followed him without trouble on his first two expeditions, but each had been simply to furniture sales.

Maggie – good girl – had contrived to learn that on both occasions he had purchased little, much less she gathered than was customary with him. He had sold a good many items, too. At lower reserves than he usually did. Another couple of useful indicators. If nothing really advancing things.

But on the fourth day, Monday, late in the afternoon, Maggie brought home the bacon. Or what well might be that.

Roanoke was visiting, she reported over her radio, one Sir Julian Deane, long ago a spymaster, a high-up in MI5, a widower, childless, wealthy, in his nineties, not in the best of health. Facts gathered after presenting herself as a market survey researcher to the lady at a more modest house than Sir Julian's on the other side of the road. And, Maggie added, excitement purling through her voice, 'there's a For Sale board up at his place'.

Got to be the one, Sylvester crowed to himself. Got to be.

He very nearly asked to see the Sugden there and then. But caution prevailed. Better put it all in writing. No need for any fancy work with by-mistake carbon copies this time, though. Alerting pig-sharp Suggers once was enough. But make the report as comprehensive as could be.

He typed away until it was nearly knocking-off time. Then, before leaving, made sure one of the cadets handed Suggers the report personally.

Jude, he thought as he flopped into the car. Think I'm entitled to a little relaxation.

At half-past two in the morning his phone rang. Blearily reaching across for it, he thought with a jet of bitterness that it was bound to be the counterfeiting apparatus inexplicably located somewhere in South Mercia. Dawn raid. On duty straight away.

And a god-given opportunity for Suggers to postpone action on Roanoke.

'Sylvester,' he grunted.

'Mr William Sylvester?'

What the hell.

'Yes? That's me.'

'*Daily Post* here, Mr Sylvester. I've got some good news for you. Very good news.'

'Uh?'

'Mr Sylvester, I'm happy to tell you you've won El Gordo.'

'Look, who are you? What is this?'

'El Gordo, Mr Sylvester. The big one, in Spanish talk. Their lottery. The big, big prize. You've won it.'

'But I—'

Then it came back to him. The ticket what's-her-name, that girl, long legs, had made him buy just as he was leaving Malaga. And he'd seen the damn thing with all the numbers on it – he'd gone overboard for both of them with the last of his pesetas – somewhere recently. Christ, at Gallitly House. Dropped it on their precious carpet. Probably still in the pocket he'd pushed it into.

The man from the *Daily Post* was yammering on. He paid some attention.

'. . . we make it out to be all of that. Close on one million pounds, Mr Sylvester. A cool million. Well, what do you think of your good fortune?'

He put the phone down.

9

The *Daily Post* call was not the only one Sylvester received that night. After the third he pulled out the telephone plug. And to hell with the Factory if that counterfeiting outfit turned out to be on their patch.

For a moment as he dropped back into bed he did say to himself 'I've won a million quid', but he refused to allow the thought to occupy his mind. He needed his sleep. He'd had an exhausting day, not made less so by his session with Jude to which generously she had added freebie extra time. And tomorrow when Suggers had OKed an obbo team for Roanoke he'd have more than enough on his plate.

He succeeded in getting off again almost at once.

In the morning he woke a few minutes later than usual. Blinking into focus the green figures of his bedside clock, he cursed, heaved back the duvet, staggered up, thinking only that if he didn't get his skates on he'd keep whoever he was due to relieve from the early shift out of his bed. It was only as he scraped his razor rapidly over his chin that the two or three a.m. phone calls came back into his mind.

Had they happened? Yes. Must have done. He'd been wide awake for a bit. So he'd won— Was it really damn near a million quid? What the hell was he to do about it?

Anyhow, no time to think of that now. DI Smithers – yes, he was on early turn – deserved not to be made to hang about. Always a bastard that shift.

In the car – vile rainy morning – he did briefly think some more. What was he going to do with all that money? Oh, all right, one or two things he'd vaguely thought he'd needed. New leather jacket. Mikey had actually been right enough there. And the flat? Would he have to get somewhere posher? But for all that, lying to that bint at Roanoke's about wanting an indoor pool, he'd said to himself his pad was grotty, it wasn't all that bad. It suited him. Was all he wanted.

Stream of thought interrupted by stupid driver in a Volvo cutting across him.

And then he was at the Factory. Sprint up the side stairs to the CID room. Flicked glanced at his watch. Two minutes in hand. More.

He banged the door open.

'Happy fortune to you, happy fortune to you, happy fortune, dear Millionaire, happy fortune to you.'

The boys were all there singing, standing in a big bunch, plus assorted wooden tops and clericals, wide grins all over their faces. And, damn it, there on the first of the desks were bottles of champagne. At this time of day.

How had they got to know? Of course, early morning TV and radio. If the papers had had wind of the business at two thirty there'd have been plenty of time for the news – suppose it is news, of a sort, Brit wins big Spanish prize – to get on the morning programmes.

He braced himself.

Have to do the right thing. Produce the big smiles. Swallow some champers. On an empty stomach. God knows how long till he could get to the canteen for a coffee and a bun. And he'd have to lay on a big party himself. This evening probably. They'd expect it. Well, at least no trouble about paying for it. Not if he was a millionaire.

And suppose he really was. Or all but.

He went through the motions. Look of dazed happiness. Hands shaken. Girls kissed. Back presented for slapping. Sloshing down a gulp of the champagne. Bending the ear to whoever had anything, however inane, to say.

Old Emlyn Evans, the Desk Sergeant, always implacably solemn, and still so now.

'I've been working it out – if what they said on Radio Four was right – about how much you've got. If you invest it at the current best rate, you'll be getting a nice bit more per annum than a Chief Constable. Not bad, boyo. Not bad. Be able to look the Old Man in the face, won't you?'

'Look him in the face?' Mikey Cross barged in. 'You'll be

65

having him looking up your backside now, eh, guv? Off on your toes before anyone can say *Archbold on Criminal Pleading*.'

The idea had not for an instant occurred to him. To resign. Leave the force. Suppose he had got enough to live on, and live well, if what old Emlyn Evans had calculated was right. But . . .

But what would he do?

'No, Mikey. Don't see why I need make a change.'

The look of appalled astonishment on grabber Mikey's face would have made him laugh aloud. Only he was too bemused by the prospect Mikey's casual phrase had opened before him. Unthought of till now. The series of prospects. Each leading God knows where.

Now Mikey, recovering a little, was bellowing for 'a bit of hush'.

He got it.

'Lads, lads. Know what? Listen, our millionaire's got no intention of hiking it to the old South of France. No, far as he's concerned there's no place like home. CID South Mercia Police.'

Incredulity all round.

'Go on, not really?'

'You mean it, guv?'

'Staying? Staying on the job?'

'Come off it.'

'Hey, you having us on?'

He hardly knew how to answer.

In the end he merely muttered 'Well, can't see any reason not to carry on.' Then he did manage to break away, heading not for the canteen where he realized he would face the whole barrage of questions again, but running head-down through the steady sullen rain to the café round the corner. That at least was likely to be free of police presence at this time of the morning.

He ordered, not a bun but breakfast. All there was. Egg, sausage, bacon, beans, fried bread. But when it was put in front of him he found he didn't want it. He could manage only a cup of tea. But that was good and hot, forcing him to sit long enough over it to start thinking again.

Damn it, he did not want to leave the force. It would be ridiculous. He had spent his whole working life as a copper. Bobbying was what he was there for, never mind about others. They might have joined for a life with a bit of excitement, or for the respectability of the uniform, or for the money and the pension, or even for the chance to exercise a bit of authority. He had joined to stop criminals. Leaving would make a mockery of that moment of decision when, just at the end of his time at college, he had heard Dad had suddenly died after all those years with guts ripped apart by that shot from the gunman he had been trying to arrest. Chucking it in would devalue every moment of his time in the police since.

But could he stay on? With all that much money?

For one intense instant he wished to God he had never listened to that silly cow Pepita and bought her and himself those tickets. Why had this happened to him? Wasn't he perfectly all right as he was?

Could he somehow get rid of it all? Of course, he couldn't. Even if he wrote out a cheque to some charity for the exact amount of the cheque he would receive himself, the fact of his having got the money would not go away. Christ, doing that would bring down on him even more astonished ridicule than blurting out just now that he would stay on in the force.

All right, so what's a bit of ridicule? A hell of a lot, when you come to think of it. Imagine going through the rest of his career with people pointing him out and saying: 'That's the gink who gave away a million quid he'd just won.' No one would trust him any longer. Not till the very day of his retirement. He'd be branded as some sort of idiot.

But, though some ridicule might go on for a while if he did stay in the force, it wouldn't be such a totally prattish thing to do that people would remember it for ever. In time, if he kept his head down, didn't flash the lolly about, they'd even forget he'd ever had it. With luck.

He heaved himself to his feet. Time to go back and face the music. And ask to see Detective Chief Superintendent Sugden, by God. There was a four-times killer to be got behind bars.

He met Sugden sooner than he had expected. Returning to the Factory by the front entrance – rain now sloshing down – he came face to face with him ponderously descending the main stairway.

'Hah, Bill. What's this I hear then? Won yourself a million on some wop lottery?'

'Seems like it, sir.'

Suggers produced a wide grin – teeth yellowed from the pipe he was seldom without – and with elaborate sadness wagged his head from side to side.

'So it's goodbye, is it? Sunny Spain or wherever. Must say I envy you. Day like this. Let me know how soon you want to go. Paperwork and all that.'

'Oh, I don't think I'll be leaving you, sir. Not when there are villains wanting catching.'

Suggers' eyes, big square reading glasses tucked into top pocket, blinked and blinked.

'Well, I suppose it's your decision, Inspector. But I can tell you, if I were in your shoes . . .'

Oh, yes. Here's one who'd be quick enough to put the feet up.

'Well, yes, sir. But I have given it some thought. As much as I've had time for. And I can't see myself throwing in the towel just because I could take it easy if I wanted.'

But now Suggers had been thinking. Slight frown lines across the wide pink forehead.

'So you're staying on, eh? Meaning to carry on just as before?'

'Yes, sir, that's about the size of it.'

'Well then, Inspector, there's something I'd better tell you.'

'Sir?'

'Yes. I've been in touch with Mr Eames at the Crown Prosecution Service, about that business of yours. The Roanoke case. And he's of the opinion, which I may say I entirely agree with, that any further enquiries would not be in the public interest.'

Sylvester felt it like a blow in the face, a totally unexpected blow.

'But— But, sir, the evidence . . .'

'There isn't any, Inspector. Just a few circumstantial bits, all of them easily enough explained. No, you had a bee in your bonnet, and you let it run away with you. That's about the size of it.'

Run away with by a bee. Christ.

'But, sir, did you read the report I sent you—'

He stopped in his tracks. Had that been actually only last evening?

'The report you had last night, sir?'

'Yes, Inspector.' Suggers blew out a hefty sigh. 'I looked at it. Of course I looked at it. But it doesn't add anything. Nothing of substance at all. It doesn't alter the situation one jot.'

He stood, two shallow steps above Sylvester on the wide stairs, looking down at him.

'I tell you what, Bill,' he said. 'Take a few days' leave. I'm sure you're owed it. Give you time to sort yourself out. About this windfall of yours, and everything else. What's it today? Tuesday. Well, why don't you take the rest of the week? Come and see me next Monday morning?'

'No, sir.'

'No? But I think you ought to have a break, Inspector. In fact, that's an order.'

'No.'

Sylvester fumbled in his pocket.

'I'm not taking any more orders, from you or anyone else. Here's my warrant card. I'm resigning. You can have my letter just as soon as I can get to a piece of paper.'

10

A flash of searing light stopped Sylvester short as, shaking the raindrops from his shoulders, he took the stairs up to his flat two at a time. A bloody Press photographer. The fellow had been lurking in the gloom just up from the landing.

The assault chased out of his head the turmoil of thoughts that had swirled in his head as he had driven home, plastic shopping-bag of personal effects removed from his desk by his side. Why the hell had he got to be subjected to this? Wasn't what had happened to him because of that bloody lottery ticket strictly his own affair?

'Get out,' he growled at the fellow, as his camera was raised for a second shot.

He turned away, managed to hoick his latch-key from his pocket while still clutching the awkward bag bulging with clutter, got the flat door open, barged through and back-heeled the door shut with a gratifying slam.

Safe inside, he let the bag fall to the floor, blundered over to his chair, slumped down, and put his head between his hands.

What had he done?

Stupid idiot. In a moment of rage hadn't he chucked in the whole of his life? Just when he had decided that this was something he could never do. But then . . . Then had he really had any alternative? For years he had battled against the attitude of Suggers and his like. And, faced suddenly there on the Factory stairs with that attitude at its worst, at just the moment when he had the possibility at last of being able to tell those eye-on-the-main-chance high-ups just what harm they were doing day after day to the service, what else could he have done?

Well, he had perhaps managed to tell them forcefully enough in his scrawled letter of resignation that police work was not just a matter of routine, of getting through the problems. Or past them, often enough. Something that over the years he had felt building up and building up inside him.

Because routine was not how he had ever seen it. Not from the first day he joined the service till that very morning. No, there were criminals going about the streets, preying on decent people. Killing them even sometimes. The way they had killed his father, never mind the years between that gunman's blasting shot and the day that had brought his life to an end. And they had to be stopped.

But what had he done now?

He lifted up his head and all but howled aloud.

He had just prevented himself ever again doing what he had believed in as the purpose of his life.

Could he take back his resignation? Say that letter had been written in a moment of anger? Hardly. What he had said in it had been altogether too frank. Someone like Suggers was not going happily to accept him after that. And, besides, he did not want to go back. He had had enough of working dragged backwards day after day by inertia and bureaucracy. Now at least he was free.

Free to do what, though?

Round and round went the thoughts as he sat there, huddled in misery. Till at last he became aware that his doorbell was ringing. Had been ringing for some time.

He staggered to his feet, more in response to habit than for any real reason. There was a woman at the door. Thirties. Good looking. Well made-up. Smart beige mac, wet across the shoulders. Big leather handbag, good quality.

'Yes?'

'Molly Mendip, *Daily Post*. I've come down from London to talk about your wonderful piece of luck. I believe one of our reporters was the first to tell you.'

He looked at her. Distantly apprehended. Something on a TV screen. A wild-life programme. Remote from anything to do with the everyday. An exotic parakeet. A hoopoe.

'Mr Sylvester?' she queried sharply. 'You are William Sylvester, the man who's just won El Gordo?'

He shook the bewilderment out of his head.

'No, look, I don't want any of this. I've got troubles enough of my own.'

71

'Troubles? What troubles, at a time like this? You're rich, Mr Sylvester. Rich.'

She had been quick to pounce.

And he, battered by what he had done at some earlier time of the morning – How long ago? What time was it? – was slow to take avoiding action.

'I dare say I am rich. But don't you go thinking that puts an end to the problems.'

'No? Come on, there can't be much that money won't put right. Think what you've got. A cool million. Enough to move straight into any house you like anywhere. Enough to go off tomorrow, today even, to anywhere in the world that takes your fancy. Even enough to leave your wife behind, if you've got a wife, Mr Sylvester, one you're tired of, and go waltzing off with the sexiest piece you can find.'

He looked at her again. Coming into focus now, for what she was. Journalist. Story hunter. Anything for a good quote.

'Are you damn well mad? What the hell are you going on about?'

'About your new life, Mr Sylvester. Your new life full of every possibility. Just tell me what, at this very moment, you most want to do.'

But now evading action had fully re-entered his mind.

'What at this moment I most want to do? Kick you downstairs, you stupid bitch. You and your goddamn newspaper.'

One step backwards. Door crashed to.

He stood there, still glaring, confronting the back of the door. Could do with a lick of paint. Been thinking that for years. Suppose all I need do now is call in the decorators. Never mind their bill. Money no object.

So what do I want to do with this no-object money? When I've actually got it.

God knows. I'm a free agent now. Could get to hell out of this town, like that silly bitch said. Set up wherever I want. Mikey Cross's South of France? But what the hell would I do in the South of France? Three weeks on the Costa del Sol and I was bored out of my mind. Bored with sun, bored with the sea. Bored with that long-legged bint Pepita.

Anywhere in the world I do want to go? Don't think so. All right to see some places, once perhaps. America. China. Italy, look at a few paintings. Operas. But settle in any of them. What'd be the point? What would I do there?

There were other rings at his bell in the course of the day. And rat-tat-tat knockings. Phone probably ringing every two minutes, only he hadn't plugged it back after last night.

And he just sat there through it all.

It was well into the evening – the room dark and dankly cold – before he stirred himself out of his thoughts-circling, eventually thoughts-less, stupor. Then he realized he was feeling hungry, or at least hungry enough to know he ought to have something to eat. He remembered that all he had had all day was that one cup of tea in the café near the Factory.

There was a tin of beans and sausages in the kitchenette cupboard. He heated it up, boiled the kettle for coffee, ate.

Real millionaire's nosh, he said to himself with returning sanity.

He made himself a second mug of coffee – Will I switch to a better brand? Nothing much wrong with this, for what it is – and decided to bring some order into his life, if only for the next few hours. Curtains drawn. Fire switched on. He realized he had grown chilled to shivering point. Phone plugged in again. Bloody papers must surely have given up now.

But barely had he straightened up from the socket when the thing shrilled out. For a couple of moments he let it ring. But then, feeling dully that life had to go on, he picked up the receiver.

'Yes?'

'It is Mr William Sylvester?'

The accent was foreign, and he guessed at once that this must be the Spanish Lottery people. He acknowledged that he was Mr William Sylvester. The voice at the far end – In Spain? In London? – congratulated him. He contrived to thank them. He agreed to send them the ticket by registered post. They would like to make the presentation on Monday week. Would it suit him to come to London? To the Dorcester. They would send a car, of course.

His first thought – a moment later he grinned at the irony – was that he'd be on duty.

'No, look, Mr— 'Fraid I didn't catch your name. But, no. No, I'm afraid I can't come up for any presentation. Not on Monday week, nor any other time. Couldn't you just send me the cheque? If I have won the money, that is.'

Acknowledgement that he had won it. Amounting at the current rate of exchange to nine hundred and ninety-nine thousand, seven hundred and sixty-seven pounds, fifty-four pence. Barely concealed contempt that he should not want to collect it in person. 'Champagne reception, Mr Sylvester. We are hoping for a big star to hand over the cheque.'

He thought: I'm never going to drink another mouthful of bloody champagne again as long as I live.

He said: 'No, I'm very sorry, but I just don't like that sort of thing. So could you please just send the cheque? No fuss. And we'll call it a day.'

Sad, very, very sad, agreement.

He woke next morning thick-headed. Before tumbling into bed he had drunk all but a drain of the remaining half of the bottle of whisky – supermarket own label – he had in the flat. Should I switch to single malt now? he had asked himself. Do I really like that? It's different, of course. But better? More to my taste? God knows. Another problem.

But, as his head cleared and he found he had half a loaf, stale but not actually mouldy, to make himself some breakfast toast – more top-class nosh – it was another problem that came to the surface. An altogether weightier one.

Roanoke. What was he to do about Roanoke? It was plain that there was no percentage in urging, from the sanctity of his civilian status, any further police action. Suggers had made it clear that anything more there was totally blocked. So was the fellow to be allowed to get away with those four murders?

But were they, after all, four murders? Suggers had consulted the Crown Prosecution people about the case, and they had given it as their opinion that there was no point in continuing enquiries. Presumably the Chief Constable had agreed with that. So was the fact of the matter, after all, that he himself had got that bee in his bonnet Suggers had taunted him with?

It could be.

Not that, he thought as he let the whole business come back into his mind, he definitely had been wrong. Rather the other way about. Every instinct he had, backed by what had seemed to be fair logical deductions, told him still that Roanoke was a murderer.

But, if the South Mercia Police, whose duty it was to apprehend

74

murderers in the territory they were responsible for, were not going to proceed, then should the fellow perhaps be allowed to get away with what he had done? In essence that was what the Crown Prosecution Service must have said: it is just possible that this man has committed murder, but the chances are so meagre that we don't advise bringing any charge. Well, if that's how the powers-that-be see it, that's how they see it.

And, look at it this way, Charles Roanoke may have gained himself a fortune by advancing by a few years at most the deaths of a number of elderly women: Bill Sylvester has gained himself a fortune by having been weak-minded enough to agree to buying a couple of lottery tickets. One of which happened to have his own name on it and the number that brought in El Gordo. If the two of them were not exactly parallel cases, they were near enough.

Oh, let the bugger go. What did it matter?

The letter-box in his door clanked open. A soft downfall of mail. Then another. For Heaven's sake, who were all these people writing to him? Most days he got nothing, or junk mail urging him to acquire things he hadn't known he wanted.

Another slithering of letters. He went to see what was happening. The postman's reddened fingers were pushing in yet another wedge. But that, apparently, was the end of it.

He stooped, gathered the whole lot together – there must be more than thirty of them, he thought – and took them back to the kitchenette table where his toast had popped up from the machine. He poured boiling water on the coffee granules at the bottom of his mug.

The moment he had ripped open the first of the letters he realized what they all must be. Appeals. Here's the rich man, let's ask him for a share.

More problems. Respond or don't respond? Respond to which, or let them all stew?

Who'd be a millionaire?

He flipped rapidly through the pile in case among them was a letter actually addressed to him by somebody he knew. There was. He recognized his mother's precise, well-formed handwriting. Sending him a letter, of course, rather than phoning. She'd always felt going out to the pay-phone at the corner was somehow telling the neighbours her business. And, God, had he even replied to the letter he had had from her just when he'd got back from Spain? It had stayed in his pocket unopened, he knew, for days. The steady nagging and the 'Why did your father have to be a policeman?', still after all these years, was something he could do without. Then he remembered. He had written a few lines. Saying nothing.

But now he'd have to read this. Presumably she'd heard about what had happened to him on the radio – she listened all day – and had written at once. He looked again at the envelope. Yes, first-class stamp. But then she didn't trust second-class, much though it hurt her to pay the extra few pennies.

Two sides of neat schoolmistressy writing. He skimmed. *I was very glad to hear* . . . But no more congratulations than that. Well, congratulations weren't what he wanted. Though God knows what he did want. Then back to the usual moaning, if with some subterranean hints that money might put some of her troubles right.

He sighed. Have to go and see her. Find out just what she does want. Go with her to the shops. Endure the chopping and changing. Pull out the cheque-book. Be the millionaire.

Better write straight away and say when he was coming.

He went back to the sitting room, decided that tomorrow was as good a day as any. Nothing to stop him going where he wanted, when he wanted now. The millionaire. The out-of-work police officer.

Then the phone rang.

Not more reporters? Hadn't they had their fill? Or was it the Spaniards, trying to get him to change his mind?

He picked up the receiver, grunted a cautious 'Hello.'

'Bill? Bill Sylvester? Colin here. Colin Taylor.'

Voice from the past. But one he had recognized – strangulated but pedantically correct – even before the name had been said. Colin Taylor. College friend. Or not exactly friend. Tagger-on. Not in the Arts Department. Business Studies. And how he had studied. He could see him now. The ever-intent face. The spectacles that seemed glued into place. But some human feelings. Must have had, because he did tag along. Occasionally. To the Union bar. To the pub. To discos. And hadn't he found himself a soul mate at one of those in the end? He seemed to remember getting the wedding invitation, a year or so after college when he'd been a Probationary Constable here. And thinking *Not on your life*.

'Well, hello, Colin. Been a long time.'

'Yes. Yes, well, it has. But— Well, busy, you know. Got my own business now. Financial adviser. And then— Well, there's the family. Three kids, two girls, one boy. Somehow one never gets around to— Old friends, and all that.'

What was he blathering on about?

Then the penny dropped. *Financial adviser.* By God, he must have seen it in the papers, or heard it on the news. His old chum – well, almost – a millionaire. In need of, what else, financial advice.

'Nice to hear from you, Colin. And what can I do for you?'

Let him think his little game hasn't been rumbled.

'Oh. Well – er – it's like this. I saw, in the paper, about your piece of luck. Well, congratulations, Bill. Congratulations.'

'Thanks. But was there something you wanted?'

'No. Well, yes. Yes, I suppose there is. You see, it occurred to me you might be in need of my— You know, services. You'll want to know about investment, tax problems. All that sort of thing. And that's right up my street. So I wondered if I could be of any help?'

'That's very kind of you, Colin. But—'

Then it struck him. He did need help. He'd not the least idea what to do with all the money. Up till now a current account had dealt with all that. In the black most of the time, if never very flourishing. But then he'd had something better to do than look after money. Catching villains.

'Well, listen, Colin, I suppose I do need some expert advice. Can I come and see you some time? Where are you, anyway?'

'No, no, old man. I'll come to you. And the sooner the better really. These things need taking care of.'

Did they? Well, he should know.

'Oh, all right then. When shall we say?'

'Well, today I'd suggest. If you're free, that is. You went into the police in the end, didn't you? Someone told me. But I expect you've taken leave now.'

'Oh, yes, I'm free. Any time. Any time.'

Colin had said at once there was a good train that could get him in by lunch-time. He asked, rather half-heartedly, what decent restaurants there were in the town. Sylvester had realized then he had a duty as a millionaire. Lunch would be on him.

77

But, a little embarrassingly, he had not immediately been able to name anywhere to go. At last, with a desperate scrabble round the corners of his mind, he remembered being told once that the best the town had to offer was a place called Le Coq d'Or. Exclusive French cuisine.

Cut above the Chinese and the Indian he went to when he wasn't making do with the canteen at the Factory. Would he have to try somewhere fancier now? Another problem to postpone.

Colin looked much as he had done fifteen or more years before, only a bit plumped out. Same intent look. Same part-of-the-face glasses. Or no. They had been horn-rims then. Now they were a subtle shade of grey. And the Fair Isle pullovers had given way to a double-breasted grey suit with a faint white stripe. Evidently financial advising paid a good deal better than policing.

Some uneasy semi-banter. Colin expansive on his back trouble and all the people he had been to about it from acupuncture to osteopathy and back again. They ordered. Colin, he noticed, picked unerringly on the most expensive item on the menu. No wonder under that well-cut suit there was a little pot-belly that had certainly not been there in lean and hungry university days.

He went for a duck dish himself. He was actually pretty sharp-set, which considering yesterday with only a tin of beans and sausages and his two slices of stale toast this morning was not surprising. He decided not to let Colin get at the wine list, and selected a red from the more modest end of the ranks. Not that it wasn't pretty unmodest in price, he thought. But go to rich men's restaurants, pay rich men's prices. Eat for show and hell with enjoyment. So, here he was in the puffball empire.

He looked at his duck as the waiter placed it in front of him. Seemed pretty good. Difficult to tell where the empire boundaries came. And whether going forwards would lead him further in or back across out.

He leant back a little in his red-plush, soft-seated chair.

'Well, tell me about being a financial adviser, Colin. What are they exactly? There didn't use to be any such things when we were at college, did there?'

Colin pursed his lips.

'Well, the profession has certainly grown in the last ten years or so. I mean, I began as an accountant myself, and then I found I was devoting more and more of my energies to giving the firm's clients advice, about their investments, what to do with what they were pulling in. And so I went freelance, as a financial adviser. I'm Fimbra registered, of course.'

'Fimbra? Don't understand.'

He did, though. Must be the organization of financial advisers. But he was damned if he was going to let this prat get away with the jargon.

'It's the Financial Intermediaries Managers and Brokers Regulatory Association, as a matter of fact. Bit too much of a mouthful to say every time.'

Point to you, old Colin.

The wine waiter brought his order. Poured with due solemnity. Despite the modesty of the choice. Puffball empire claiming another swatch of territory.

'So, what advice have you got for someone who's just come into more money than they know what to do with?'

The advice was complex. And very soon Sylvester decided that he wasn't actually being told the best thing to do with the money. He was being forced to listen to – or, rather, to sit and watch – a man riding his hobby horse as if the Grand National winning-post was only a flurry of whip-strokes away.

He wondered about stopping him. Thought he might as well let him go on. The whole spiel had nothing really to tell him. Nothing that had any real bearing on the problem of what actually he was going to do with all the money, what use he was going to make of it. Yes, he had at the beginning of the lecture more or less grasped that there were uses that large sums of money could be put to. Investments of various sorts, entered into in various ways. 'It must be made to work,' was a much repeated refrain. 'Money must work.' But it had soon become apparent that the only work Colin was interested in for his million was whatever would make it get bigger and bigger.

At last, as the desserts trolley was wheeled away, Colin seemed to have run down. As he looked at the chocolate-drowned profiteroles in front of him, the eyes behind his grey-framed glasses glowed moistly.

'Well,' Sylvester said, 'that's all been most enlightening. You'll put it in writing for me, I hope. And, of course, send me your bill.'

Someone, at that moment, tapped him sharply on the shoulder.

He turned, with a flicker of irritation.

It was Roanoke.

Roanoke.

'Inspector Sylvester. I thought it must be you, though I didn't think policemen ran to lunch at the Coq d'Or.'

Recovering from the initial surprise, Sylvester realized that there were people in the world, in the town even, who didn't know about what had happened to him. Roanoke kept himself amused in the mornings, no doubt, with richer, more salacious pleasures than reading the papers.

'Oh, you'd be surprised at some of the places we have to descend to in the course of duty.'

A dart of coldness in the blue eyes pinched up by the florid cheeks.

'Yes. Well, I'm glad I've seen you. There's something I've been wanting to say. It's come to my notice that you've been going about asking questions about me. I had thought I'd explained, even more than was necessary, when you and that slob of a sergeant came calling the other day.'

'I don't think that's a proper description of Detective Sergeant Cross, sir.'

No need to let the swine know he was no longer a colleague of Mikey the fly.

'That's as may be, Inspector. But what I wanted to say to you was this: if I get to hear you are indulging in any more impertinent enquiries into my private affairs, I shall know what steps to take. And, I promise you, you will find them unpleasantly effective.'

He turned sharply and strode out.

11

Sylvester sat there, lost in thought. Roanoke's contemptuous demand – it was nothing less – had made him, the moment it had been spoken, determined to do exactly the opposite. For the time it took Roanoke to stride out of the restaurant, he actually forgot he was no longer Detective Inspector Sylvester, no longer the police officer Roanoke had assumed him to be. Nobody, but nobody, was going to tell him what his duty—

Then his mind readjusted itself. That demand had been directed to a nothingness. He could not, however much he might want to, go on pursuing enquiries into the man's activities. He no longer was a person charged by society to, in the words of the oath he had taken at the start of his service, 'preserve the Queen's Peace'.

But the very fact of Roanoke having attacked him reaffirmed his belief, hardly dented by what his superiors had thought, that the man was a murderer. A four-times murderer. And worse.

Worse, it struck him now for the first time since his sudden decision on the stairway at the Factory, because Roanoke still, surely, was planning a fifth murder. He had in all probability selected his victim. Sir Julian Deane. Old. About to sell him most of his furniture. About to retire to somewhere like Astwood Manor or the Old School at Oxleigh.

Could he stand by and let what had happened to Mrs Bathurst, Miss Pettiman, Mrs Forth, and Miss Gallitly happen to a person he could protect?

But could he protect him? By going to Detective Chief Superintendent Sugden? Or even the Chief Constable? He knew what reception he would get there. Branded as obsessed as soon as he opened his mouth. Then could he go to Sir Julian and attempt to warn him? But, if what he had learnt about Roanoke had failed to impress the Crown Prosecution Service, his airy train of logic was even less likely to affect Sir Julian, already on good enough terms with Roanoke to have sold him his furniture. And there was no other way that he could see.

'Who was that?'

It was Colin. He had forgotten his very existence.

He brought himself back to reality.

'That? Oh, a fellow I got across when I was still in the police.'

'Still in the police? You mean you've resigned? Already? You didn't tell me that. Still, I suppose it makes sense. But what's your position over your pension? Have you thought of that?'

'No, Colin. No, I haven't thought what my position is over my pension.'

'Well, you should, you know. I mean, the sum may not amount to a great deal, but it is money. It can be put to work.'

'Yeah. Yeah, well, add that to what you're going to write to me about, eh? And now, you know, I think I must be on my way. Got a lot to do, one way and another.'

'Yes. Yes, I'm sure you must have. But do give urgent consideration to the various courses I've suggested, won't you? The sooner we get cracking the better. I don't like to think of all that money lying idle.'

The cheque for all that money came next morning together with another batch of appeals, the ill-written envelopes of individuals now as well as the careful typing of charities. He dumped the lot in the kitchenette bin. If he was going to give to some charity, and he supposed he ought to, he was going to choose one he wanted and in his own good time. But he did take the cheque round to the bank almost at once. The long line of figures on it had seemed to stare at him challengingly. The sooner he huddled the big stiff pink sheet out of sight the better. So, first into a paying-in envelope. Then into the secret depths behind the narrow slit of the Creditpoint.

Did he feel it was somehow dirty money? No answer.

Then he set off for Nottingham where his mother still, more than fifteen years after his father's death, lived in the narrow terrace house in which she had spent all her married life. It was a journey that made him more miserable with every mile. He knew what he would be in for at the end of it. Recriminations.

He had been subjected to them ever since his decision to join the police.

'Why? Why have you done this, William?' the new-made widow, years ago, had charged him the moment the last of the people who had come to the funeral had departed, sweet sherry and paste sandwiches settling in their stomachs.

'Good God, Mother, can't you see —'

'William! I won't have language like that in my house, and on a day like today too.'

'No. I'm sorry. But surely following in Dad's footsteps ought to be something that pleases you.'

'No, William. It does not please me. Your father was a good man, after his lights, but he was never going to rise up in the world. Not even if he hadn't been unable to work. I had hoped for better things from you, and you know it.'

Impossible to tell her then that he had suddenly seen those better things, the promised career in industry, being an executive, as ashes. Bitter tasting.

But it was more than that, the antagonism between them, he admitted to himself as he jockeyed through the traffic of West Bridgford. It was all the days of his boyhood in that atmosphere of scrimp and make-do she had seemed pinchedly to delight in. Her revenge – he saw that again now, had seen it long ago – for having married a man whose lack of money had stopped her being the teacher she might have become.

Yet all the cheese-paring had not really been necessary. That was what, looking back, was so galling. All right, a police constable's pay in those days had been much lower in the scale than now. Yet it was enough for some reasonable indulgences on occasion. But there had never been any. 'Money doesn't grow on trees, you know' and 'I'll have no waste in this house'. So, the turned shirt collars, the darned and re-darned underclothes, the patched trousers. Scrupulously patched, but patched. The holidays spent at home. The never-bought sweets. The few toys. The whole stunted life.

And, as he had expected, once he had arrived at the narrow terrace house in the Meadows, things were as they had been in those distant days. She had known he was coming but she had not baked a cake. Instead there was the lunch of two careful portions of corned beef with two tomatoes each, bread spread with just enough margarine and tea with enough in the pot for two cups for each of them, calculated to the last dribble. He spent the time at the table coaxing out of her ideas for what he might buy her with his new-found wealth.

Then there was the trip he had anticipated, shopping at Jessop's. And, as he had anticipated as well, in the end everything on the list he had screwed out of her had been rejected. With the single exception of a new teapot. 'You know ours hasn't poured properly ever since your father knocked it off the table in one of his fainting attacks.'

He put off till the last minutes of the visit telling her his other piece of big news, that he had left the police. He knew it would please her more even than if El Gordo had brought him not one but ten million pounds, and he did not want to have to listen to the expression of her pleasure.

'Oh, William, I am so glad. It was never the right thing for you. Mind, I don't say that the police isn't respectable. I would never have married your father if I hadn't thought that. But it isn't the sort of thing you should be doing, and I was afraid, you know, that you'd go on being pig-headed about it and want to stay on. Even after getting all that money.'

'Well, you've had your wish. I've given the service up.'

'And good riddance. I've never said that to you before, William, but it's what I mean. Good riddance. There can't but be something nasty about police work. Your father never saw too much of that side of things, as only a uniform constable. But detectives. I know the sort of nastiness they get their fingers caught in, and I'm heartily glad you've escaped it all at last.'

For a moment he wanted to say to her, to shout it, that his father at the end had seen more than enough of 'that side of things' at the point of a shot-gun wielded by a yobbo. But he managed to hold his tongue.

'So what do you think I'm going to do now, then?'

'Well, I've been thinking about that. You could do anything you wanted, with all that money behind you, couldn't you?'

There was a wheedling note in her voice that sent his hackles up.

'If I did know what I wanted.'

'Well, William, what I thought was this. Why shouldn't you go back to the university? A lot of people of your age do nowadays.

Mature students they call them. You could study for a higher degree. Perhaps in the end write a book. You could even become a professor.'

'Mother, I don't think academic life would suit me now. Not after—'

He checked himself.

'But it's so well looked-on. It would be just right for you, William.'

'No, Mother.'

And back on to her face, which had been a little softened, came the old censorious look.

'Well, I can see you mean to have it your way. As always. But you tell me, what are you going to do? You can't just idle your time away, you know. That money won't last for ever.'

He had had no answer to that. Beyond pointing out a million would easily last him for ever. And that he scorned to do.

Driving back over Trent Bridge, his mood had been even blacker than when he had arrived. So what it was that abruptly reminded him of his Auntie Violet he hardly knew. Perhaps it was no more than a reaction against the penny-pinching that had just been so vividly brought back to him. Because Auntie Violet – not strictly an aunt, but the widow now of a cousin, a small-time coal merchant – was the antithesis of all that his mother stood for. He had never seen much of her as a boy. His mother's disapproval of her whole way of life had been too vehement for more than the most occasional contact between the two families across the width of Nottingham from the Meadows to Bulwell. But he remembered as a thing set apart one visit he and his father had made.

There had been in the backyard of the tiny house the strong, sharp, yet sweet smell of coal sacks and shiny encrusted blackness on every surface. But, when he had come in for tea with his hands soot-covered from fingertips to wrists there had not been the outbreak of sharp scolding that would have descended on him at home. Auntie Violet, plump, high-coloured face, wearing a satiny dress in some colour verging on the garish – Had it been purple? Had it been rose-pink? In his memory it was sometimes one, sometimes the other – had burst into peals of laughter, pointing at him with one plump finger. Her mirth had not even stopped when, in his dismay, he had clutched at the white tablecloth and left an uncompromising black handprint on it. He supposed he must have been swept to the kitchen sink and had his hands washed, but he could not remember. All he could call to mind was sitting up, a few minutes later presumably, at a table laden with good things, crumpets, jam sandwiches, two different cakes, and being told to tuck in.

But hard times had come to that blossomingly cheerful lady. Coal deliveries had been less and less needed as central heating had become more widespread. Then Uncle Fred had died, and she had found herself left very poorly off. She had not had the best of health either. So much he had gathered from her annual Christmas cards, their only communication once his father had died. She was now in an old people's home. One decidedly different, he guessed, from the well-regulated comforts of Astwood Manor or the Old School at Oxleigh.

He looked in his rear-view mirror, saw the road behind was momentarily free of traffic, swung round in an abrupt U-turn.

St Wulfstan's Alms-houses were, Sylvester thought when he had at last tracked them down, not prepossessing. True, the terrace of dark-brick little cottages was set back from the road by a garden. But that was a far cry from the neat benches-dotted, flowers-crammed one at the Old School or the sweeping lawns of Astwood Manor. Here what did grow looked winter-bitten before its time, and the network of paths between the grudging beds was sour with tussocky grass.

He went up to No 7, hoping he had remembered the right one from the succession of Christmas cards since he had shaken the dust of Nottingham from his feet. There was a knocker on the door, bright-rubbed brass. He gave it a brisk rapping.

After a moment or two the door opened. Auntie Violet. He had got it right. Older by a good few years than when he had last seen her, she was yet unmistakable. Still well plumped-out, still wearing a bright-coloured dress – blue with splodgy yellow flowers, rather than the rose-pink or purple she wore always in his memory – with two cardigans, one on top of the other, a yellow and a green. And, despite lines of pain cutting into the flesh, her face still shining with outgoingness.

'Billy.'

She had known him at once.

'Come in then, come in. I got it nice and warm, chilly old day like this.'

She turned and led him into the single room of the little house. It was he saw, unable to prevent himself pausing in the doorway to observe, crammed with all sorts of pieces of furniture, a tall leaning cupboard, two painted and chipped chests of drawers, a pair of armchairs, the worse for wear. And it was not home to one person only. Propped in one of the two beds, there was a woman perhaps fifteen or even twenty years older than Auntie Violet. Shrunken, frankly dribbling, plainly in her last days on earth.

'This is Marigold,' Auntie Violet said with bouncing cheerfulness. 'Say hello to her, poor thing. She can't hear a word, but she likes people to show an interest.'

Dutifully he stepped in, leant towards the far bed, put a large smile on his face, nodded like a wobbling teetotum.

'That's right, that's right. Give the old dear something to think about. And now sit here by the fire. Got a nice bit of a blaze. Can't bear folk who won't put a bit of coal on a fire. Never could.'

The fire, in fact, was roaring away, and, in spite of the narrowness of the grate, it was making the crowded little room stiflingly hot. But he didn't mind. It was all so different from the frigid kitchen where a few hours ago he had faced his mother over corned beef, two tomatoes, and bread thinly spread with margarine.

Auntie Violet lowered herself, giving a wince of pain, into the armchair on the other side of the fire.

'Wondered if I'd be seeing you, Billy me lad. When I heard on the radio someone called William Sylvester had won a million quid.'

He felt an immediate pang of guilt. He ought to have thought of Auntie Violet, poorly off, in a charity home, and wonderfully kind to him as a boy. She ought, despite the years since he had actually seen her, to have come to mind as soon as he had learnt he was a rich man. Or certainly when those wedges of begging letters had come sliding through his letter-box.

'Well,' he said, 'here I am anyhow. And—'

He glanced round the tiny furniture-crammed room, at the

ancient old woman in the second bed, at what was obviously a commode close up to it.

'Listen,' he said, 'I'm rich now. All of a sudden a millionaire. So what can I do for you, Auntie? You've only to say.'

'Now that's nice of you. Really nice. But, you know, there's nothing I really need.'

She looked about as if searching for something in the little, low-ceilinged room that might be missing.

'No,' she said. 'I'm happy enough here, you know. Oh, I dare say it isn't much. It's not what I was used to when you came over with your Dad. But I'm all right. I got me pension. I can always buy meself any little bits and bobs of things I might take a fancy to. No, it's nice of you, dear, but I don't think there's anything.'

He felt ashamed. With his mother, coming away from Jessop's having rejected everything bar that one new teapot, he had felt only irritation. But Auntie Violet, patently, had been speaking the simple truth. Despite her cramped surroundings, despite the presence in the little room of that dribbling creature in the far bed and the commode beside her, she was happy with her lot. There was nothing, it seemed, that the rich man could do for her.

But there was.

She gave a sudden loud chuckle. The sound he remembered from those boyhood visits.

'I know what you could get me, though,' she said. 'A nice bottle of port. They don't like you to have drink here, the Superintendent and the Matron. And it isn't easy for me to sneak out and bring something in, not with my legs the way they are, even if I could afford it. So, before you go, slip down to the off-licence and bring me a bottle of Sandeman's Ruby. Haven't tasted that for years.'

'It's a deal.'

Damn it, he had difficulty keeping the tears from his eyes.

She settled herself more comfortably in her chair.

'Now then,' she said, leaning forward, face glowing with pleasure, 'tell me all about it. Right from the beginning. Did you have to go to London to collect the cheque? Some dolly-bird actress give it you? Smacking big kiss and all that?'

Again he felt ashamed. Was that what he ought to have done? Accepted the gift from the sky with open hands. As Auntie Violet would have, taking the good as cheerfully as the bad. Should he have agreed to the Spaniards' request? Gone through the act, smiled, laughed, kissed the star they had found to hand over the cheque, kissed her again for the photographers if they wanted, shaken the champagne and let it squirt out all over the place, drunk some, drunk a lot, said the right things, said them over and over again?

He shook his head.

'Well, no,' he said. 'Tell the truth, I didn't feel I wanted to go in for all that. It hasn't really sunk in yet, you know. That I've got all that money.'

'Yes. Well, I suppose it must take a bit of getting used to. After the way you were brought up. I won't say a word against your Mum, but she was a terror for meanness. How is she though? Still where she was, down the Meadows?'

'Still a terror for meanness.'

He grinned.

'And you still going to your police station, are you?'

Once more a flush of shame. She so plainly expected he would be carrying on.

He made a face.

'No, Auntie,' he confessed. 'Chucked it in.'

'Oh, you shouldn't have done that. Not all of a sudden. Go to your head, did it? Being the millionaire?'

'No. No, it wasn't like that. I wouldn't have turned it in for that reason. It's too much part of me. No, I'll tell you what happened.'

He had not meant to. But suddenly he had felt the need to justify himself. To this warmly genial judge. But a judge none the less.

So, taking his time over it, he told her almost everything. From the moment he had read half-on, half-off Peter Maffin's letter to the Chief Constable right up to his row on the stairs with Detective Chief Superintendent Sugden. It was, he supposed, a breach of confidence. But he couldn't see Auntie Violet telling anyone else. And it had lifted a burden, speaking aloud all his thoughts and feelings ever since that first interview with Charles Roanoke.

That had surprised him, the relief of confession. But he had felt it like a sodden weight being lifted from his stooping shoulders.

'Yes,' she said at the end of it all. 'I can't say as I blame you, chucking it in and writing that letter you did. Sounds a right old fool, that Superintendent Whatsit. Still, you didn't ought to have lost your rag like that, really. Hasn't helped, has it?'

'Well, no, Auntie, it hasn't. But I'm damned if I can see what I can do about it now.'

'Yeah, there's not much, is there? I mean, you can't go investigating all on your own, can you? You wouldn't have the right. And then you'd want to have all those forensics and whatever they're called to back you up, wouldn't you?'

'Yes, I dare say I would, sooner or later. So it seems I'm stuck.'

'Then you'll just have to put up with it, me lad. There's plenty in this life you can't do nothing about. And there's not much point in moaning about it.'

He looked at her.

She had plenty she could do nothing about. And, more, she was plainly not going to let this rich man come and lift her out of circumstances she had taught herself to accept. Bar buying her that bottle of port.

He pushed himself to his feet.

'Thanks anyhow for listening to all my troubles,' he said. 'Troubles of a millionaire. I'll nip along now and get that port. See you in a few minutes.'

He bought, when it came to it, half a dozen bottles and had them put in a box to leave at her door. Because, despite the weight he felt had been lifted from him by his visit, and despite the warm pleasure seeing Auntie Violet once more had given him, he had a notion that he would not be coming to Nottingham again all that soon. However much he felt that he ought to. One way or another his trip had given him a bad conscience. Though why he was unable to say.

12

The days that followed were not easy. He had nothing to do. He felt he was swimming in a sea of uncertainty. Objectless. Every now and again, as he sat for hour after hour staring at nothing, he thought what he ought to be doing was plunging into the sort of things people who had won big money always seemed to say they would do. Have the holiday of a lifetime, whatever that was. Buy a big house. But what would he do in a big house? Get a new car. But where would he go in it?

He felt, in fact, he could not go anywhere. A ridiculous fear of being recognized, of having to act like the millionaire he was and not like the unobtrusive detective inspector he had been until so recently, kept him almost imprisoned. Occasional sorties he had to make, to buy bread, coffee, take-aways, and sometimes a six-pack. But even then he avoided the places he had been used to going to, and slipped like a sneak-thief along to somewhere he wouldn't be pointed out as a rich man making a parade of slumming it.

Up above a street corner he passed on one hurried, skulking night expedition, to get a new supply of cash from the machines at the bank, an advertisement for one or other of the football pools caught his eye. *You'll Never Work Again*. He shuddered. On his next cash-gathering trip he made a long detour.

From his bookshelf every now and again he pulled down one of the handful of novels kept from college days. But, classics of the English language though they were, not one of them held his attention. And the odd paperback, bought more recently, was no more gripping. He even took, after a little, to reading the appeals that continued to come through his letter-box. But he could make no sense of them. None seemed any more important, any more harrowing, any less footling than any of the others. His heart, he thought, had become sealed up in an iron box, or anaesthetized by that massive injection of wealth.

One of the letters, quick to come, was from Colin Taylor. Long and detailed, and urgent. But all the advice and the figures in it made no impact. He left it on the table beside his chair for a whole day, then tossed it into the bin.

At every hour, dully, he found Auntie Violet was on his conscience. And his mother. There was nothing either would let him do for them, for their very different reasons. But he felt, with itchy uneasiness, there must be something. Why else did he have all the money? What was he going to do now that he did have it?

And there was Roanoke. But each time the thought of the man came into his head he pushed it away. As Auntie Violet had said, there were plenty of things in life that nothing could be done about.

Then in the evening of the second Monday, dumping the great heap of Sunday papers he had ventured out to get the day before, in the hope of finding something in all the welter of them that would mean something to him, he suddenly thought *Jude*.

He had not, in all the days of his sodden unthinkingness, experienced the least sexual impulse. And it was not now any upspringing of libido that put the thought of her into his mind. It was rather that he saw her, in a dart of something new, as being outside it all.

All right, she had taken to her way of life because it brought her in much more than she could have made otherwise. And she spent what she got, too. Often, chatting, she had boasted about some shopping spree she had indulged in that morning, laughing till she was exhausted at the variety of things she had bought. But, for all that, her life was one altogether outside the world of salaries, savings, taxes, investments, garnered riches. Money to her was something in the hand, a necessary means to enjoyment, nothing else. It was not a life he could ever lead himself. But, perhaps because what she told him of it rose so naturally from her personality, while he listened he found that whole way of going on totally sympathetic.

It was the thought of this, rather than any prospect of sexual relief, that made him jump from his chair, grab a coat, and hurry out. The image of her bright as a painting in his mind. No great brain, but alive in every inch, conscious of herself from swinging swath of auburn hair to feet springing into eager stride.

But, if he had believed that by going to Jude he would really enter a world where he was no longer a millionaire but simply a man, a body with needs but no attachments, he was to be disappointed.

'Well,' she said the moment she saw who it was her maid had installed in the room. 'So who didn't tell a girl they were fuzz?'

'Fuzz? But how d'you . . . ?'

It was simple-minded of him.

'Oh, go on. Your name in the paper, picture and all. And what you do, of course. What d'you think?'

He smiled ruefully.

'Yes. I'd forgotten.'

'Forgotten you'd got yourself a million quid? Come on.'

'No. No, I can't forget that. Sometimes wish I could, tell you the truth. No, I meant I'd forgotten the papers would have eventually got round to knowing what my job was. What it used to be, actually.'

'Oh, so you've turned it in, have you? Well, suppose you couldn't do anything else really.'

'No.'

He sighed.

'No, I don't think I could've done anything else in the end. You can't really have a detective who's a bloody millionaire.'

'Well, cheer up. Now you are a bloody millionaire, d'you want to give a girl a few quid extra? Have the works. Whatever you like. I got a lovely policewoman's uniform. That turn you on?'

He looked at her.

'No. Nice thought, but I don't actually want anything else than the usual.'

'Glad it ain't gone to your head then, all that dosh.'

She held out her hand for her payment. He hauled his wallet from his pocket, suddenly flushing with sweat at the thought that, rushing out as he had, he might not have enough in it. The millionaire.

However, it turned out that he had, just. And when she came back after tucking it away he found his urges were after all fully in place. *Licence my roaming hands to go, Before, behind, between, above, below.* Donne's lines, rising up from long-ago learning, almost always swirled round and round in his head each time he visited Jude. They did so again now. Triumphantly.

But at last the two of them lay, sweat-shiny and exhausted, side by side. One of the things he had liked about her almost from the time he had first, in the words of the Police (Discipline) Regulations, indulged with her in 'discreditable conduct in a serving officer' was that, unless someone else was waiting, she didn't just get up and walk out the moment the business was done.

They had in their time had many a long talk lying there on the bed, for all that he had never, cautiously, told her what it was he did or even what his name was. But the curiosities of human behaviour, both sexual and social, had provided plenty to chat about. The extraordinary things some of her clients wanted, like the man who had to have sticky cakes thrown at him before he could get aroused. Or the enormous sums, as much as five hundred pounds, some of her clients were prepared, or even delighted, to pay for not particularly extraordinary services. Amounts balanced only by those Jude herself happily admitted spending in her shopping sprees on objects she often found, coming home, she didn't really want. Clothes, shoes, hats, handbags, bits of jewellery, perfume, things to put on her car, toys, dolls.

He had expected their talk now, when he had begun to emerge from his satisfied stupor, to be no different, even though she had at last a name for him and knew what his occupation had been. But it was different. Because, now that she did know who he was, she talked – nothing more natural to her – about what had happened to him.

'Here, you know what you said?' she began, breaking the soporific silence. 'About you wanting to forget you've got your million quid. You mean that? You are a funny bugger and no mistake.'

'Yes, I did mean it, funny bugger or not. Christ, think what it's done to me. There I was happy enough, doing my job. Job I wanted to do, and—'

'Bloody pigs.'

She gave a deep-throated chuckle.

'All right, there's some coppers who've got a thing about you lot and aren't above using the law to give you a hard time. But, remember, when you get beaten up, or when a pimp gets hold of one of you, who it is who comes riding to the rescue.'

'Sometimes.'

'All right, sometimes. We're not perfect.'

'Yeah. But all the same, now you can do whatever you like, all that moolah, I don't see why you want to moan.'

'What I said. I was happy before. I didn't mean to win that damn thing, El Gordo. I only bought the ticket to please some girl in Spain.'

'Now don't you go telling me about other women.'

He barked out a laugh.

'All right, all right. But it's true what I was saying. I just bought the ticket to get shot of the last of the pesetas. Less trouble than going to change them at the bank.'

'Yeah, I can see that. But when you'd gone and won, well, then you ought to be bloody chuffed about it. Get yourself some nice things. Have a good time.'

He gave her a pat on the thigh.

'Done that.'

'Oh, go on. That the best you can manage? Why aren't you up in London, doing the clubs, fancy restaurants, anything you like?'

He looked up at the ceiling for a moment. Thinking.

'Well,' he said, 'truth is, all that sort of thing's all right. And I dare say when the mood takes me, if it does, I will give myself a treat or two. But, damn it all, I can't go doing that and nothing else for the rest of my life.'

'No? Think I could. Not that I'll ever get the chance.'

For one wild moment he thought about making over the whole of his million to her. Bar perhaps enough to keep Auntie Violet in port. But he knew it couldn't be done. She wouldn't, much though she liked having money, let him do it. If only because she'd be afraid he'd come back next day wanting to reclaim it all.

Then she sent a short sharp laugh up into the air.

'You know what? I couldn't go on giving meself treats and nothing else either. Not week after week, month after month. You know what I'd find meself doing after a bit? Coming back to the old trade. I would, you know.'

'Yes. I think you would. Damn it, it's what you do. It's your profession, same as mine was the police. And you're bloody good at it, too.'

She actually blushed then.

Rising up on one elbow to look at her when she had said nothing, he had seen she was blushing. With pleasure.

'I mean it,' he said.

'Yeah. You wouldn't say it unless you did. Not you.'

'No, don't think I would.'

'And you know what?'

'No?'

'I've a pretty good idea you're just the same yourself.'

'What? What d'you mean?'

'I wouldn't be surprised to be told you're a bloody good copper.'

He didn't blush. But he lay in silence, absorbing it.

'Yes, actually,' he said eventually. 'No boasting, but I think I am a bloody good copper.'

He sat suddenly up.

'Was,' he said. 'Was. Was. Was. Was a bloody good copper.'

'Well then, why don't you go back to it? What you done? Written them a letter saying goodbye? You could always take it back.'

'Not so easy,' he said, slumping down beside her again. 'For one thing I don't think if I did go back I'd be as good a copper as I was, not if everybody knew I was a rich bastard sort of playing at it. And then, well, in that resignation letter of mine I told my boss a few truths about himself.'

She gurgled with laughter.

'Bit of up-yours, eh? What was he, your boss? Snooty devil?'

'No. Just anything for a quiet life. Keep your head down. Never offend anyone higher up. Hope for one last promotion, if you've not blotted your copybook. Then retire on a nice fat pension.'

'Well, that's not all that bad. Why did you want to go telling him all the things you did?'

'Oh, I suppose because he'd just that moment stamped right down on an investigation of mine. Into someone who's bloody committed four murders.'

He should not have come out with it. He was still under an obligation of confidentiality. But the pent-up frustration had been too much. As it had been when he had been with Auntie Violet.

And, in fact, if he said no more, his secret would be safe enough with Jude.

'D'you mean that?' she asked now, however, a sharpness in her voice.

'Oh, yes. It's the truth. Mind, he had some reason on his side, my boss. I suppose I'm the only bugger who believes the fellow I was after has done what he has done. But I'm sure of it. Positive. With or without hard evidence.'

'But murder. Your boss can't just let it go.'

'Oh, yes, he can. He's done all the right things, you know.

96

Trust him. Got all the OKs he could need from higher up. And, well, it's true enough, there's nothing I could have gone to court with, up to now. Nothing at all.'

'But all the same . . .'

He groaned a little.

'Oh, yes, all the same, I'm damned sure in myself that that fellow over the years has committed four murders. To get himself the victims' money.'

'But it can't be proved, that it? I mean, what did he exactly do, this feller? Not bash them over the head? Who were they anyhow?'

'Shan't tell you. Mustn't tell you. But, no, he murdered them, if he did, with some poison or other. And, what's worse, I haven't the least notion which.'

'But hasn't anyone else? I mean, the doctors and that?'

'No. Death certificates all hunky-dory. I'm out on a limb about it.'

'But you're sure all the same?'

'Oh, yes. I'm sure.'

She sat up suddenly. Upright from the hips. Sparking.

'Then I'll tell you what you ought to be doing with all that money of yours. You ought to be spending it finding out just what that feller did do. And seeing him put away at the end of it.'

Slowly he raised himself up on to both his elbows and looked at her.

'Yes,' he said. 'Yes. You're right. It'll be difficult. Bloody difficult. Lot more than when I was in the force. But, by God, you're perfectly right.'

13

Next morning, inhibitions about being pointed at as the winner of a million pounds now ragged away like fog before a nor'easter, Sylvester drew out from the bank a hefty wad of notes. Then he marched round to a second-hand car dealer, questioned more than once in earlier days. From him he bought, disdaining bargaining, the grottiest vehicle on the premises that still could be relied on to go at a decent lick. His only other stipulation, not spoken of, was that the car should have a decently large rear window with the seat below wide enough to crouch on. Looking out, unobserved by passers-by.

Driving away, blue clouds fuming from the exhaust, he gave a wry smile. Hardly a dent in his million bank-roll to acquire a vehicle the very look-alike of the Force's occasionally highly useful 'Q-car'. But the smile faded. Look-alike car, yes, but under the dashboard no radio to summon up all the backing the South Mercia Police could provide.

From an Oxfam shop he bought next what he had been quietly snubbed by whey-faced Maggie Adams for suggesting to her. One flat cap, one battered trilby, plus – Heaven help me, he thought – a matted green-and-white woolly hat. To these he added a bleached-out mackintosh, minus two buttons, and an ancient tweed jacket.

The detective inspector investigating officially certain allegations about that respectable antiques dealer, Charles Roanoke, Rotary Club acquaintance of Detective Chief Superintendent Sugden, had had to take care not to seem to be badgering the man. But now he was released from all such restraints. Provided only that his elementary disguises prevented Roanoke noticing him, as from experience he knew they almost certainly would, he could keep as close surveillance as he liked.

In sleepless hours during the night he had cursed himself over and over for having let Roanoke go unwatched in all the time since he had marched out of the Factory. He had told himself it was asking too much to have realized immediately that resigning as a detective would not put an end to the calling he had held for so long. But he had not felt his guilt absolved.

What if Roanoke had already contrived to get Sir Julian Deane to make a will in his favour? The fellow could already be making preparations to administer his poison. Whatever that was.

He could even already have made away with his victim.

The thought had twisted up, snake-like. Only to be quenched with a douche of common sense. No, it was highly doubtful there had been enough time to complete the process gone through with Miss Gallitly and the others. Besides, in all that heap of Sunday papers he had waded through he had seen nothing about the death of a well-known former spymaster.

Yet he forced his grotty vehicle along till it shuddered as he made his way out to that big mock-farmhouse. Catching sight at last of the spot he already had in his mind's eye, a patch of verge under a low-sweeping ash tree some two hundred yards from the white farm gate, he came to a screeching halt.

From here he could see almost all the richly gravelled drive of the house. No tomato-red Bentley out on it, but that might still be in the big garage beside the Range Rover.

For a moment he saw again that cool interior, vivid as a remembered nightmare. The shapes of piled antiques looming dimly. The crimson gleam of the goblet of wine on the bench beside the man as he had stood there with his shot-gun 'distressing' that flour-chest into greater value. Even the harsher red of the fire-extinguisher on the wall.

At once uneasiness asserted itself.

Against all better judgement, he slid out of the old car. A last-second return of caution made him duck back in again, pick up the limp trilby, cram it well down on his head, wrap himself in the almost buttonless mackintosh.

But he went towards the house almost at a run.

Stopping to look from the last yard of resiny-smelling evergreen hedge that stretched along from the gate – some bloody farmhouse surrounded by evergreens – he at once conceived the notion that he was already too late to catch Roanoke leaving. The doors of the garage were closed, but either of the man's two vehicles could have been driven off long ago. And the windows of the house were all reflecting blackly the bleak day outside, and surely on a morning as dank as this anyone as prodigal with his possessions as Roanoke would have lights on everywhere.

How much longer should he give it? Must be half-past ten or more. He glanced at his watch. Twenty-five to eleven. Well, Roanoke, if he had no particular appointment, might well not leave the comforts of home till, say, eleven. Or even twelve. A long wait ahead. But no way could he risk going right up to that wide front door and giving the fancy black iron bell-pull a tug. Not after that encounter with Roanoke in the Coq d'Or.

But then, just as a cold drizzle of rain began to add to his misery, his dilemma was solved. A little red Post Office van drew up at the gate. The driver rummaged for a moment to his rear and emerged with a fat parcel. Up to the front door. Jerk on the bell-pull. Minute or two waiting. Fed-up shrug of the shoulders. One more tug for luck. Another short wait. Tramp back to the van with the parcel.

Sylvester stayed where he was till it was evident the postman was not going to return with a form saying an attempt at a delivery had been made. No doubt the fellow knew that if he didn't succeed in leaving the parcel one day he would be able to the next. Fat parcels were likely to come often enough for someone like Roanoke.

As soon as the van had disappeared round the bend of the road he marched in through the gate.

He had plainly lost Roanoke for the day. But the chance to get a good look at the man's lair with no little poppet from the Alhambra Theatre to cause complications was well worth having.

He headed for the back of the house. Would Roanoke have left a window carelessly open? And, if he had, was this former police officer going to indulge in a little unauthorized entry? In his early CID days he had cut corners that way more than once. Why not now? A look at the fellow's books, bound to be some-where inside since he had no other place of work, might tell him a lot.

But, no. Not worth the risk, or not without plenty of careful planning. If by some chance he was spotted now and found himself under arrest, Detective Chief Superintendent Sugden would take

100

a personal delight in seeing him put firmly in the dock. Where, then, Charles Roanoke would never stand. As he ought to. As one day he would.

But still worth a prowl round that could be explained away if necessary.

He made a survey of what lay ahead. The garden – grounds, he guessed, Roanoke would say – ran far down from the house. Long lawns, dull with the rain but still brownish from the summer. Beds of roses, eight of them in a double row, large and square, with petals, pink, red, yellow, white, scattered on the sodden earth. Beyond, an orchard, its trees now all but bare. Finally a hawthorn hedge separating the place from autumnal fields stretching sullenly into the distance.

Tucked away in the far corner there was a wooden building, something between a summerhouse and a large shed.

Worth a look?

It was big enough for Roanoke to have put things in he might not want seen by casual visitors, like his little actress friend or the men who had installed his pool. Furniture dubiously acquired? Even stored documents?

He walked down through the drizzling rain between the big rose beds and on into the orchard, squashing under his feet the speckled brown remains of fallen apples and pears. Unpicked and disregarded.

'Now what'd you be wanting?'

He came to an abrupt halt.

For a long moment he was unable to make out where the voice, dark corncrake countryman's accent, had come from. Then he saw. There was a man sitting cross-legged sheltering from the fine rain in the long grass at the corner of the summerhouse-shed. Leather-tanned face, cut with deep lines, unshaven. Anything between sixty and seventy-five. Thin frame. Time-grimed corduroy trousers. Old anorak, faded almost to colourlessness, over a check shirt scarcely less new. Pale blue eyes staring unblinkingly.

'Ah. I came to see Mr Roanoke. But he doesn't seem to be about.'

'Think he'd be down 'ere pickin' his apples, what's left of 'em, did yer?'

In a flash of guesswork Sylvester decided to make of that a joke to be shared.

He gave a cough of a laugh.

'Well, no. Can't really see him doing is own fruit-picking. Not unless he was in a hothouse.'

'Ah.'

For a little he thought this was the only reply he was going to get.

'See you know 'im then.'

'Yes, a bit. Enough not to see him doing that sort of work.'

Again a pause to consider.

'Reckon he makes all that money of 'is pluckin' other things'n fruit.'

'Fat customers, eh?'

''Bout the size on it.'

'You work for him? You seem pretty much at home in his— What d'you call it? Bit big for a garden.'

'Grounds. That's what 'e likes to say. Grounds.'

So he had been right. He felt a bite of pleasure.

'Nah. Lets me take what I wants off 'is trees, an' 'opes as 'ow I'll keep an eye on the place. That's all I has to do wi' Rogue Roanoke.'

The little wiry old man got to his feet.

'Arthur Arkle don't work fer no man,' he said. 'Not since 'e learnt what was what, 'e don't. An' not fer no money neither. That's what makes all your trouble. Money. I won't 'ave it. Not a penny on it.'

Deep rural philosophy. Well, why not?

Encouraged by that 'Rogue', he decided to plunge deeper. Here was somebody it might be worth cultivating.

'As a matter of fact, I'm very far from being a friend of Roanoke's.'

'Thought as much. Way you came a-prowling down 'ere. 'Oping to find somethin', were you?'

'Yes, I was.'

'Ah. You won't, though. Rogue's too clever fer that.'

'You don't seem to like him.'

'Tried to give me a fifty-pound note once.'

He had been thinking, before Arthur Arkle had made clear his hatred and fear of money, of offering him, not fifty pounds – easily though the new-made millionaire could have run to that – but some sum. Now he realized the offer would have brought any co-operation between them to an abrupt end.

102

And, impractical though such a money-rejecting way of life must be, he could sympathize. Easily enough. The weight of his million was heavy still.

'Listen,' he said. 'You were quite right in thinking I came here to find out what I could about your Rogue Roanoke. He's a bad lot. Bad as they come.'

The watery eyes in Arthur Arkle's tanned, lines-etched face twisted shrewdly up.

'You a copper? Thought you might be.'

'No,' he barked out.

He drew in a breath.

'No, I'm not a copper. I was till recently, tell the truth. But I'm not any more. Or not . . . But, all the same, I do have what you might call a copper's interest in Mr Roanoke. And I think perhaps you can help me.'

'Oh, aye?'

'Will you? You believe me when I say he's bad? Not just bad but dangerous?'

'Might.'

'Then you'll help?'

Arthur Arkle shot him a sly glance.

''Pends what help you want, don't it?'

'Only to keep an eye on him. More of one than you do already. A lot more even. From when he first shows his face till when he takes himself to bed. If you can.'

'I can do that all right. If I wants.'

'I hope you will want. I'm not going to be such a fool as to offer to pay you. But if there's anything I can do for you, let me know.'

'Arthur Arkle don't need nothing. He's a porridge man, he is. An' that's enough fer 'im.'

'A porridge man?'

For that he got a look of derision.

'You 'eard o' porridge, I should 'ope. Well, I eats it. Good fer you, that is.'

'It's— It's all you eat? All you want?'

'Bit o' his fruit sometimes. An' blackberries an' such.'

'Well, all right. I couldn't do it. But if you can, well, good luck to you.'

Those might have been words said simply to get on the right side of a potentially useful snout. But, he realized, they had been more. Laced with a flicker of real envy.

103

It seemed Arthur Arkle had taken in what had lain beneath, too. For a long moment he stood in silence, a look of far-away consideration in his watery blue eyes.

'I'll be seeing you time ter time, then.'

It was a bargain struck.

14

Before he left, Sylvester had asked Arthur Arkle one question. He had not had much hope of a useful answer. But he had been lucky.

'I don't suppose you happen to have heard where he was going today?'

'Did though.'

'Oh, yes?'

'He were taking one o' them fancy birds of 'is off with 'im. Heard 'im tell 'er. *"Got to call in at the Clinic, have to drop you there."* Don't know what 'e meant by it, but that's what 'e said.'

But Sylvester had known what Roanoke meant. The Clinic could be only one place. The Rotherfield Clinic.

The Rotherfield Clinic, established on the outskirts of the town some eight or nine years. A rival to the private hospitals of London. Drawing patients from a wide area round. Just the sort of place where as distinguished and wealthy a man as Sir Julian Deane would go when he was seriously ill. Just the sort of place that would be a happy hunting ground for Charles Roanoke.

Before he had gone half a mile on his way, however, he realized he would need an altogether different appearance if he was to get inside somewhere like the Clinic with no valid reason. He reviewed his wardrobe.

Well, yes, he had a suit. Only he had had it for fifteen years. At least. Served its purpose at suit-wearing times. Crown Court witness-box. Occasional smarter-than-usual party, when he could bring himself to go. But hardly up to presenting himself as— What? Concerned nephew of a wealthy aunt about to need medical care? Should do.

So he drove to the town centre, put his horrible vehicle into the spiralling multi-storey car park next to a big department store.

105

And emerged from the already bloated Christmasiness of the place some half-hour later wearing a very good suit, plus new shirt, new silk tie, new black shoes. Conscious, too, despite all the noughts in his bank balance, that the suit had hit his credit card for a good deal more than the £225 sports jacket and £99 trousers he had seen down in London in the days before he had won El Gordo.

He went back up to his dirt-encrusted Q-car, tossed into it a store bag stuffed with his old clobber, took the urine-smelling lift down to ground level again and secured a taxi from the nearby rank. Last touch of the well-padded appearance.

There was a porter's lodge at the Clinic, the porter in a uniform he thought more suited to some slinky foreign army. But without a murmur the man gave him directions for the administration office.

Not that he had any intention of finding his way there without getting conveniently lost.

Lofty corridors, parquet-floored, more reminiscent of the head-quarters of some major industry than a hospital. Wood panelling. Modernistic chandeliers punctuating progress. Discreetly closed doors. With little beige-wood painted signboards beside them. Name of patient: name of doctor or surgeon in charge.

A doddle.

In three minutes he found *Sir Julian Deane – Dr Foster*. But this door was half-open and from inside, he heard with a sudden quickening of his heartbeat, a familiar voice. Braying, confident, smooth, amused and amusing. Roanoke.

Roanoke, as before at the Old School, taking care to be where he could easily be seen or overheard by any passer-by. Taking his precautions.

So had he already persuaded Sir Julian, childless Sir Julian, not to leave his wealth to some institution? It was possible. Clearly possible.

Then was Roanoke, at this instant, despite that half-open door, doing whatever it was that he had done with Miss Gallitly and the others? Ensuring that death came before any change of mind could affect his prospects?

But what could what he was doing be? What had it been?

What wouldn't he give to be able to step inside, somehow invisible, and see exactly what was going on.

Yet he could think of nothing cleverer to do than use the old trick. He dropped down on one knee by the wall and jerked undone the lace of one of his new shoes. Thank God, he had resisted the salesman anxious to get him into a yet more expensive pair, pumps with little gold chains across their insteps.

At least Roanoke's voice was clear enough.

'Oh, Julian, that's priceless. And he really did that? A Minister of the Crown, however awful the party he belonged to. Marvellous.'

Sir Julian's response to this piece of flattery was inaudible. No more than the croaking of an enfeebled voice.

But the intimacy of that 'Julian'. Already, in just the time since Maggie Adams had reported Roanoke buying the old man's furniture, the fellow had ingratiated himself that far.

'And, you know,' the hearty, confident voice came bouncing out of the open door, 'that rather reminds me of an experience of my own. I was asked a year or two ago by— Well, perhaps I'd better not give you a name. Not that you won't easily enough know who I mean. With your knowledge of the world. But let me, all the same, call him Lord X. Lord X, never married – you and I can guess why – bags of family money, and fair game for any half-baked socialistic nonsense going. Well, he wanted to sell a picture. Give the proceeds to the Society for Undermining British Life or something. And do you know what the painting he offered me was? The tattiest piece of Soviet realist art you ever saw. Dreadful beyond words. Gift to him from his masters, no doubt. But, hanging next to it – next to it, would you believe – there was a super little Cotman, been in the family since it was painted, I dare say. So you know what I did? Well, I didn't see why a shit like that should possess part of our country's heritage. So I told him I'd pay him what he was asking if I could have that little landscape I rather liked as part of the bargain. And he fell for it. Fell for it, hook, line, and sinker.'

A faint cackle of feeble mirth from inside the room. And this time the words were just audible.

'Oh, my dear chap, they're everywhere, that sort. You know who's just along the corridor here?'

'Not a Socialist peer?'

'No. Worse. That fellow Toth. Tomas Toth. Came over from Hungary, where I dare say he was as Red as the next man, without a penny piece. And now he's a sight richer than you or me, my dear fellow.'

'Oh, Julian, the age of the gentleman has gone. Gone.'

'I'm afraid it has.' Sylvester was more attuned to the thin voice now. 'But when I think of a fellow like that, able to come here, to this place, to do his dying. Leukemia, they tell me. Well, I hope it gets him, and gets him soon. That's—'

But, from round the corner behind, the click-clicking of approaching heels. Swiftly Sylvester retied his shoe, pushed himself upright, set off at a deliberately uncertain pace, peering at the name-plates on each door he passed.

'Are you looking for someone?'

A nurse. Uniform combining the up-to-dateness of an atomic station with the tradition of Florence Nightingale in the Crimea. And distinctly pretty.

'I'm wanting the administration office actually. But I think I've gone astray.'

She laughed.

'You certainly have. You want to go back to the turn there and then take the other corridor. It's the door right at the end.'

'Thank you. I'm sure I shall find it now.'

He set off in the direction indicated. And, as soon as he had turned the corner, stopped. Listened to those clicking heels. Waited till the sound had ceased. Cautiously went back.

Not safe to risk more than a minute or two more of eaves-dropping. But any extra gleanings might be useful.

Roanoke's voice in full spate.

'. . . I must say I cannot understand how sensible men can let themselves be, I can only say, taken in. Oh, I know, my dear fellow, some of them were your colleagues, or junior colleagues at least. Your friends even. But I have to say it. They're naïve. Naïve. After systematically distrusting the Reds for twenty years and more, suddenly to declare that all along they were really angels, whiter than white. I mean, it's ridiculous. Sheerly ridiculous.'

Then an answer. Now inaudible.

But Roanoke's rejoinder made it clear that there had been no disagreement. As if there would be.

'Absolutely so. Absolutely so. And, my dear chap, soon as you're on your feet again you'll be able to tell them. Letters to

The Times. Words in the right ears. Things like that can't but count. And, of course, you can rely on me to give you all the practical help.'

Voices now from along the corridor. Earnest discussion.

He turned and marched confidently towards them. Two doctors evidently. Ongoing brisk exchange of medical terms. They passed him without a glance.

Outside, he paused to review the situation – if only because, unused to the carelessness of riches, he had failed to tell his cab to wait.

It seemed that Roanoke had altogether wormed himself into Sir Julian's good opinion. Had even got himself enlisted as his assistant when he had recovered. Not that he would recover. Not if he ever made a will in Roanoke's favour.

The man had to be given credit for the speed he had worked. He must have cottoned on in hardly any time to Sir Julian's embittered feeling that all his efforts as a defender of the realm from the menace of Communism – not so long ago a real enough menace – had gone for nothing. And he had played on that with such skill it was hard to withhold a touch of admiration.

But how to counter him? How to watch him at his every visit to the Clinic so closely that his method of murder would come to light?

As a detective of the South Mercia Police, if he had had a boss as dedicated to putting villains behind bars as himself, all the resources needed would have been there for him. The means to bug Sir Julian's room. Even with a camera working through a wall-probe. The Force would have got hold of that if the case was seen to be urgent.

But he was only Bill Sylvester, private citizen.

And millionaire. The thought came to him in a light-flood of revelation. Sophisticated bugging could be bought, if you had enough money. And people to install it.

He had once successfully dealt with a case of electronic eavesdropping. At a branch factory of Ultra-Radionics. Unfortunately the two villains whose services a rival concern had – precisely – bought must still be serving the sentences he had got them. Not for hire.

But then he remembered – mind zig-zagging – there was another villain, or at least doubtful character, that very case had brought him into contact with. Ex-Detective Constable Marshall Wilcox, expert on bugging. Probably as a moonlighter on the other side of the fence on occasion. Certainly, six months or so after the Ultra-Radionics case he had met his come-uppance. Handling stolen goods. And bloody lucky to have got away with just being 'required to resign'. But now he was a private investigator.

Somewhere in Birmingham, if he recollected right. He had been asked to sign a reference for him. Had declined. Had refused point-blank when asked again. Had seen the reference signed George Sugden, Detective Chief Superintendent.

But Marshall Wilcox now it would have to be, little though he liked the idea. Beggars can't be choosers. Nor can millionaires. Not at least if they're in a hurry.

Marshall Wilcox Associates – Matrimonial Investigations – Process Serving – Electronic Surveillance.

The plaque was of stainless steel. The letters on it engraved black. But the place was in one of Birmingham's seamier areas, next to a tired-looking launderette. An even tireder porn-book-shop opposite.

Wilcox saw him with suspicious speed as soon as he had been announced by a bright blonde javelin-breasted receptionist.

Broad-shouldered, spreading belly, shambling movements, large face reddened by weather or drink, nose a mini-map of blue veins. And gold bedecked. Broad strap of watch on one wrist, thick dangling bracelet on the other, signet ring biting into flesh of meat-red finger, wide tie-clip just above the Prince of Wales check waistcoat. Across that, heavy gold chain running from pocket to pocket.

He suppressed a desire to ask after those 'Associates' on the plaque outside. Instead enquired neutrally: 'How's it going then?'

'Lovely. Going just lovely. Why I stayed so long in the force I'll never know. 'Ere, cigar?'

He pushed a box across his large black-ash desk. A small peeling of the veneer at the nearest corner.

'No. Still don't. Thanks.'

'What, not even now you're a blinking millionaire? Thought you'd of spread out a bit.'

Box flipped open, cigar taken out. Cut. Gold cutter. Lit. Gold lighter.

Always a spender, Marshall Wilcox. Collecting shiny objects like a sodding jackdaw. Was his undoing. Video cameras it had been at the time he'd come unstuck. What was it that had emerged? Five thousand quid's worth in less than two years, eighteen months. Probably doing much the same thing again now, only with the gold bits. And got himself in too deep.

But use him while he's still around to use. Millionaire beggars not choosers.

'So you know about my piece of luck then?'

'Seen it in the paper. Didn't see you on the box, though. Thought there'd be something about the ceremony. Dolly actress pressing the flesh. Her flesh on lucky old yours.'

'No. I got them to send the cheque.'

'What, old Suggers not let you off duty? You ought to of chucked it in, like me.'

'Oh, I have, Marshall, I have.'

The look of wariness that had been behind his eyes ever since the door had opened faded like an extinguished electric fire.

'Well then, that's nice. Two ex-coppers together, eh? No awkward questions that got to be asked. Yeah, that's really nice.'

'Well, I am here on business actually. Little job I was hoping you could do for me.'

'What, you got a missus tucked away somewhere none of us knew about? Want her traced, do you? Papers served? Something else you got in mind now? Newest model, complete with quadraphonic sound?'

'No, nothing like that. Just the sort of thing you're particularly good at. Piece of bugging.'

The wary look came back into Wilcox's bloodshot eyes.

'You have left the force? You're not having me on, Mr Sylvester?'

Sylvester suppressed a smile.

'Oh, no. You needn't have any worries there. I'm no longer an officer of the South Mercia Constabulary. I promise you that. And, as a simple citizen, I suppose I'm as entitled to bend the law as the next man.'

'Well, yes. But . . . Well, but, Mr Sylvester, that's not like you. If I may say so.'

It took him half a second to answer.

'No, Marshall. It isn't like me. Or not like the Bill Sylvester

111

you knew. But circumstances change, you know. A million quid changes them quite a lot. And, for reasons I don't really want to go into, I need to know everything that goes on in a private room at the Rotherfield Clinic. You know the place? Can you help me?'

Now a new look of apprehension came on to Marshall Wilcox's large, flabby-with-good-living face.

'Good God, guv, you don't know what you're asking. I do know the place. Private. Privacy the whole name of the game there. In spades.'

'Yes, I dare say. But all the same I want to know everything that's said in that room. I'd really like to have a camera in the room next door, only there's no question of getting the co-operation. And I'm prepared to pay, Marshall. Much as it takes.'

Look of calculation now. One man who should never play poker.

'Well, if you really mean it. But it'll cost you. Arm and a leg. I couldn't do it no cheaper, not even for you, Mr Sylvester.'

'That's all right, Marshall. Just send me the bill. You know I've got the money.'

'All right. But what's it all about? Why're you wanting to know what goes on in there? I mean, bit of a mystery when you come to think about it.'

'Yes. Well, just don't think about it. Let me give you the details, and you get on with whatever it is you do.'

Real Gresham Gallitly stuff. The demanding millionaire. Order and it shall be done.

He was learning.

15

It took Marshall Wilcox three days before he had anything to report. Sylvester had waited patiently. Bugging a resort of the super-rich was not something that could be done in five minutes. Not even if Gresham Gallitly had given the order.

But when the special delivery postman handed him the first of Wilcox's fat envelopes to sign for he ripped it open almost before he had shut his door again.

He ran his eye rapidly through the dense pages. Three short visits from the nurse on duty at hour-long intervals. Nothing there. Except perhaps confirmation, from a touch of anxiety behind the routine questions, that Sir Julian Deane was not far from the end of his life.

But now: afternoon session with Roanoke, the caring visitor.

He skimmed away, wincing occasionally at the typist's many misspellings.

Ah. Something worthwhile here.

Oh, yes, Julian, I meant to ask. Have you thort thouhgt any more about that idae I had?

Yes. Yes, I've been giving it . . . But I'm tired, you know, my dear fello. Tired.

Oh, I know you are. And, believe me, I simpathise. But when something important is there to be done is as well, isn't it, simply to go ahead and do it. And the Fodation, the Julian Deane Foundtion for World Freedom, if anything was ever worthwile, it's that.

I know. I know, my dear chap. And I promise you . . . Tomorrow. Yes, tomorrow.

Well, I'm going to hold you to that, Julian. I'm going to be really tuough.

So, no will changed yet. Plain enough. But certainly coming soon. Everything left to – Christ, he's got a cheek – the Julian Deane Foundation. And who'll see to it one way or another that he gets his little claws on every penny that goes to that bogus institution? Charles Maurice Roanoke.

He skimmed further along.

Nothing much more. The talk now little different from what he'd overheard himself three days before. Mention of Tomas Toth. Roanoke covering his bets?

One of the nurses was telling me the felloe never gets any vistitors.

Sir Julian gasping spitefully.

That will teach him to bring his comun communisttic ideas here.

Roanoke chiming in with a few vicious platitudes.
Turn the page. Roanoke departing. Fulsome talk of return tomorrow. And—
He blinked. Stared.
Two nurses in the room now. Short, sharp medical exchanges. And then—

He's gone, hasn't he, Sister?
Yes. Mite have come any time. Heart the way it was. Straiten him out a bit, Nurse, and put a pilloe under his chin. Sheet over the face. I'll tell Doctor.

Gone. Dead. Sir Julian dead. Just like that.
So . . . So Roanoke missing his chance once again. Quarry simply dying on him before he'd managed even to bring him down.
Ironic.
And not only ironic for Roanoke.
He felt as if he equally had been checked in the hunt. If Roanoke had no victim in sight eventually to use his unknown poisoning method against, there was no chance of discovering what it was he did. Had done to Miss Gallitly. To Mrs Bathurst, Miss Pettiman, Mrs Forth.

But where would the fellow turn now? Would he make yet another attempt? Or would he decide the moment had come to give up? Luck against him. So chuck it in, the dangerous game.

Because, never mind how often he had got away with it up till now, a damn dangerous game it was he was playing. And he must know it. So would he decide to be like anyone else? To admit his reaching for wealth had been too ambitious? Surrender? Settle for less?

But he knew Roanoke was not the sort to settle for less. Could have told that, he thought, the first moment I set eyes on him, standing there in his garage in that aggressively patterned check suit, burgeoning behind its waistcoat, with in front of him that time-worn flour-chest just made more valuable – no, more expensive – by having been shot full of fake wormholes.

No, Charles Roanoke would still be hunting.

And then he knew where the hunter would look first for his game. In the room at the Rotherfield Clinic not a door or two away from Sir Julian's. Where, near to death from leukaemia, lay the Hungarian entrepreneur who had made so much money out of – what was it? – radios or something. Some new electronic gadget sold at half the price of any rival machine. Tomas Toth.

Marshall Wilcox seemed to have got himself a new typist. Fed up with the blonde with the javelin breasts? But at least now the stuff coming out of Toth's room at the Clinic was easy to read.

Couple of pages of the routine visits from the nurses.

Just one more little test, Mr Toth.

What for? What for? You've had nearly all the blood in me already.

Doctor's orders, Mr Toth.

And I'm feeling hundred per cent OK. Think I'll go home. That helicopter of mine out there at the back still?

Oh, yes, Mr Toth. But I don't think you'll be getting into it for quite a while yet. Not till after Christmas at the very best. Your trouble can go into remission, but, you know, it's always liable to come back. And at any moment.

Don't believe you, Nursie.

Well then, we'll see what this test has to tell us, shall we? Now just bend your arm.

Quite enough of that.

Ah, unexpected visitor. Unexpected for Mr Toth. Expected by yours truly. And recognizable enough, even without the self-introduction.

Oh, yes, you're Charles Roanoke, and you happened to hear, visiting someone else, that Tomas Toth was in a nearby room. And, oh, yes, you've been a great but distant admirer of his enterprise, and you couldn't resist the chance of paying your respects. If you're feeling up to a visitor, that is.

Oh, come on, boot him out, Mr Toth.

But, no.

Sit down, sit down. Glad to see the friendly face. All those people I know, all the people Tomas Toth has given big, big champagne parties for – nice things to eat, all from Fortnum and Mason, flown up that afternoon – they don't come to see old Tomas when he's ill. Who wants to see someone going to die? That's what they think here, you know. That I'm going to die. They don't tell me to my face. They're not the sort to do that. But I know what they think. And they've let all the people ringing to ask know it, too. So they don't come. But why blame them? I don't, not one little bit. People want to live. I want to live. I want to enjoy.

Oh, that's quite right, Mr Toth. It's what I always say. Let everyone enjoy the good things of this world. Never mind, if you've had a poor start. Get rich. I don't think that's incompatible with a good Communist upbringing.

Good Communist. No such thing, Mr What-you-called. I tell you, Tomas Toth had one and enough of Communist shit when he was a boy. To each according to his needs. Tomas got more needs than most. Big needs.

I'm sure you had, Mr Toth. All I meant, you know, was that being brought up in a Communist country doesn't mean you've got to stay poor all the rest of your life.

Communist country? Hungary wasn't never a Communist country. What you saying?

No, I think we're at cross-purposes. What I meant was you having spent your early days under Communism. I can't tell you, in fact, how absolutely heartening it is to know that there is somebody in this world who was able to buck the system in the way you did. It's wonderful. Wonderful.

Christ, if only I was back in the Force. Maybe this isn't strictly evidence. But it'd be enough to go on. More than enough. Buttering up those two poor old sods in totally different ways. Obvious. Absolutely obvious what the bugger's up to.

Or – don't overdo it – absolutely obvious he's having a go for their money. But murder's another thing. And how did he bring that off before? Not a clue in all this bumf.

He skimmed along again.

Jesus, enough to make you sick. The bare-faced flattery. And Toth seemed to be falling for it. Hard-headed businessman he may have been, must have been to have made all that money. But bloody Roanoke twisting him round his little finger. You have to give it to the sod.

That's enormously interesting, Mr Toth. But— But there's one thing that does alarm me, I must admit.

You don't want to go being alarmed, Mister. You want to enjoy. Enjoy. No use you thinking: this going to be bad for me, this good. If you like, you got to do it, you got to have it. That's why I got my helicopter. Because I like to have one. No use thinking: will I crash in it, will it get me there really quicker? No. You see a helicopter. You think, that's nice. You get.

Oh, yes. Admirable. Admirable. But all the same I do confess to one niggle.

Don't have no niggles, Mr— Mr Whatever. Did I niggle when my poor wife wanted to have friends for tennis? No. I get you a court, I said. And what did I do? Got three. Got three. Case the first wasn't right, case she wanted more friends to play. But poor Lily. Dead. Poof. Dead. But she wouldn't want her Tomas to be sorrow. No. Enjoy. Enjoy.

But all the same, Mr Toth, we do all have to die one day, and that's what worries me. What's going to happen to your— To your empire – it's nothing less – when you come to – er – that.

Tomas Toth not going to die. Can't be, yet. Feeling hundred per cent, Mr Your-name.

Well, of course you're not going to die yet, Mr Toth. Of course, you're not.

The bugger. Knows bloody well the man's got leukaemia.

Terminal. That's what the nurses gossiped to Sir Julian. Terminal leukaemia. And yet he has the sodding cheek . . . No, worse, the damn cruelty, to say to the fellow he's not going to die yet.

But all the same, Mr Toth, what's going to become of Toth Industries, if— Well, if anything should happen to you?

If Tomas Toth – what they say? – kicking the bucket, yes? Well, he don't care one bugger what happens then. Tomas not here to enjoy: nothing happen, nothing left. No, no. While I got I enjoy. Enjoy making plenty of money. Enjoy making plenty mini-videos, people want to buy. Mini-tellies. Enjoy. Enjoy spending what I got. Getting things that's nice. You seen my cars, Mr Can't-remember? TOTH 1, TOTH 2, TOTH 3, 4, 5. Got 'em all. Because I enjoy to have, yes? I enjoy people to see.

Oh, yes. Excellent, excellent. But, you know, I can't bear to think of all that you've done just disintegrating one day. What you want, you know, is what I might call a successor. I'm so sorry you never had a son. A son to carry on the line. Or a daughter, even.

Oh, wanted. Wanted. My Lily wanting bad. And, by fuck, we trying. Night after night. That bed it nearly was falling in pieces. But no go. Nothing. Not never. So what you got to do? You got to say some things just can't get to be. So enjoy what can. Enjoy, enjoy, enjoy.

But— But don't you want to think it'll all go on after you?

Poor Roanoke. Almost makes you laugh. Come up against a tougher nut than he counted on this time.

He read on.

Nothing much different. Roanoke backing off. Live to fight another day. That'd be it. And at least, as he at last said goodbye to his new friend, he promised to come again next day. And offer accepted. Even eagerly.

So see what tomorrow brings, then. Or what today is bringing, in fact. Because even now the little machine Marshall Wilcox has got hidden somewhere in the Clinic grounds in radio-reach of the mini-bug he somehow got lined up on Tomas Toth's sick-room must be whirring away. Recording this day's doings.

*

But next day it was Marshall Wilcox himself who came to the door, gold bracelet chinking, gold chain across sprawling stomach, black briefcase with gold, gold clasps clutched in one meat-red hand. And a good deal earlier than his special delivery packet had been due.

'Yes, Marshall, what is it? Your machine up the spout, or what?'

'Nothing like that, guv. Nothing like that. You're paying a hell of a lot for this, and you're getting the best. Promise you that.'

'So to what do I owe the honour . . . ?'

'Saving you money perhaps, Mr Sylvester. You see, there's been what you might call a development.'

'Oh, yes? What development?'

'It's like this, guv. I was over at the Clinic, making sure everything was OK. Charging you for the time, of course, but I reckon you can afford it.'

'Yes, yes. But what's happened?'

'I brought you the tape, guv. Listen for yourself.'

Well, Mr Toth, something of considerable interest.

Smoothy voice. But authoritative. Who? Ah, the consultant. Person who'd ordered that test Toth agreed to so reluctantly. So what was so interesting?

The cytological findings were always subject to a certain amount of doubt, of course.

What the hell's that long word? Cyto-whatsit?

Ah, the layman's commonsensical attitude. Cytology, Mr Toth, is the study of the function of the cells, their multiplication and so forth.

The cells that were multiplying me to death. That it?

Yes, that is more or less it. But I am happy to tell you that they prove not to have been – er – multiplying you to anywhere at all. The diagnosis was somewhat complicated by the fact that you were suffering from pneumonia. But it's plain now that you have been the victim of nothing more serious than a variety of mononucleosis. You're a fit man, in principle, Mr Toth.

That I could have been telling this past week. I was enjoying life, Mister. Enjoying. And going to bloody well go on enjoying.

Sylvester smiled.

Poor bloody Roanoke. Foiled again. If it wasn't someone dying on him before he'd screwed a new will out of them, it was someone miraculously coming back to life. Or misdiagnosedly coming back. Call it which you want.

But where was he to go now? Where are both of us to go?

16

One thing, Sylvester thought, I can't sit back doing nothing – like one of the idle rich.

If he could not see immediately how he was going to get his man into the dock now, he could at least try to make sure the fellow had not already found another target. There might well be some other person whose furniture he was buying before they went into a retirement place that he had lined up. A second string to his bow. Wouldn't put it past him. Not for a minute.

So, next day, Saturday, he was out in his Q-car, well before full daylight, parked on the verge of the road some two hundred yards from the big mock farmhouse. A good half-hour, he reckoned, before the earliest that Roanoke was likely to leave.

And there he waited, crouching out of sight of any chance passer-by on the car's back seat looking out of its wide rear window. It was not until just after nine that lights appeared at the house. And, bar a visit from the postman, that was the only sign of life he saw all day. Roanoke never stirred. Hungry and cold himself – he had failed to bring more to eat than a squashy pizza from his fridge, and some whisky remains that proved only intermittently warming – he pictured the big man sprawled in front of a logs-piled fire, sports programmes on the TV, bottle of his – what was it? – Something-or-other Chambertin at his elbow. But only when it got dark again did he abandon his watch.

Next morning, heaving back his duvet to the chill of 6.30 a.m., he almost decided to wrap it round himself again and stay where he was. He could hardly see Roanoke turning out early on a Sunday, and besides it looked as if the day ahead was going to be foul. Rain was bulleting against his window.

But a few minutes after seven he was once more in place in the Q-car, and twenty minutes later he saw – bounce of self-justified pleasure – lights come on in the farmhouse.

Roanoke left, in his Range Rover, half an hour afterwards.

Following had been extremely tricky while in the near-darkness of early morning; he had had to use his headlights. Only because Roanoke, too, was driving with lights was he able to keep the smart grey vehicle in sight at all. But as soon as there was enough light, sluggish and intermittently darkened by squally showers though it was, he ventured closer. Near enough to be in no danger of missing some unexpected turn.

But where was Roanoke going? Some arrangement to view an invalid's furniture at a time suiting them? Very unlikely. But not safe to give up the pursuit.

And now, on a main road, the Range Rover was going at a speed that was taxing his battered old vehicle to the utmost. Twice he thought he had lost his man. But on each occasion, by sticking hopefully, hopelessly, to the road, when Roanoke had been slowed down by dawdling traffic he got within sight again.

They ended up in Boston. The bells in the tall tower of its church – the Stump, didn't they call it? – ringing good people to church. But Roanoke was not a good person. The first distant taste of sea air had brought an ominous recollection. Roanoke was not only evil but was also the new owner of a boat. A £30,000 boat, if he remembered the gossip he had picked up from antiques-dealer acquaintances.

So was the fellow making a dash for safety? Had something alerted him? Suggers, after all, forced for some reason to set enquiries on foot?

And, yes, as the Range Rover snaked quietly through the town, his guess at its eventual destination seemed more and more likely. Eventually it was brought to a halt outside a pub looking down on the Witham, its slaty water almost choppy from the ferocity of a buffeting east wind. If this was a getaway, Roanoke was going to have a bloody rough time of it at sea.

He took the Q-car just round the next corner, parked quickly, walked carefully back.

Roanoke was down at the river, just boarding a powerful-looking white-hulled boat. The *Sunburst*. Presumably he'd named her – she looked brand-new – himself.

Must cost him a packet keeping her here, bang in the centre of the town. And what the hell to do if, in a few minutes, the engine broke into thunderous life? Run to the nearby bridge? Leap down from it on to the boat's deck? Wrestle with the villain, pin him down, hear a gasped-out confession?

Well, more like, just watch him nose his way down river, and say goodbye for ever to a four-times murderer. Nothing else to do, when you came down to it.

But the boat's engine never fired. After almost an hour, while overhead rain-heavy clouds raced under the high wind and from time to time spilled their chilly contents in pinging, hard showers, the unpounced-upon villain emerged and made his way back to his vehicle.

So apparently all he had been doing was contemplating a trip out to sea. Flex the muscles of his fancy craft. Bluster through the waves. And, when he had waited that hour for the weather to take a turn for the better and had found it had not, he had decided to let caution prevail.

As he did when engaged in acquiring his too quickly arrived at bequests.

Oxfam mac soaked through as comprehensively as if it had been made of paper, Sylvester put himself squelchily into the driving seat of his ancient, if reliable, vehicle.

On the Monday Roanoke was no early bird. It was gone half-past eleven before he took the Bentley out of the big garage. Once more Sylvester saw that cool interior, the crimson of the wine in its goblet, the harsh red fire-extinguisher, the looming pieces of furniture, the check-suited, gun-cradling man.

Waiting until the big car was just out of sight, he scrambled over the seat of his own battered vehicle and was after it in less than a minute.

An effort pretty much wasted, as it turned out. Roanoke drove into the town, found a space for the Bentley in the big car park where till a few years back twice-weekly markets were held – *Bought a bloody good pair of shoes there once* – walked round to an exercise gym, newly opened, and disappeared inside.

Sylvester, illegally parked in the street, had followed, hung about outside, walking past the place once and pausing just long enough to read its advertisement detailing all the apparatus you could use for a subscription of £500 a year. When, an hour later, Roanoke came out he was poised to follow. Aged mac, shapeless trilby.

Short walk to the Coq d'Or, scene of their last face-to-face encounter witnessed with surprise by Colin Taylor, unconsulted financial adviser.

For a little Sylvester lingered just beyond, wondering how long it would be safe to leave Roanoke inside. But then a girl – short skirt, long legs, mass of brass-blonde hair, great waft of heady perfume – passed by him and in her turn swept into the restaurant. He made a bet with himself: latest bit from whatever had followed the Lloyd Webber–Tim Rice show at the Alhambra that – what was her name? – Susie Frank had been in. If so, Roanoke would be safe for a good two hours.

He hurried back to the Q-car – no warden had pounced – and drove as fast as he could go to the farmhouse. High time he had a word in safety with Arthur Arkle, porridge man.

Nowhere to be seen as, without going through the pretence of tugging at the fancy iron bell-pull, he walked down the sodden lawns and on through the orchard. Rotten pears and apples reduced to mush now. But, at the far end, he saw a thin trickle of smoke rising up from beside a big old oak tree at the corner of the first field beyond the hedge.

Glance this way and that. And, yes, a gap. Not easy to slip through, even shoulder first, but possible. From it, a path, or a track through the grass at least. And, tucked beneath the oak, visible now an ancient railway carriage.

Three minutes later he was tapping on one of its doors, amused to see, in faint still gold-coloured paint, it bore the number '1'.

Arthur Arkle's leather-brown face came thrusting out of a rattled-down window at the far end. Watery blue eyes peering unwinkingly.

'So you come, then.'

'Yes, said I'd be in touch.'

'Ain't got nothin' for you, though.'

The window rattled up and shut with a thump.

Sylvester stood there for a moment. Then decided the transaction had been all that was necessary. If disappointing.

With time now to spare, he drove back into the town at a respectable speed, put his vehicle into the car park this time, though at a distance from Roanoke's Bentley, stationed himself again on the far pavement a little way along from the Coq d'Or.

Just fancy a plate of that duck I had there. But better things to do with my money. Like standing here pretending to be window-shopping. Thank Christ, (a) it's not bloody raining, (b) shops happen to be the sort a gawper might gawp into.

Place selling some sort of water-purifying system. Clever trick device in the window. Tap apparently suspended in mid-air with a twisting stream of water, very crystal-clear, running perpetually into a bowl beneath. Could buy one of those thingies, not miss the price. But, even if it's half as efficient as that trick tap implies, would it be worth it? Lengthen your life by two or three months? But, even so . . .

Time to stroll on. Never do to attract the attention of a passing wooden-top. One who doesn't know me. Get done for loitering with intent. Intent to steal one expensive and doubtfully useful water-purifier.

Jeweller's. Well, yeah, more reasonable for passing plod to ask a few questions. But equally somewhere your honest citizen, if a jackdaw type, might pause to slaver over what they couldn't afford to buy. So nice long stay here. And nicely polished window reflecting entrance to the Coq d'Or, stand at the right angle.

And, after rather longer than it was sensible to have gazed at the glittery stock, that entrance at last disgorged Roanoke. Proprietorial hand placed firmly on – guess who – Miss Heady Perfume.

Sylvester, after seeing they had turned in the direction of the car park, beat them there by a good three minutes. Followed the Bentley, soon sure it was heading back to the farmhouse. Halted long enough to see it turn in through the open gate. Decided events inside would keep the two of them busy. Drove home.

Looked as if Roanoke had not found a new target yet. But there must be some other way of getting at him. Four-times murderer. There had to be.

Like – why not? – go back to the very beginning?

The Dringfield and Westmarch Dogs Refuge looked no different from the way it had when with a sulking Mikey Cross he had been there to investigate its secretary's anonymous letter accusing Charles Roanoke of murder. Pro Bono Publico even took as long to respond to his ring at the tarnished brass bell as he had done back in September.

And for the same reason.

125

'Sorry, sorry, in the lav,' he jabbered out even before he had got the door fully open.

Then, taking in who was standing on the pock-holed tiled front path, his face fell, comically as a clown's with descending trousers.

'Police. But— But— I told you everything I knew. I mean, I thought that whole business had been forgotten. If I made a mistake, I've said I was sorry.'

'Relax, Mr Maffin. I don't think you did make a mistake. And I'm not the police. Not any more.'

Peter Maffin, same baggy flannels, leather-patched jacket, pale pinched face, owlish spectacles, looked simply puzzled.

'If I can come in, I'll explain.'

'Oh, yes, yes. Excuse me, I should have . . . But, you see, I thought . . .'

Sylvester urged him into the bare office. Sheepdog with a stupid sheep.

The room might have been back in September, so little had anything in it changed. The piles of yellowing pamphlets on the plywood shelves looked precisely as untidy as they had then. The big old typewriter was in just the same position as when, to scare Maffin, he had rattled off *The quick brown fox jumped over the lazy dog.* Perhaps a few more fly-specks had arrived on the bare bulb at the centre of the ceiling.

Could there really be a way to Roanoke here? But try. Nothing else to do.

'Mr Maffin, when we last saw each other I'm afraid we didn't exactly end up on the same side of the fence.'

Peter Maffin replied to that with an uneasy grin.

'At that time, of course, I was a police officer and it was my duty to see that, as we said in the Force, there was to be no breach of the peace on your part.'

'But— I mean, I would never have—'

'Oh, yes, I've no doubt you wouldn't have done anything foolish. I knew it at the time. But the official line has to be followed.'

'Yes. Yes, I suppose so.'

'But now things are different. I resigned from the police some time ago.'

A sudden look of enlightenment on Maffin's round-spectacled face.

'Oh, yes, now I know. You're the chap who won a million

126

pounds, aren't you? That Spanish thing. I read about it in the local rag, and I thought I recognized you. But your photo, if I may say so, wasn't very good, and I never properly caught your name before. That is— Well, then – er – when you were here before.'

'Yes, I quite understand. A detective inspector can be pretty intimidating, even to someone perfectly innocent.'

'Well, yes. Yes, you sort of were. And your sergeant.'

Weak grin.

'I dare say. Sergeant Cross had his uses, but he wasn't exactly sympathetic.'

'But why have you come to see me now, Insp— Er— I'm afraid I still don't recall your name.'

'Sylvester, Bill Sylvester.'

'Well, why then, Mr Sylvester, have you come? I can't— You don't perhaps want to make a donation to the Refuge? If you could spare us something from that – er – million, I assure you we'd be very grateful.'

'Well, I might do that, Mr Maffin. Yes, I might. But what I came out here for was to ask if by any chance there had been anything, when I was here in September, any little extra point, you never got round to mentioning.'

Frightened look flitting back.

'But I assure you I did my best. I really think I told you everything. Except— Well, somehow your sergeant – Did you say Sergeant Cross? – was rather off-putting, actually.'

'Yes, I thought that might have been the case. So there was something you might have added, was there?'

Here? Now? The way in? But, likely as not, just some idiotic nothing.

Feeble smile on the owl-spectacled face.

'Well, it was only sort of an idea. I mean, please don't think that right from the start when I wrote that letter I wasn't doing my absolute best. To— To assist the police.'

'I'm sure you were, Mr Maffin. I'd be inclined to say you're one of the few members of the general public with a conscience.'

See if a bit of flattery helps spoon it out. Whatever it is. Did before, if I remember. Something about the CC being impressed.

'Well, yes. One does try to act like a good citizen.'

Worked.

127

'So tell me, please, what was it you didn't manage to get round to before? You said you told me everything except. Except what, Mr Maffin?'

Maffin swallowed.

'Well, you see, I'd promised. I made a promise to my friend – er – Nurse Dexter, that I wouldn't repeat it. She said that talk of that sort only led to trouble all round.'

'Repeat what, Mr Maffin?'

Like blood from a sodding stone. But press on.

'Yes, Mr Maffin?'

Two gulping swallows.

'Well, it was just after Margaret Bathurst had died. She was very upset, Nurse Dexter. And she just came out with it.'

Can this be it? Might be, might be. Just that one detail about how that first victim died. The way in? At last?

'Yes?'

Keep it calm. Gently, gently.

'Well, what she actually said was that if Mrs Bathurst had been a younger woman and in possession of her full health, she would have wondered if her symptoms didn't indicate something.'

Something. Something. Oh God, why can't the fellow bloody cough it up. But slowly. Slowly-slowly, or I'll lose the bugger.

'Yes, I see. But just what symptoms was she talking about?'

'It's— It's hard to recall exactly, after all this length of time. And you must remember that it was only just one passing remark.'

'Yes, yes. I take all that into account. But, after all, you were the one to make those suggestions of something not being right in the first place. So if you want it all to be followed up, you really ought to do your best to remember what Nurse Dexter suspected, however long ago it was.'

'Yes. Yes, I know.'

Pallid smile now. And a deep breath.

'Well, it was like this. I think. In her last hours Margaret Bathurst showed signs of being very over-excited. Unduly. Yes, unduly. And there was evidence, too, of some trouble with the kidneys. I think it was the kidneys. And then— Well, then there were the convulsions that finally brought the end.'

'I see. And Nurse Dexter thought these were symptoms of poisoning? By what, Mr Maffin?'

This could be it. A clue to just what it is Roanoke uses. Then find out where he gets it. And proof of an illegal purchase, say. This could be the beginning of his come-uppance. Start of the final trail.

But Maffin's face crossed with doubts.

'Well, that was the whole trouble really. What the symptoms indicated.'

'The trouble? How?'

'You see . . . Well, you see they are some of the symptoms, at least so Nurse Dexter told me, that occur in cases of— Well, of poisoning from cocaine.'

'You mean Mrs Bathurst was an addict?'

What was the fellow saying? Was this in the end all total nonsense?

'No, no, nothing like that. She just thought, Nurse Dexter, that someone had given Margaret Bathurst cocaine. Somehow. Quite soon afterwards, of course, she made sure it could not have been so. But, before, she had made that unfortunate remark. So, of course, she made me promise to forget I'd ever heard it. And I tried to. I really did. But you can't forget something like that. And when you were questioning me I wanted to tell you. But— But, well, you were rather hard on me, and then there was that Sergeant Cross. Looming. He didn't say very much, but I felt all the time I was being . . . Well, menaced.'

'Sergeant Cross often had that effect.'

'So, you see, that was why I didn't tell you. That and my promise to Mary. To Nurse Dexter. You won't go to her and say that I broke my word, will you?'

'I don't think I'd be likely to get any more information from Nurse Dexter, even if I did.'

'Well, no. No, Mary knows how to keep silent when she thinks that's best. Definitely.'

17

Cocaine. Was this the poison Roanoke was using? Certainly, it would be the sort of stuff a man with money to flash could get hold of without much trouble. Recreational drug, as the publications called it. Recreation of people able to pay for it, whether the cash came from the bank or breaking-and-entering.

But if Roanoke had made use of it, and four times one after another over the years, surely some doctor would have been alerted. Dr Hardew, attending three of the cases at Astwood Manor, was plainly no slouch, for all his obsession with high-priced electronic medical aids.

If he remembered rightly, too – and he must get hold of a Glaister or some other reference book and check – the presence of cocaine in a fatal quantity showed up at a post-mortem from severe degeneration of the liver. Quote, unquote. So wouldn't there have been signs indicating an autopsy?

Then there was the question of administering. The stuff could be injected. But how could Roanoke have injected those old ladies with cocaine? Ridiculous. And it could – check again – be ingested. Lovely medical word. But it took, if he had it correctly, quite a large amount to be fatal, ingested. And how could Roanoke, who had been so careful not to be with Miss Gallitly at the Old School anywhere near meal-times, have contrived to get her, or any other of his victims, to ingest? Very unlikely.

So, after all, going back to Peter Maffin had hardly advanced things.

But all the same, cocaine. It could be. Now, any way of finding out if Roanoke was a user himself? Might account for the damn cockiness.

How about Miss Heady Perfume still at this moment probably rollicking about in some big bed with him? Maybe they'd both snorted beforehand. No, better. Go for Off-with-the-old. The one before. Susie Frank. And it shouldn't be too difficult to track down an actress lately in work, if still not on tour somewhere. At the worst it might mean laying out a few quid more than the twenty he had donated – Jesus, the way the rich lived – to the Dringfield and Westmarch Dogs Refuge.

The London restaurant Susie Frank had suggested in snapped-up answer to his invitation – 'Near my little flat', which Sylvester translated as 'bed-sit' – was slightly less high-priced than Roanoke's Coq d'Or haunt. But only slightly. Yet Sylvester, looking down the menu, felt he could hardly complain. He had calculated all along that to get the dirt on Roanoke he would have to treat Susie to what she saw as the best.

Costly business, this being a one-man police force. Especially with Marshall Wilcox at this very moment totting up yet more for keeping obbo on Roanoke. But millionaires can't be choosers. And it had cost nothing to track Susie down. One call to the *Stage* newspaper, letting it be understood he was the South Mercia Police, and he had learnt where the Lloyd Webber–Tim Rice show was now playing. One call to the theatre, conveniently within reach of London. And an eager Susie accepting an invitation.

Susie – God, how silly she was – did not, like Colin Taylor, begin by choosing with an accountant's accuracy the most expensive item on the menu. But she did hover infuriatingly between *Quail egg and bacon salad* and *King prawns and rocket with passion-fruit vinaigrette*. Marked emphasis on the passion-fruit.

And this is just for starters – pun, pun, pun. Then, asked what she would like to drink, tremendous pout and actually breathing out: 'Champers is lovely always, isn't it?'

So he wasted little time in dragging the talk round to her stay with Roanoke. Not difficult. Her conversational powers consisting mostly of leaning over the table to give him the benefit of puffily bra-projected breasts.

'Oooh, he was ever so nice, Charles.'

Nice enough to offer a snort?

'I can imagine how nice he was.'

'Well, you know, he's rolling in it. Rolling.'

He braced himself, and took advantage of that wide-eyed delight in Roanoke's wealth to push things on to an intimate plane.

'Bet that wasn't the only rolling that went on out there. Many a roll between the sheets, eh?'

'Oooh, you are naughty. Naughty but nice.'

God, was whatever this bloody meal was costing not going to be enough? Would he have to get the sodding girl to bed before she'd tell him anything worth hearing?

Well, at least bedding a witness, if it did come to that, could be done now he was a detective inspector only for the purpose of getting information from the *Stage* newspaper.

Still, try again.

'Oh, come on, sweetheart. What did the two of you do all the time? Swim up and down in that pool of his?'

'Oh no, it was only me that used the pool. When he left me all on my own, the morning you called round.' Advance of two breasts cuddled together. 'And caught me almost in the altogether.'

Let that one pass.

'So what did you and your friend do when he was there? He give you a good time?'

'Between the sheets, you mean? Well, I will admit there were goings-on there. And not too many sheets about it. Big mirror over the bed. And a very naughty picture on the wall.'

Abruptly she spluttered into giggles.

Hell, I'm not going to get a blow-by-blow commentary, am I?

But he wasn't.

'It was ever so funny once, as a matter of fact.'

'Oh, yes?'

What was coming now?

'Yes. You see, a girl found herself in some rather peculiar positions there, and once when he was – well, you know – busy down below I found I was looking up right under that picture. He said it was a real antique, and ever so valuable. Victorian. But it looked just like a dirty picture to me. And I don't mean all covered in grot neither.'

How much of this was he going to have to put up with? And was what she'd seen under Roanoke's Victorian erotica going to be worth hearing about? Well, try to bring her back to it.

'But behind the dirty picture, you were saying . . . ?'

'Ooh, yes. Almost forgot what I was telling you. Well, it was a safe. You know, just like on the films. Hidden behind the picture.'

*

132

The whereabouts of Roanoke's safe was all he got out of lunching lickerish little Susie. Besides a hefty bill. Much hovering between *Grilled halibut with samphire and beurre blanc* – remembered reference to Shakespeare's 'one that gathers samphire, dreadful trade' falling on totally deaf ears – and *Rib-eye of Scotch beef marinated in orange, virgin olive oil, and garlic, with wild mushrooms.* Great giggling over the virginity of the olive oil. But nothing more. And his own attempt to have beef unsoaked in orange juice and oil greeted with hostile contempt by the waiter.

And not a hint about Roanoke as a cocaine user, neither one way or the other. Absolutely easy though he had made it for Susie to talk about that.

But, in the train on the way back, he decided the single scrap of information he had acquired might prove worthwhile after all. If Roanoke had a safe he took pains to hide, then it was likely to have in it things needing hiding. Could he get a look at them?

Break into the place? *Millionaire on Burglary Charge.* Not if there was any other way. And there was, by God. Intensive mental flip through remembered record-sheets. And, bingo. Ratty Peters. Ideal for the job.

Ratty. Professional safe-breaker. In and out of prison most of his life. But for the past few years, far as he knew, reformed. Or at least feeling himself too old to go on. And, if his last impressions of him were correct, not enjoying the affluent old age his exploits might have brought him. Largely because when whatever mob he was working with had made a good haul he invariably began spending his share fast as he could go. Leading, almost as invariably, to arrest caught with recorded-numbers notes.

So now ripe to operate once more. If paid enough.

Must go to the bank tomorrow. Do something about getting the million – what's left of it – earning some interest. If not through any of Colin Taylor's complexities.

Ratty – Sylvester had recalled his address without difficulty: he had been there giving it a spin more than once – was well named. Jockey-shaped, nose with a little extra white tip, eyes switching always this way and that. Somewhere in his sixties now, and coughing with it.

On the doorstep.

'Mr Sylvester. I ain't done nothing. What you want to come

round 'ere for? There ain't even been anything for me to 'ave done.'

'Just a friendly call, Ratty. Happy Christmas, and all that.'

'I know your friendly calls. I'm down the nick before I got time to draw breath.'

'No, no, Ratty. This is friendly, hundred per cent. You're not talking to the Bill any more, you know.'

'What you mean?'

'I've resigned, Ratty. Turned it in. Come on to your side of the fence, if you like.'

'Honest? You ain't a copper no more? But why, Mr Sylvester? You was all copper always. Not like some.'

'And now I'm not. Never again. I came into some money, and I found I was fed up with the likes of Detective Chief Superintendent Sugden. That's all.'

'Well, come in then, Mr Sylvester. Come in, though Gawd knows what you're 'ere for. Want ter share a bit of that money you come into?'

He cackled with laughter. Sylvester withstood the waft of rotten-teeth breath. Opportunity to be seized.

'Well, Ratty, as a matter of fact I have come to offer you a few quid.'

The look of disbelief on the rodent-like features was purely comical.

'In exchange for a little job of work I'd like you to do.'

Comical look vanishing.

'What work? I'm a pensioner, I am. Don't need to work never no more.'

'Your usual sort of work, Ratty.'

'Here, you don't mean a blagging? I ain't done nothing like that since I don't know when.'

'Well, since about three years back, as I recall. Bristol cigarette factory, night before pay day. Very nice job on the safe.'

'Your lot never could put that down to me.'

'But it's not *my lot* any more. I told you.'

'So what you want then? You can't really mean you want me to do a peter for you.'

'But I do, Ratty.'

'Listen, I'm going straight now.'

Inwardly Sylvester sighed. He had hoped it would not come to bullying.

'Yes, Ratty, you're going straight, and how well off has that left you? Comfortable in your old age, are you?'

He took a slow survey of the room. One armchair in greasy moquette, once patterned red and green, right arm curling from its true position. A gas fire, turned low and popping intermittently, scarcely warming the place. Above, on the narrow mantelpiece, a single cheap Christmas card, already sagging a little. In front, a teapot with a large white chip on its brown surface. Table covered with oilcloth, stained with dozens of rings. Packet of sugar and milk bottle on it, one empty unwashed cup and a half-bottle of whisky with a drain left in the bottom. Two hard chairs, one with a crack in its top bar.

Enough. Point made.

'Well, Mr Sylvester, I has to take the rough with the smooth. Don't everyone?'

'No, Ratty, they don't. Some people get themselves the smooth for ever. And it's one of them I have in mind for your attentions.'

'Look, no, Mr Sylvester. No. I couldn't do another stretch. It'd be the finish of me. I cough something terrible, Mr Sylvester. In the night. I can't hardly sleep.'

'So you want to move to somewhere less damp. You want to be able to go to bed every night with whisky coming out of your ears.'

He saw temptation beginning to eat inwards.

'It'll be worth a couple of thousand to you, Ratty. You could do with that, couldn't you?'

'But why d'you want somebody's peter done? That's what I can't understand. You, Mr Sylvester.'

'Never mind why, Ratty. Just think of the money. What it could get you.'

Long moment of hesitation. Then he saw it coming. The look of worked-up resolution hardening the rat-like features.

'Suppose I must, then. Seeing as it's you, Mr Sylvester. So where is it?'

'Big house just outside the town. Owned by a chap called Roanoke.'

'Roanoke. The antiques feller?'

'Yes, that's him. Know him, do you? You didn't ever do a job for him, by any chance?'

'I did not. He's straight, far's I know. But, listen, I sussed that place out once. And I tell you this, I ain't going anywhere near it now. Not for a couple of grand. Not for ten.'

Jesus, what's gone wrong?

'Why not, Ratty? For Christ's sake, it's only an ordinary private house. No guards. No dogs. Should be in and out for a smart operator like you.'

'But don't you know about it? Thought you'd be bound to. Wired straight up to your nick, or what was your nick. Touch a window there and half the coppers in the county be breathing down your neck.'

Damn, damn damn. Of course, Roanoke's place would be ranked 'Very High Class' on the Burglary Computer. And, yes, a friendly word with Suggers at one of those Rotary dinners and he would get all the extra service he could ask for.

So what to do? Well, don't let Ratty off the hook for one thing.

'Oh yes, I dare say you would have caught it, at the time you sussed the place out. Because then you didn't have a friend who'd got access to all the security details. But now you have, Ratty. Now you have.'

But had he? What access did a retired detective inspector have to any security details?

Ratty's eyes, now, were flicking from side to side even more rapidly.

'No, honest, Mr Sylvester, I can't risk it. Not at my age. Them days is done. Straight up.'

But he was the best bet, possibly the only one. Don't let up on him.

'For fifteen hundred quid, Ratty? You could get yourself a lot of home comforts for that.'

Look of calculation plain to see. With the total dropping down five hundred by five hundred with each objection. Dutch auction. But he had to be made to toe the line. Poor devil.

'Well, if you can get me the info, Mr Sylvester. But only if. And every last detail, mind. Then I'll think about it. Can't say fairer than that.'

'Then you'll do it, Ratty. Make no mistake about that. I'll pop in again after Christmas.'

18

What the hell was he to do? All very well to say to Ratty Peters he'd get hold of full details of Roanoke's security arrangements. But how was he to do it? If he asked someone he was reasonably friendly with at the Factory – and there were a few of those – they would want to know why he needed the information. Might even wonder if he'd joined the other side. At best his pursuit of Roanoke would become common knowledge. The place was worse for gossip than an old ladies' tea-party. Eventually, his request might get to the ears of Detective Chief Superintendent Sugden. Then the fat would really be in the fire.

Did this mean he ought to give up the whole business? Christ, already he had used his wealth to force wretched old Ratty to agree to do what plainly every instinct told him was stupid. Stupid and dangerous.

All wealth corrupts, and one million quid, less a few hundred, corrupts not far from absolutely.

So was it back to letting Roanoke get away with it?

No.

No, after what he had realized about himself talking to Jude that day he knew he could not just put aside his detective's instinct. In the police or not, that's what he was. A detective. And there was nothing else for him but to go on doing what that demanded of him.

Even if, by using the means at his disposal, viz. one million pounds, he did things to poor buggers like Ratty Peters that his ordinary self would have drawn back from. Because he had no ordinary self. Or not one that mattered when the chips were down. What he had was a detective self. And with it and through it he would track down Roanoke. Track him down for what he had done. Track him down before he could commit murder a fifth time.

But how to get hold of enough information about the security at the man's big house? Enough to give Ratty a decent chance of getting the contents of that safe for him to examine and then see replaced? And it was as much in his own interest as Ratty's that no one should ever know what had been done. If Ratty was caught, there was nothing to stop him saying who put him up to the job. *Millionaire In Burglary Conspiracy*.

So how to get that information out of the files at County Constabulary headquarters?

But he knew the answer. All along he had known the answer, though he had refused to let himself acknowledge it. There was one man at the Factory who could give him the information, and who yet would never let a soul know. A man who could be bribed. Bribed to commit an offence under Police (Discipline) Regulations, and because he had been bribed be effectively silenced. Mikey Cross.

'Mikey, fancy meeting you. Happy Christmas.'

'Oh, hello, Bill. Same to you. How you getting on then? Managed to get rid of that million yet?'

'Not quite, Mikey. Not quite. At least there's enough left to buy you a drink.'

Look of surprise on those grabber's features.

Would have been a look of crude suspicion if he had known he had been laid in wait for over the past half-hour, followed till he was far enough away from the Factory for the offered drink not to be supped in the pub round the corner where every other customer was a police officer.

'Very nice of you, guv. Bill.'

'Shall we go over the road there? Don't know it myself, but it looks all right.'

Pint apiece. Important to drink the same tipple when friendliness was to be established. Where there had not been much friendliness before.

Stick to gossip till the pint opposite was all but drained.

'We have another?'

'My shout.'

But not said with much conviction.

'No, no. I'm not a millionaire for nothing.'

Two more pints.

138

'Bit of luck, actually, bumping into you like that, Mikey.'

'Oh, yes?'

'Yes. You can't think how galling it is, out of the force, when you find something niggling at you that you've forgotten when you could have found out in five minutes by dropping in on the Collator.'

'Should've thought you'd got better things to do than think about things at the nick.'

'Oh, well, you know, something starts to bug you, and before long you find you can't get to sleep at night tossing it around in your mind.'

'Not my trouble, mate. Only thing keeps me awake is the old woman wanting a bit.'

Produce coarse hearty laugh. Let it all rest for a few moments. Sup the ale.

'But if you could just find out this thing for me, I'd be very grateful.'

Dark look of suspicion. Wrong choice of phrase. *I'd be very grateful*. Patronizing. And Mikey quick to resent it.

'Could you stand another pint?'

'Never been known to say no.'

Christ, what some people will take provided it's free. I'm in danger of sodding bursting myself. But nothing else for it.

Over to the bar. Back. Walking carefully.

And no more messing about.

'I'll tell you what it is, Mikey. It's that fellow Roanoke we once went out to talk to. About a letter someone sent to the CC.'

'Don't remember. Oh yes, I do, though. We went to see the bloke that wrote it after. Snobby bastard. Talked fucking Latin.'

Glare, hardly concealed, saying *And you talked Latin back*.

'Yeah, that's the fellow. And I took to wondering the other day about his house.'

'What that place with the dogs?'

'No, no. Roanoke's house, and all those antiques he's got there. I was wondering what security he had.'

Mikey shook his head in amazement.

'Can't bleeding leave it alone, can you? What you want to go worrying about some rich bastard's security for? If he gets done, he gets done. Who cares?'

Choice of paths here. Could seize on what he's said and pretend

139

this is all out of ex-detective's care for Roanoke. Or could bite the bullet and let Mikey know I want to see something inside the place. Keep Ratty's name out of it, of course. And Mikey will be safe enough if he takes the bribe. Which he will.

So which way? But no choice really. A cynical, greedy, self-regarding sod like Mikey's never going to believe anyone who's left the police will go on caring about beating crime.

'No, tell you the truth, I just want a look-see inside that bastard's place.'

'Oh, yeah? What for would that be?'

'Let's say I've taken against him, and I'd like to be hundred per cent sure he's the villain I think he is.'

Mikey's head shaking to and fro again.

'I said you couldn't leave it alone. Of course the feller's a villain. How else he got rich so quick? But you don't want to go worrying your head about him. Or any other villains, come to that. Christ, mate, you're a bloody millionaire. You ought to be able to think of better things to do than going in against some other rich git.'

Thank you, Mikey Cross, for that *rich git*. And gloves off.

'Listen, Mikey, why I want to get inside Roanoke's place is my own business. But I need to know exactly what security there is there. Every last detail. Now, are you going to find out for me or not?'

'No, I'm bloody well not. I'm not going to go sticking my neck out for you.'

'And who said it's only for me? It's for cash, Mikey. Money, dough, spondulicks, shekels, bread.'

Pause to work things out. But not for long.

'How much?'

From just outside Roanoke's garden, where he was making sure no unexpected visitor turned up, Sylvester could see Ratty at work. With a chisel he was methodically removing the putty from the window of a ground-floor lavatory. Hands, clearly visible in the hard mid-morning light, dead-looking in their thin white surgeon's gloves.

In a few minutes, lifting out the whole pane in front of him, Ratty would have access to the hollow security bar behind. Inside that, according to the plans Mikey Cross had got for them, there ran one of the house's numerous alarm wires. Ratty would drill a small hole in the bar and then with a steel-cutter slit up its whole length before, taking extreme care not to touch the wire, cutting with his mini-hacksaw round top and bottom and removing the bar complete.

Ratty had given him a run-down in the days while they had been waiting for word from Arthur Arkle that they could have the place to themselves. Next he would burn away the insulation of the wire with a cigarette-lighter. The ancient one he had produced had been the only tool of his former trade he had not required money to replace.

The minutes went by. At methodically regular intervals he looked each way along the road. Twice cars passed. But it was obvious from the speed they were going they had no intention of coming to a halt. Tucked away as he was beneath the drooping ash-tree there and wearing his colour-drained Oxfam mac, their drivers would almost certainly have not even seen him.

At last, at the lavatory window, he saw the tiny flare of Ratty's lighter. Come and gone. Then come and gone again. Now Ratty would be clipping a length of bell-wire to top and bottom of the bared alarm wire. Cut that, and, taking care not to tug away the clips on his safety loop, jockey-like Ratty could comfortably slide inside.

In.

Long wait now. And bloody cold in the bone-cutting wind.

He imagined Ratty going from room to room inside, cautiously making sure everything was as he had been told it would be. Slipping up the stairs. Trying the door of the big bedroom. Creeping in. Glancing perhaps at the ceiling mirror that had reflected Roanoke's activities with Susie Frank. Lifting down the Victorian painting she had said was dirty but not covered with grot. Then work on the safe.

How long would that take? Ratty had said three-quarters of an hour, if it had to be done so that the contents could be put back and no one the wiser. But he might need longer. Or be lucky and do it in less. At least they had as long as they needed. Roanoke had told Arthur Arkle he was going up to London, had asked him to keep an eye open.

Nice piece of irony.

But what if Roanoke changed his mind? Risk had to be taken. At least the road either way was silent now.

Should he give Ratty a call on their two-way radio? Another

bloody costly item. Expensive business being a successful criminal. Though presumably Ratty and the people he had worked with thought it worthwhile. Not that Ratty had really found it so.

But, no, better not use the radio. Leave Ratty to get on with it undisturbed. If he found anything amiss he'd be quick enough to call himself.

Glance at his watch. Jesus, only five minutes since Ratty had gone in. Clap hands together to get the blood circulating. Gloves against the cold, and against leaving prints anywhere. Check the road. OK. No one walking along from either direction. Not that these days anyone seemed to walk anywhere, not when they could go by car.

How's Ratty getting on? Comical to think of his bent back, head down at his work, reflected in that big mirror where Roanoke's back had been reflected. Also head down at his work.

Another check on the road. No change.

What about Arthur? Might he have the curiosity to come and see why he'd been asked when Roanoke was going to be safely out of the way? Seemingly not. Tucked snugly in that first-class carriage of his, then. Someone free of all the human vices. No curiosity about other people's goings-on. No hankering for money and what it could bring. Why couldn't we all be like that? But we weren't.

Give Ratty a call now? Come on, he said he'd need three-quarters of an hour, and he hasn't had half that yet.

He settled down to wait. Aged mac letting the wind go right through. Patience. Wait. Wait, wait.

You could blot everything out of your mind, if you made the effort.

'Mr Sylvester.'

Ratty's voice from the transceiver, muffled in his pocket, startling him into alertness.

He hoicked the little box out.

'Hearing you, Ratty. Trouble?'

'Nah. Piece of cake. You can come for the stuff now.'

'On my way. What've you got? Any little packets of white powder by any chance?'

'Just bleeding papers, Mr Sylvester. And not many o' them. 'Ope you think it's all been worth it.'

'We'll see. Meet you at the window.'

*

142

Ratty's turn to act as watchman outside now.

Out of the wind in the scanty shelter of a pair of french windows at the back of the big house, Sylvester went systematically through Ratty's haul. Bank statements, a single account book, a few miscellaneous papers. Gloved hands fumbling. But worth taking every precaution against leaving dabs.

Increasing depression. All right, the bank statements confirmed Roanoke was now well overdrawn, though he had been solidly in the black till fairly recently. But, beyond some authentications for antiques which looked dubious, nothing to indicate any wrongdoing.

Until a single sheet of notepaper – it was headed with a reproduced pen-and-ink sketch of Roanoke's so-called farmhouse – floated out of his grasp as he waded through the account book. He scrabbled it up.

But that was no more than infuriatingly tantalizing.

Headed *Campaign*, it simply listed dates, sets of initials and sums of money. But the first initials were significant enough.

M.B. £61,798.

E.P. £248,675.

M.F. £2, 876.

L.G. £0000!!!!

Then there had followed *J.D.* and *T.T.*, both viciously scored through. Margaret Bathurst, Miss Pettiman – Elspeth? Edith? Eunice? Which had it been? – Mrs Forth, Miss Gallitly. Roanoke's fury at his failure there and, more recently, again with Sir Julian Deane and Tomas Toth.

But after these there was one more set of initials. With no sum of money against them, and no date. And so scrawled as to be almost indecipherable. R.A D. or R.A.O. Or even, since the top of the last letter was not quite closed, R.A.U. Or just possibly – there was a tiny dash under the letter that might, or might not, be deliberate – R.A.Q.

19

Odd how people felt the need to write things down, even if in code, that were much better left unwritten. But it was something noted in more than one investigation over the years. Let alone those mass murderers who had kept diaries cataloguing everything. But, give bloody Roanoke credit, that tell-tale piece of notepaper did use only initials, and it had been tucked away in a hidden safe inside a well-secured building.

But who was R.A.D., R.A.O., R.A.U., R.A.Q.? One thing was clear enough. He, or she, was Roanoke's choice as his next victim. With some luck of course, following Roanoke day by day ought to lead to wherever he was beginning his new campaign. It could be done easily enough, either on his own or using Marshall Wilcox.

Christ though, that bill from him had been well padded-out. Give him a talking-to? No, better not. His sort cut all the corners they can unless they have plenty of expenses to show.

But Roanoke's campaign, was it in fact already well advanced? Somewhere. At some nursing home or retirement home or even at the Rotherfield Clinic again. The victim, whoever they were, might already be lying not far off death. A death that would be rapidly hastened the moment a will had been altered. But finding where that was happening might take days. Even weeks.

It had been a long wait till this visit of Roanoke's to London had come up. He could have been seeing R.A.D., male or female, at their home all the time. Marshall Wilcox's reports following him had not always stated the names of the owners of such houses as Roanoke had called at, presumably on most occasions simply buying antiques in the normal course of his business. And, then, his campaign over R.A.D. – if that D was right – need not always have been conducted person-to-person.

144

He imagined Roanoke's smooth tones, suitably adapted to his listener, issuing from a telephone. Hearty, or malicious even, or pussy-cat soothing.

A telephone.

He gathered up the papers, carefully put down on step of french windows in the exact order they had been in. But where precisely had the *Campaign* sheet come? It had caught his eye as it had fluttered down, but it had not been at all clear what had released it from the pile.

Well, just have to risk it. It certainly looked as if it had simply got muddled in at some stage.

He took out his transceiver.

'Ratty. You there?'

'Receiving you. Over.'

How he loved the jargon.

'I've finished. Meet you at the window. I want just one more small thing, then we can pack up.'

'And a bloody good job, too.'

At the window, with its wide loop of bell-wire dangling, he at once asked Ratty his question.

'Listen, when you were looking round – and, remember, you're not to nick a single bleeding object, or you don't get that second lot of notes – did you by any chance see anything like a phone index? You know, a little book to put numbers in.'

'Here, you're not going to go phoning someone from inside?'

'No, no. I just want a quick dekko at the phone numbers he keeps.'

'OK. I think I seen it. Back in a sec.'

He was as good as his word. Roanoke's index, typically, turned out to be an elaborate leather-covered affair with a button to release the pages for each letter of the alphabet.

Clumsy gloved finger on *D*. Only two entries: *DOCTOR, DENTIST*. Bugger, the fellow didn't seem to make any great use of his expensive toy. Try *O*. Only one entry. *Old School 263 7229*. So some of his cajoling was done on the phone. Poor old Miss Gallitly.

Quick. The *Q*. Nothing. Well, to be expected. So, *U*. And nothing again.

Damn, damn, damn. Good idea leading nowhere.

No, wait.

'Listen, Ratty, when you put this back have a shufti and see if the local phone book's there. And, unless it's in a very prominent place, I'll have it. Bit of a risk. But I'm going to need it for some time.'

'Then you're lucky, Mr S. I seen it. Tucked away at the bottom of the London ones what he's got and the Yellow Pages and all that.'

'Marvellous. So just you sneak it away and shift the pile a bit. Even if he does find it's not there eventually, he won't suspect anybody's been inside. Not if that's the only thing missing. And it had better be, Ratty. It had better be.'

'All right, Mr Sylvester. All right. I'm not a bloody thief, you know.'

'Of course not, Ratty. Who would ever have thought such a thing?'

'But what d'you want the phone book for, then?'

'Just in the hope there may be something in it. That's all.'

'You're the boss. Wait 'ere and I'll bring it you before I shut that safe so nobody won't never know it's been open. And then, mate, I'm going to bleeding scarper.'

'Don't worry, don't worry. I'll go out to the road again and guard your back. How long will you want?'

'Ten minutes inside, ten more put the window back proper.'

It seemed a long twenty minutes. For some reason, while he had kept calm enough all during Ratty's long stay in the house getting the safe open, now he was jumpy with nerves. Standing under the drooping ash, he could not resist abandoning his duty of watching the road to flip through the D names in the stolen phone book. Would he on the very first page find someone with R as a first initial and a tick or mark against them? Would this last gamble pay off?

Dabbs, Dabby, Dabney, Dabrovski, Dabson, Dace, Dacey, Dacie. No sign of any marks.

A car whirled by. He looked up. But it was disappearing harmlessly at the other end of the road.

Dack, D'Costa, Dacre, Dadd. Dadd, R. Ah. Little tick. But, no. *Dadd, R, Fishmonger.* Presumably just the man Roanoke ordered his salmon deliveries from. But he had ticked the name.

146

He did do that. So . . . *Dadswell, Dagg, Daggart, Dagleish*. Another car, in the opposite direction. *Dailey, Dain, Daines, Dainty, Dale*. Heck of a lot of Dales.

He bent his head, zipping down the column.

'Right then, what are you doing here?'

He looked up. Heart thumping.

Two flat-caps, standing legs apart, hands on hips. Enjoying it. Their damn patrol car, which they must have brought to a quiet halt shortly after seeing him, stationary a couple of hundred yards further along.

Christ, what to do?

'Oh, hello, lads. Don't think I know you, do I?'

'Going to be a cheeky bugger, are we?'

God, totally wrong foot.

'I— I'm sorry. You see, I'm CID. That is, I was. Was CID. Thought you might have recognized me.'

'You and the Emperor Napoleon? Now, what's your name?'

'It's Sylvester. Bill Sylvester.'

Out with the pocket-book. And, before there was time for more explanation, name entered. God, when his book's inspected it'll be seen. And the location. It could eventually get to Suggers' ears. He'll know then I'm still after his pal Roanoke. And he won't like that. He could make things bloody awkward for me. At the least.

And, Christ, what if these two take it into their heads to search me? Find the transceiver in my mac pocket? They'd guess in a minute someone must be inside a house near by, and Roanoke's is the only one. I must look pretty much like a villain, in any case. Loitering with intent. Bloody poor-man's Oxfam mac.

He gave the two of them a smile. A weak smile.

'Listen, I really was in the CID. Truly. Till not so long ago when I won a million quid in a lottery and resigned. You may remember?'

'Hey, yeah. Yeah, I do. That was you, was it? DI, weren't you?'

'That's right.'

Jesus, I'm sweating with relief. Bloody sweating.

He coughed.

'Look, could you do me a favour. It's like this. I wouldn't want anybody like DCS Sugden to know I'd been a loitering-with-intent suspect. He'd fall about laughing. So, could you make sure, far as you can, that no one sees that entry in your pocket-book?'

Long look, still edged with suspicion. And quite rightly. Bit of an odd request, say the least.

'Yeah, all right, sir. Sorry to have pulled you up.'

Sir now. Get rich, get respect.

'No, quite right. I'd have done just the same myself in my day.'

'Good morning then.'

'Good morning.'

He watched them amble back to their car. Take off.

Would they do what he'd asked? Or had he actually drawn attention to himself more than he needed?

Well, nothing to be done about it now. And at least Ratty hadn't been sussed.

And he had got Roanoke's phone book. And there might be a mark in it somewhere against a name with one or another of those sets of initials. It would be a long task, plunging through all the D names and O, U and even Q. But it might be worth it. Roanoke had put a mark against that fishmonger.

In the end the rich detective employed one of the needy to do the laborious work for him. Miss Ursula Hankinson, found under *Secretarial Services* in the Yellow Pages. The signs of her neediness all around her in the shabby second-floor flat, workplace and living accommodation combined. Once-white paint greyed with age. Wallpaper with a design of small roses in ordered rows almost obliterated into shadowy beigeness. Carpet showing its threads. Solid dining table with an ancient office typewriter like a sit-up-and-beg bicycle, set in front of a hard chair with a small pad of cushion tied to the rear struts. One-bar electric fire giving just enough heat to bring out an odour of stale face-powder. On the wide windowsill, beside a single gas-ring, a glass bowl containing a dozen wrinkled prunes in their dark juice.

'Yes, Mr Sylvester, I can undertake the work.'

Thin to gauntness, tweed skirt battered into a state of matted nullity. Cream-coloured blouse fastened to the neck. Lined face with the powder visibly thicker in the lines. Grey hair held severely in place by a tortoise-shell comb.

'Fine. And as soon as possible?'

'I cannot begin until this afternoon. I do my shopping every morning from twelve till one. It's almost twelve now.'

148

'Um. Well, I am in a hell of a hurry, actually. Could you switch round, shop later this afternoon – if I paid a bit over the odds?'

'My charges are fixed by the hour.'

'But, I was saying, this is really pretty urgent and I'd gladly pay extra. Shall we say time-and-a-half?'

'No, I'm sorry. I cannot alter my arrangements.'

Jesus. By the time he'd gone back to the Yellow Pages, if there was a copy somewhere here, found another likely name, one with a certain promise of confidentiality, used the pay-phone in the lino-floored entrance corridor down below, gone round to wher-ever it was . . . And, besides, her charges were ridiculously small.

'Very well then. What time shall I call back this afternoon?'

'I never see clients after five o'clock.'

'Then I'll be here at five-to. All right?'

'That will be perfectly satisfactory.'

It was perfectly satisfactory. When Sylvester entered the dreary room again, at seven minutes to five, Miss Hankinson handed him a slip of paper on which, neatly typed, there was a short list of the D, O, Q, and U names Roanoke had ticked, with their addresses and phone numbers. Together with a bill made out in full detail.

He scrabbled money from his wallet. Paid.

Was made to wait while she found change. And to wait longer while she scrupulously receipted the bill.

But at least it gave him a chance to check the list. Only five names in all.

'You're sure these are the only ones marked?'

'I am accustomed to detailed and accurate work.'

Boo snubs to Mr Careless Rich Man.

He looked down at the sheet again. There could be no doubt. Four tradesmen, including *Dadd, R, fishmonger*. And then one other.

Upward, R.A. The Manor House, Feston.

Upward. But wasn't there a Robert Upward, fabulously rich, owner of one of the big department-store chains? Yes. So this almost certainly was him. Right sort of wealthy man's address, though Roanoke's connection with him might be only as a cus-tomer for antiques. And the three initials. Exactly corresponding to that *Campaign* sheet. Yes.

And, surely, still in time.

20

'This is Mr Upward's manservant speaking. I am afraid you cannot speak with Mr Upward. He is not here. I regret to say he is not at all well.'

No surprise.

'I see. I'm very sorry to hear that. Is he in hospital? A clinic? I'd like to write.'

'Mr Upward's present address is Astwood Manor, Astwood, South Mercia. I am sure he would be most pleased to hear from you.'

Astwood Manor. Happy hunting ground. For some. And no distance.

By a quarter to six he was parked, waiting, on the verge opposite. Mid-winter darkness all the thicker for a shower just over. Up at the house warm lights shining from one or two windows yet to have their curtains drawn. As he waited, one by one the curtains were closed. Flicked across, he thought, in something of a hurry. By, if luck was with him, the person he wanted to see. Princess Green, little lively black retailer of gossip.

And, promptly at six, she came tittupping down the smoothly gravelled drive in the light from the lamp over the big front door. A bundle of bright blue in her shiny, hugging mackintosh. As she crossed the road, he flicked on his interior light, put his head out of the window.

'Come to give you a lift again.'

She peered towards him. Then a grin lit up her face. Big teeth white in the faint illumination from the car.

'Come to hear more about what goes on back there, more like.'

'You guessed. Hop in.'

'What if I say no?'

He gave her a broad smile.

'But you're not going to, are you?'

'Well, I s'pose I could tell you a thing or two about old Ma Milton. And about her hubby. Could tell you more than that about him, dirty old man.'

'All the dirt. I'm happy.'

He opened the passenger door. She was in with a single wriggle.

'Anyhow,' she said, as he slid the car into the road, 'what's the pigs so interested in out here? Lot of old cats bickering. Can't be that.'

She plumped herself round to face him.

'You ain't going to arrest one of 'em, are you?'

'Well, to tell you the truth, I'm not in a position to arrest anybody any more.'

'What you mean?'

'I've left the police, sweetheart. Just a simple nosy-parker now.'

'No, you ain't,' she suddenly shot out. 'I know what you are. Saw your picture in the paper after you come out here. You're the millionaire.'

'Quite right.'

How many more times would he have to admit to it? Those two flat-caps this morning. Now Princess.

'So what you doing picking me up, then? Going to carry me off to your secret yacht?'

'Love to, sweetheart. Only I haven't got a yacht. Not even a secret luxury flat.'

'Well, you're a rotten one. What you done with all your money, then?'

'Nothing, darling, sorry to say. You see, I've been busy.'

'Oh, yeah?'

'Yes. And that's what's brought me out here, matter of fact. You remember back last September I wanted to know all about an old lady who died at your place, lady called Mrs Bathurst?'

'Dawder. What she saved her fifty-pees for. Dogs Home. I remember.'

'That was it. Well, would you be surprised to hear there's a possibility her death was not what it seemed to be?'

Moment to work it out.

'You mean, murder? What, at Astwood Manor? You got to be joking.'

'No, sweetheart. I'm not. Or I'm pretty certain I'm not. Which is why I want to chat with you.'

'Yeah. But all the same . . . I mean, you saying there's someone out at the house what's a murderer? You can't mean old Ma. She's so worried about everything being respectable, she'd never so much as pinch one of the old dears' teaspoons. And as for the Major, all he thinks of pinching is my bum.'

How dangerous will it be to confide in this chatty little piece? Worse, how fair?

But best chance of finding out how well Roanoke's entrenched. If he is. So, have to do it.

'No, it's not anyone living in the house. It's a visitor. And, mind, I haven't got any proof. So this is strictly between you and me, right? No talking to the boyfriend. No talking to your mum.'

'Here, you ain't having me on, are you?'

'Do I sound like it?'

'Well, no, you don't. That's what I don't like.'

'I'm sorry, sweetheart. Believe me, if I could see any other way of finding out quickly what I need to know I'd go for it.'

Long silence. Car flicking along the wet surface of the road.

'All right then. What you want to know?'

He could hear her take a big, big swallow.

'Right. Well, first of all, is there a new patient at the Manor called Upward, Robert Upward?'

'Him. Yes, o' course. Even more of a millionaire than what you are, ain't he?'

'He is. Times about a hundred. So, does he have a lot of visitors?'

'Well, no, not a lot really.'

She sat thinking. He took the car at an even pace down whichever road first presented itself. Princess didn't seem to notice they have ceased to take the quickest route into the town.

'Just two of 'em. Far as I can remember. Only regulars anyhow.'

'Two?'

'Yeah, there's what he calls his manservant. Comes every morning, just for a chat as far I can make out. He don't do nothing no more. Nice old boy, though, when you get to know him.'

'And the other?'

'Oh, him. It's Mr Roanoke. He's been coming to see a lot of—Here, it ain't him, is it? Smarmy sod. It could be. Yeah, I could see him doing that. But he ain't, has he? I wouldn't like to think I'd met somebody what'd done that.'

152

'Well, that's just what I don't know. Not for sure. Maybe it's all a false alarm, so don't let it worry you. But, all the same, I would like to know as much about his visits as you can tell me. If only to eliminate him.'

He did not in the end learn a great deal. But what he did discover did nothing to eliminate Roanoke. As he had known all along that it wouldn't.

Yes, he began coming to see Robert Upward as soon as he had moved in, with some of his favourite furniture. He came, so he said, to look after that. Polished it. With 'some special stuff'. And, yes, they seemed to be big buddies, the two of them. Always talking and talking, though old Mr Upward was a bit past it really.

'Does he come always at the same time, Mr Roanoke?'

'Yeah. Yeah, he does. Just after lunch.'

'And how long does he stay?'

'Well, till it's nearly time for their teas. You know they has bread and butter, cut all thin, and their own little teapots, and a biscuit or two. Not a proper tea. Four o'clock.'

'And he never stays while Mr Upward has his?'

'No. Funny that. But he don't.'

'So, tell me something else. When Mr Roanoke's there, is the door of Mr Upward's room closed or open?'

'It's open. Always. How d'you know that? Old Smarmy says it has to be because of the smell o' the polish he sprays on the furniture. Sort o' flowery. And pongs all right.'

'Right. One other thing then. If . . . If a friend of mine, or someone I know at least, should come to the house and want to spend a few minutes alone in Mr Upward's room while he's out of it, could he do that? Without anyone except you knowing? What'd be a good time?'

'Going to bug the place, are you?'

Bright as a button.

'Yes. That's it. Could you fix that? I'd see you didn't lose by it.'

'Here, no. I don't want money. Not for doing something like that. If it really is to stop a murder. And it is, ain't it?'

'Yes, sweetheart. It is.'

Crack. Slap-bang into a moral dilemma. Warn Robert Upward?

Or give Roanoke rope, watch him every minute, hope to catch him in the act?

For a moment Sylvester longed to be back in the force. Colleagues to consult. In the way they'd discussed many a time dilemmas like his. A snout gives word of, say, a pay-roll robbery. Shooters going to be carried. Arrest the gang straight away, hoping at least to catch them on firearms charges? Or wait till they're on their way, and be that much more certain? Or wait longer, till they've gone in? Catch them coming out with the loot. Get a case that no brief, however clever, will get them out of. And maybe find some poor sod of a watchman bleeding to death? He'd welcome the thinking even of Detective Chief Superintendent Sugden now. All right, view dictated by what would look best in the record of Detective Chief Superintendent Sugden. But something to argue against. Clarify the mind on.

But he had nothing. No one.

Who did he trust enough to put the facts in front of? Old college chum Colin Taylor? He'd work it out on best actuarial principles. Profit and loss. Not bloody likely. Auntie Violet? There was someone whose approach to things he would trust. He could get over to Nottingham in an hour, and take her a new supply of port. Better than just getting Jessop's wine department to deliver, as he had done at Christmas. But terribly unfair to thrust a life-and-death decision – what it very well might amount to, no getting past it – on someone as old as her.

Who else? Nobody. Or, yes. Yes, there was someone whose opinion he respected. Jude. For moral considerations go to a prostitute.

Licence my roaving hands . . .

Only, when it came to it, they weren't roving to much purpose. He rolled off.

Jude, lying flat beside him, turned her head and looked up.

'You been with other women? Spreading it about, all that lolly you got?'

'No, been keeping my goodies for you. Or, actually, seem to have forgotten all about goodies these past few weeks. Other things on my mind.'

'Well, you ought to watch it, you know. You don't want to let anything get to you to that point.'

154

She laughed.

'And I'm not saying that 'cos it's bad for business. It's just true.'

'I suppose it is. Well, I know it is really. In theory. But when it comes to doing what you know is best for you, it isn't always so easy. If something bugs you, it bugs you.'

'Is it your murderer you were telling me about? If he is a murderer.'

'What else?'

He sat up.

'And I'm bloody sure he's a murderer. And you were the one who told me I ought to do something about him. You can't complain now if I don't do what I'm here for.'

'I'm not, darling. I should worry. You've given me the money, haven't you?'

She rolled over and heaved herself up.

'Don't mean that,' she said. 'I worry about you. Honestly. We're friends, aren't we? Known each other a long time now.'

'Yes. Yes, we're friends. And, to tell you the truth, that's what I came here for. Talk to a friend.'

'All right, want to tell Auntie Jude all about it?'

'I shouldn't really. Shouldn't put my troubles on to your back. But I must talk to someone.'

'Talk then, darling. You haven't put anything else on my back, after all.'

She lay down again. Stretched out. He lowered himself beside her.

'It's like this,' he said. 'I've reason to believe, as we used to say in the police, that a certain gentleman is contemplating another murder. In fact, I'm bloody sure he is. He's got friendly with a guy who's very rich—'

'Like you, darling?'

'Like me multiplied by a hundred.'

'Lumme. He doesn't want to pay a girl a visit, does he?'

'Too old. Too ill. Because that's the way my friend likes them. Old and ill, and ripe to be cajoled into leaving him big money. Then he moves in.'

'Well, what's the problem? You tell this old geezer what your friend's up to. Save his life.'

'And leave my friend to do it all over again with someone else? Someone I don't get to find out about? He's been unlucky twice, for various reasons, in the last few weeks. Something I happen to know. So he's badly in need of a lot more money. Now.'

'But didn't you say he'd made a hell of a lot out of the murders he's done already? And you did mean he had, didn't you?'

'Yes, I meant it. And he ought to be bloody well off, after all he inherited from two of those murders. But he still thinks he's in need of more. Well, he is in a way. He's got bills outstanding, and he's got no intention of cutting his standard of living. Another thing I happen to know.'

'So what you're saying is, if you save this rich guy's life your friend's just going to go and murder someone else?'

'Yes. Exactly it.'

'And what's worrying you, so's you can't do anything about what you come here for, is whether to keep mum to this multi-millionaire – Cripes, fancy you knowing someone who's that – and hope to catch your friend in the act. Or whether to warn the old bugger. He is old? Really old, is he?'

'Yup. And you've hit on one of the things that counts. Trust you. If someone's not far from dying anyhow, isn't it all the fairer to risk their life? In what you might call a good cause?'

'Except they're not being given the choice. It's you what's deciding for them. Or not deciding.'

'Right again. It's down to me. I'm the one who's got to decide. One way or the other.'

'And you have, haven't you, really. You've decided to use the poor old multi-millionaire like one of them goats you see on the telly, tied up so the tiger'll come and get shot.'

'Yes. Yes, I have.'

He sat up and got off the bed.

'Well, thanks, darling. I had an idea you'd straighten me out.'

'Wasn't me. It was you, talking. But you not going to have your money's worth, now your mind's made up?'

'Well, no, darling. Don't think so. Somehow it'd be callous.'

'Yeah. Know what you mean. Well, see you again.'

'You certainly will.'

21

This time he was not going to leave it all to Marshall Wilcox and his tapes. Phone call to Astwood Manor. He pictured Mrs Milton on the other end, Major Milton, shadowy figure at her side, ready to excuse any wealthy resident's 'little eccentricities'. Standing impeccably upright, both of them. Had she really worn a corset? Certainly had looked like it. Telephone held at the tips of her fingers, as if slightly deplorable. But necessary. *Full facilities for care.*

'Yes, there is, as it happens, a suite vacant.'

Knew that. Courtesy one Princess Green. But asking just for 'a room', not exactly millionaire-speak. Have to watch it.

Price per week announced, discreetly. Enormous. He accepted without a murmur. First tricky bit coming up.

'As a matter of fact I know your charming place. I was, until some months ago, a police officer, and I once had occasion to visit you.'

'I don't think I recall a policeman . . . Are you sure it is not some other establishment you have in mind?'

Quick, start the play-acting. And make it good.

'Oh, no, it's definitely Astwood Manor I want. It's – I'm afraid it's rather difficult to explain. It's— Well . . .'

Lay it on. Verge of a nervous breakdown. Remember DCI Jock Withers. When it all got too much for him. Sitting there incapable of deciding to do a blind thing. Poor sod.

'Mr Sylvester?'

'Oh. Oh, yes. Yes, well, you see, it's rather difficult. But recently . . . Well, I came into a very large sum of money, and— And, of course, I left the police. But I found the responsibility . . . And my doctor – well, the man in Harley Street he sent me to – said complete rest. And— And straight away I thought of you.

157

Of Astwood Manor. Your— Your atmosphere of calm. And— And— Dignity. Yes. Yes.'

'Well, we do endeavour to keep the unpleasant aspects of the world at a distance. We feel it our duty.'

Chatelaine.

But hooked, by God. Hurdle Number One got over.

Marshall let in to the place by Princess next day. Bugs installed in Robert Upward's suite. Sitting room, bedroom, bathroom, the lot. And Marshall round at the flat with what looked to all appearances to be a simple, but expensive, portable CD player. Hidden inside, radio receiver for the bugs, even more expensive. *It is the duty of the wealthy man/To give employment to the artisan* remembered quotation.

Flopped out in dramatic fashion on the chintz-covered *chaise longue*. Book lying unread on lap. Trollope. Should have been *Barchester Towers* for this place. As seen on TV, respectable and dull-sounding. But only *The Way We Live Now* in the flat. Much too tough, story of old money-spinning Melmotte. Another millionaire in trouble. Still, dark blue Oxford University Press binding OK for tone.

So all well so far. Bit of a bad moment at the front door. Forgot Princess was likely to answer. Thought she'd burst into giggles. But one 'Good morning, my name's Sylvester,' and she picked up her cue a treat. 'Oh, yes, sir. You're expected. I'll call Mrs Milton.'

No trouble with that corseted old bat. Desperate hesitation at door of the suite as if just making up my mind to enter was too much. And, reaction prompt as a knee jerk, the quick look back down the corridor to see if discreet help was at hand. Then, inside eventually – she sodding gave me a gentle push – *Peace, just perfect peace, that's . . . That's all I want.* Couldn't have been quicker to accept. If the money's there, do your own diagnosing. Right up till the first cheque bounces.

But will I be able to keep it up? For as long as it takes? Day after day. Weeks maybe.

On the low table at elbow distance the 'CD player'. Ready at any interruption to have its murmur from the suite just below extinguished.

So far only occasional throat-clearings. Once something that had sounded like a suppressed moan. Poor bugger.

Should be almost time though. For the furniture-polisher's arrival.

Ah, tap on door. Must be.

Yes? The failing voice.

Then brisk click of door opening. Marshall certainly not skimping on the apparatus. Might be actually in the room.

Good afternoon, good afternoon. I trust things are a little brighter?

Exuding confidence. And heartiness. If a subtly different brand from that employed on Tomas Toth. Bit more restrained.

Kind of you, my dear fellow. But . . . Well, shall we say, no change?

Perhaps you'll feel more the thing when this weather gets better. I don't think you ought to attempt to go out while it's as cold as this.

I haven't in the least attempted to, I promise you. Indeed, I doubt whether I shall ever go out again.

Oh, come now. I can see you in the spring going all over the place.

No, no. One should face facts, you know. That's why I've seen to my will.

Changed his will? This it? The death warrant?

Well, I must admit I'm glad to hear that that's done. One should never leave something like that. My own was made long ago. Everything to the Victoria and Albert, where I learnt all I know about fine furniture. Since I've no family, worse luck.

The Victoria and Albert, eh? Well, that's not much different from the way I was letting it all go back to the nation. Since I've no more family than you.

Jesus, only just in time then. If he's wangled a new will out of the old bugger, he'll be putting the next stage into operation before long. So, watch him. Watch him every moment he's down there below. Listen. Listen to every word he says. Every tiny scrape of sound.

159

You're in danger, Mr Upward. Deadly danger.

But now you've carried out our plan. Satisfaction creaming under the voice.

Oh, yes. Yes, I'm sure you were right. There ought to be more people in possession of resources who can act at once when people are in distress or even—

Knock at this door. Discreet tap, rather. Who's this?

Flick switch. End of murmurs from below.

'Come in.'

Make the voice dull. Hesitant.

Door open.

Nurse Dexter. Even more solid-looking in uniform. Round face with its button nose more intent. And, out of her snug little nest of a flat, noticeably more purposeful.

This will be a sight more tricky.

'So it is the Inspector Sylvester who came to see me at home.'

'Nurse Dexter. How— How nice.'

'I didn't quite believe Mrs Milton when she told me. But she says you came into a lot of money and left the police. Is that so?'

Boot on other foot, all right. Under interrogation.

'Well, yes, it is. I— I won almost a million pounds. In the Spanish lottery. What— What they call El Gordo, the Fat One.'

'Did you indeed? And am I to understand it's been too much for you? Nervous breakdown. Doesn't sound quite like a detective inspector to me.'

What's she trying to do? Have me chucked out as an impostor? Be funny. In a way. If it wasn't for what I'm here for.

'Well, Nurse, I wouldn't have thought myself it would have— Have hit me the way it has. Not till it happened. But— But a million pounds, terrible responsibility. Burden. Yes, a real burden.'

'Well, I can understand that. I dare say if I was ever so foolish as to go in for one of those things and won, I'd find it too much for me. But I know what I'd do about it.'

Flash the anxious look. Wish there'd been time to look up more symptoms.

'What would you do about it, Nurse?'

'I'd give it away. Just as quick as I could. There's plenty of charities could do with a million pounds.'

'Yes. Yes, I did think of that. But then . . . Oh, it was so difficult. I mean, which to give it to? And ought I to keep some back? For . . . For my mother. And I've got a relative, my Aunt Violet, who's not at all well off. In an alms-house.'

Christ, I'm sounding like a fucking cry-baby. But probably right for my condition. God knows.

'Yes. Well, I dare say it takes different people in different ways. Not my job to tell you what you ought to do. I've just come to take your temperature.'

From under the bib of her starched white apron she whipped out a thermometer, thrust it towards his mouth.

Open. Wriggle under tongue. Silenced.

Meanwhile what's happening down on the floor below? Surely Roanoke won't be using his poison already? Whatever poison it is. However he contrives to administer it. Certainly there wasn't any sound of the door being closed after him. So presumably taking his usual precautions not to seem to have any opportunity.

But, God, if he is doing it now. Somehow killing the old man. And me up here, just one floor above. Letting it happen. Jesus, I'd never forgive myself.

Damn it, how long is two minutes? Nurse Dexter, standing there like a bloody pillar, looking at her fob watch. Come on, for Christ's sake.

'There.'

She darted forward, slid the thermometer out of his mouth, gave it a single sharp glance.

'Nothing much wrong with that.'

Should he have contrived to bump his temperature up? What was it the boys at school used to do, get out of not having done their homework? Eat soap? But he was the one who'd always done his homework. A doddle.

'Well, I'll see you tomorrow. Unless you do feel ill. You've only to ring, you know.'

'Yes. Yes, thank you, Nurse. And nice to see you again.'

Door closed on her sturdy back. Flick on Marshall's trick machine.

Oh, my dear chap, it all seems so long ago.

What? What? What seems long ago to Robert Upward? And how does he sound? Worse? Yes? No?

Come on, no panicking. He doesn't sound any different than he did five or ten minutes ago. Not dying little by little, right there somewhere below.

So Roanoke waiting. Of course. Wouldn't be such a fool as to kill his fat calf within a few days of that will leaving him whatever it did. Big sum so as to be able to dole out to deserving cases on the spot. If, from those few overheard words just as Nurse Dexter knocked, I got it right. And presumably whatever sum that was has not been put into some trust. Or Roanoke wouldn't have sounded so pleased.

Long silence in the suite below. Bar the wheezing of the old man's breath.

Both of them presumably pondering those last sad-sounding words. *It all seems so long ago* Even Roanoke at a loss for some cheerful rejoinder.

And the sod would have to go on coming up with the cheerfulness for some time to come. Can't cut off the ego-massaging as soon as the will's made. Easy enough to change a will back. Nor can he use his poison yet awhile. But what is it? What the hell is it? And how long will he wait? Months? No. Won't want to risk old Upward having second thoughts. Forming a trust after all. So weeks? Well, yes, could well be.

Bloody hell. But he dared not be missing from his end of the bug every minute Roanoke was in the suite below, and in the hours after he'd left, too. Because – judge by the other cases – the fellow uses something that has to be administered only once, even though its action must be delayed.

Now the old man beginning again. With a sort of moaning, rattling preliminary sound.

Yes, to think there was a time when I devoted my every waking thought – good many of my sleeping ones, too. I dare say – to devising ways of adding money to money.

Pause for breath. Roanoke unable to produce reassuring comment. And no wonder.

That's what I was doing, you know. Piling up the money. Piling it up. See how high I could make my personal heap. Having *Forbes Magazine* personally delivered overnight, just so as to see how far up the list of the world's rich I'd got.

Wheezing laugh. Roanoke joining in. But feebly. Unsure whether it's the right response.

Yes. That was it. A game. Nothing else. I'd no use for the money. You can't spend more than so much, even on works of art you buy to have stored for you somewhere. Even on nonsenses from Asprey's or wherever.

Yes, they do produce some fearful diamond-encrusted objects, I must say. Though I suppose if they've customers for them, you can't blame them.

Remark ignored by the multi-millionaire.

Damn it, my dear fellow, I didn't even have a family to leave the money to. No friends either. Dangerous things, friends. Acquaintances, yes. Had hundreds. But I was damned if I was going to leave a penny piece to any of them.

Long pause. Thinking presumably. Sound of wheezing very clear. Roanoke probably contriving a deep-thoughts face, too.
Now that moaning, rattling preliminary once again.

And quite suddenly they all collapsed, my dreams. No reason. No reason I could ever discover. Just one day think-ing: Why am I doing this? So I stopped. Just let the money stay where it was. Couldn't think what else to do with it. Old age? May have just been old age creeping on. I don't know. And then, just the other day, was it, you came along, my dear fellow.

Hope I've been a help.

But, for once, tentative. What else could he be?
Almost feel sorry for the shit. Very tricky situation for him. Put a foot wrong, and . . .

Yes, my dear chap. You made me see what a fool I was being.

Christ, though. You had to hand it to Roanoke all the same. To have persuaded that canny old money manufacturer not to let that huge fortune of his slide back into the coffers of the State but to leave him directly – directly – whatever chunk he had done. As somebody with resources who can act at once in cases of need.

Or, put it another way, money to do what you like with. And with Robert Upward safely in his grave, no bets about what Charles Maurice Roanoke would like to do with it. None at all.

And I doubt if it'll be chickenfeed either, what he'll get.

Extortionate weekly fees apparently brought freedom to play at being ill as long as the cheques kept being written. His own 'little eccentricity'. Not that Nurse Dexter, each day when she took his temperature, did not convey stout disapproval. However unspoken.

Small price to pay.

Small returns, too, for those regular cheques. Roanoke visiting Robert Upward daily. But nothing more to hear than the sound of his furniture polish being squirted on and acres of uninformative tittle-tattle being chuntered out. Brought to an end, every day, as tea-time approached. Chat about antiques. Chat about the weather. Chat about what was in the papers. Chat-chat-chat about anything but Upward's new-made will and the uses the money would be put to after his death.

Do you know, my dear fellow, what it was that started me off?

No. It was one particular incident, was it? This is extraordinarily interesting.

Butter, butter, butter.

Faint laugh from the ancient body near its end. Nearer than it thought, unless the secret of what Roanoke intended should come into the 'CD' listener in time, and action could be taken with proof there to be grasped.

Oh, no. Not an incident. Not an incident at all. Just . . . Just my name.

Your name?

Upward, my dear chap. Upward. In those days, long ago, plain Bob Upward. But, thinking back as I do so often now, I realize I somehow got it into my head that I had to go, precisely, upward. Up and up and up.

And you did. I don't suppose anyone went so far up

from such— Well, frankly humble beginnings.

Not humble, my dear fellow. Low. The lower depths. Isn't that what they say? Well, it was true in my case. It was my mother's name that was Upward, you know. God knows who my father was.

And from those – er – depths up you rose. A phenomenal achievement. I don't hesitate to say it.

But it's not true, you know. Not really true. It wasn't an achievement. It was a fight, and not a fair fight either. No holds barred. How else do you think I got out of that cesspit? My mother, with her stall selling second-hand rags no one who wasn't desperate would think of wearing.

Yes, yes. A long haul.

But I saw how to do it. I learnt. And inch by inch I clawed my way up. Upward. Upward.

Another feeble cackle of laughter. It seemed almost too much for the frail body.

Would Nature do Roanoke's work for him?

And then it was not inch by inch but foot by foot. Yard by yard, if you like. Yards of materials bought cheap, and at forced prices too, and sold dear. Damned dear.

Oh, come, you're being absolutely over-modest.

You'd like to think so, wouldn't you? You'd like to think your respectable acquaintance—

Friend, friend. Surely friend?

Very well, if you like. Friend. And you'd like to think he'd never done a dishonest thing in his life, wouldn't you?

I'm sure he hasn't. Or not seriously dishonest.

And you believe you can make all the money I did, the pile on pile of it, honestly? You should have seen me at it. You should have seen the things I did to create the impression I was richer than I was. To make credit when I needed it. The briefcase I opened to show it was stuffed with cash. And the cut-up newspapers at the bottom. And, later, the meetings I made a point of going to by helicopter. And never paying the account. The way I made my housekeeper come bursting in to complain the new cook was using Château Lafite at God knows how many hundred pounds a bottle.

No laughter now. But enjoyment at disconcerting his apparently respectable friend.

If only he knew . . .

But the talk seldom as illuminating. The weather. The news of the day. The assiduous enquiry about the old man's health.

But every word picked up. Every chuckle from Roanoke. Every wheezing breath from Robert Upward. The sound of the briskly cheerful tap on the door, never earlier than half an hour after the old multi-millionaire's lunch. No sound ever of the door being closed. However carefully. For however short a time. Invariably faint noises from the corridor outside, click of heels, distant chatter, long-case clock on the nearby landing whirringly chiming each separate quarter. Even, in lulls in the talk, its ticking. And for five minutes every day the squirt, squirt, squirt of Roanoke's special polish being applied. With commentary on the supposed beauty of the piece being treated, and its value in thousands or tens of thousands.

Could it be that? The polish spray? Was it . . . Was Roanoke slowly poisoning the old man with that?

Rat-tat on his own door. Princess. Bringing tea. Own little pot, bread and butter, two biscuits. Chocolate. Which no one else got, she'd told him, except the kitchen staff. And he got served first, too.

From below he heard Roanoke launching into his *Have to be off, client to see* spiel that got him clear before any poisonable food was in the room with him.

Flick off the machine.

'Hello, sweetheart. Chockie bikkies again. Aren't I lucky?'

'Didn't ought to have nothing. You ain't no invalid.'

'So I'm not. But you keep your little mouth shut about that. Or else.'

'Else what?'

Flirt of bottom.

'No, listen, darling. I told you. I'm not here as a joke. God knows, I sometimes begin to wonder if I've made a mistake coming after all. But I haven't. I haven't. I'm here for a bloody good reason. So don't you say a word to anybody. OK?'

'Yeah. Go on, you can trust me. 'Cos, if it's what you said, I don't want to know nothing about anything.'

'Good girl. But actually there's something I'd like you to do for me.'

'Here, it ain't nothing to do with 'im, is it? I told you, I don't want to have nothing to do with 'im. Not if he's what you said.'

'No, no. He won't ever have to know you've done what you've done. And it's quite simple.'

Look of distrust. Almost comical in its exaggeration.

'Relax, relax. Listen, you tidy Mr Upward's rooms in the morning, the same as you do mine, yes?'

'Yeah.'

'Well then, all I want you to do is: tomorrow take something with you that'll scrape the polish off one of his own bits of furniture somewhere. Scrape it, where you're sure it was sprayed today, but where any mark you make won't be obvious. And bring me what you've got off. Couldn't be easier, could it?'

'Well, all right, since it's you. But I know you pigs. Promises, promises, and then nothing like what you said.'

'But I'm not pigs any more, sweetheart.'

'Oh yeah? Once a pig always a pig. That's what I say.'

You're right, too, darling. And there are times I bloody wish you weren't. Could be off sailing the seven seas or doing anything I liked, Mr Rich. If I wasn't a pig, pig, pig.

Laboratory analysis. London firm he remembered the Force sometimes contracted out to. Lot of jargon. Meaning: furniture polish, plain and simple if a bit heavy with the flowery scent. Nothing else.

Not worth the supposed invalid's taxi trip to the flat to collect. But one other letter inside the door. Ignored in the expectation of what he might learn from the fat London-postmarked one.

Typed name and address. And on the back – crest of the South Mercia Constabulary.

Last administrative detail? Shouldn't be. All dealt with weeks ago. Late invitation to a New Year's party? Never.

Dear Mr Sylvester,

I have been trying to get in touch over the telephone, but your number is never answered. I would like a word with you, however, as soon as possible. Kindly ring my secretary to make an appointment.

Yours faithfully,

George Sugden, Detective Chief Superintendent.

22

Going up the familiar stairs. Stairs where he'd actually told Suggers he could stick his job. It was giving him the willies, damn and blast it. Should have told Suggers' secretary that if 'Detective Chief Superintendent Sugden' wanted 'a word' he could bloody well come to him. Only that would have meant Astwood Manor.

As it is, not sure about leaving while bloody Roanoke's there. Why couldn't Suggers have been free at some other time? Or me been less curious?

But ought to be OK. For Christ's sake sprawled there listening to their talk for three solid weeks now. And not a hint of anything being done. Gone through every variation in the weather. Followed the pair of them telling each other what they'd both read in the paper at breakfast till every detail of House of Commons wrangling was hammered in like lines of Shakespeare. Almost become a bleeding expert on antique furniture. So why should it be any different today?

'Ah, Bill. Come in, come in.'

So 'Bill' now? The bugger must be feeling uneasy over whatever it's going to be.

'Nice to see you, George.'

That had got to him. Muscles of that massive deep-pink face stiffening as if they'd had concrete poured into them. Always had made a point of not Georgeing him. Left that to his equals in rank. Equals or above, like the Big White Chief when he'd wanted to create an atmosphere of informality. Or, out of the building, the privilege of a Mikey Cross.

'Er— Take a pew, Bill. Just wanted a word.'

'So you said in your letter.'

'Yes.'

Pause. Glasses on. Glasses off.

'Well, it's like this, – er – Bill. It has come to my ears that you've been— Well, shall we say, hanging about outside Charles Roanoke's place.'

Those bloody flat-caps. Thought at the time it might be a mistake to ask a favour. Just drew attention to it. And gave them the chance to sneak. Pair of tittering schoolgirls.

Suggers groping for his pipe.

'Now you and I know perfectly well that there was some— Some misunderstanding over Mr Roanoke back last autumn. And, thinking it over, when I eventually got to hear, I came to the conclusion I ought to— Well, have a word.'

'So you said in your letter, George.'

'Yes. Well, I don't want to make this official, but let me put it this way. It really won't do, you know. It really won't do.'

'What won't do, if I may ask.'

Massive sigh. Papers on desk flutter.

'You're not making this easy, you know.'

'Oh, but I would. If only I knew what it was you're trying to get at.'

Thump. Two meaty hands slammed on to the desk.

'All right, Sylvester, if you want to play silly buggers, have it your way. Now, I'm giving you a warning. One warning. Steer clear of Roanoke, or by God I'll have you for threatening a breach of the peace. I'll have you inside if I have to.'

So what now?

Take notice of Suggers' warning? Back off? Jesus, no. Try once again to get it into this thick head that Roanoke is the one who should be put inside? No, if he wouldn't listen to Detective Inspector Sylvester he wasn't going to listen to Mr William Sylvester-no-clout.

He stood up.

'All right. I note what you've said.'

And out. Before any more moralizing tempted him to Aggravated Bodily Harm.

Flick on Marshall Wilcox's toy the moment he'd slammed the door behind him. Ear to the speakers. Not much sound emerging.

And why should there be? Why shouldn't everything be as it always was at this time of day? Tea things retrieved by Princess. Three hours or so till dinner, either in the dining-room or if 'feeling not quite the thing' in your own suite. Two hours till drinkies. If that was the way this life took you.

So what sounds to expect from Robert Upward's suite? An occasional throat clearing. A fart or two, to be frank. Pages of a book turned. A groan.

And what was coming up? Throat clearing. Fart. Groan. No page-turning. But then Upward did not always read at this time of day. Sometimes he dozed. Gentle snoring. Today perhaps there were a few more groans than usual, but not so many as to be alarming. If he was in any real discomfort he'd ring for Nurse Dexter or whoever was on duty. He'd done it before. He was not doing it now.

Click over Marshall Wilcox's cunningly hidden little switch and put some music on. Respectable set of CDs supplied by Marshall. Classical. Evidently judged to be what he would listen to. Compliment? Or snide comment? Stuff for the well-padded cissies.

Anyhow nothing wrong with some music till it was time to eat. Up here tonight. After the afternoon's humiliating confrontation – nerve-stretching, too, with those absurd premonitions – laborious conversation with old pussies, female and male, asking too much. So, exercise rich bastard's privileges. Spend the evening lost in Beethoven with possibly the last chapters of *The Way We Live Now* and the meal on a wheeled-in trolley.

But he would have had to have been deafer than any of the ancients in the dining room not to have heard, above the limpid water-runs of the Moonlight Sonata, the sudden howling from the floor below.

He told himself it might not be coming from Robert Upward's suite. But even as he flicked the switch over to the bug he knew what he would hear.

It was not pleasant. It lasted in all for an hour and a few minutes. Not long after those first yells Dr Hardew had come to join Nurse Dexter. And it had soon been plain he knew there was nothing he could do. Robert Upward had been gripped by convulsions. Coupled with other symptoms – Latiny names just caught amid the noise – it was plain he was in his last hours.

Death took place at nineteen minutes past nine.

Well, we did all we could.

170

Nurse Dexter, her voice loud in the sudden quiet.

Yes. It had to come some time. It might have come at any time. It came now.

It was a pronouncement. With all the gravitas of the enranked medical profession.
But Nurse Dexter proof against it. Or almost.

Doctor, you don't think . . .
What, Nurse?

Was there a splinter of anxiety, after all, in that shot-out question?
Be beautiful if he could see the fellow's expression. Or, better still, his whole body. Spot one of those tiny signs of uneasiness. Lie detectors. The tautly crossed legs under a table. The twitch in a thigh. The sudden glint of sweat on the back of a hand.

Well, Doctor, wasn't the onset of convulsions rather unexpected?
No, no. Nonsense. Typical, in fact. Typical. Perhaps somewhat more vigorous than in other cases, but nothing untoward. Nothing at all.
Yes, Doctor.

But, easy to hear over Marshall Wilcox's ultra-expensive apparatus, that 'Yes' was not Yes.

Now, listen to me, Nurse. When a man of Upward's age, who is already suffering from a number of related conditions, expires with some abruptness it is simply what is to be expected. But, if that man happens to be extremely rich, there is always the possibility that some busybody, the Press or a distant relative, anybody, will attempt to say that there was foul play. Without any reason whatsoever. So in such circumstances it is particularly important that no breath of anything out of the ordinary is allowed to reach the public. I hope you understand me.
Oh, yes, Doctor, and I know you're quite right. I would

never had said anything outside these four walls. It was only a passing remark.

A remark better not passed, Nurse.

Yes, Doctor.

What was he to make of that? Of course, Robert Upward had been poisoned. Murdered. But did Dr Hardew know it? Or just suspect it? Or had he, almost before suspicion had arrived, a tiny purple stain, already made up his mind? Unless it had been inescapably thrust in front of him, was he going to push the notion out of his head?

And Nurse Dexter? Plainly she had not such control over her thoughts. She had suspected all was not right. Would she, even, remember that the police officer who had once come to her asking about other deaths was now in a suite on the floor above?

And what would she do? Would she, after a night's sleep, decide to defy Dr Hardew and come to him? Or get in touch with the Coroner and suggest an inquest was necessary? Or would she succumb to Dr Hardew's view as a man of the world, of the world of the wealthy? She wasn't exactly to be blamed if she did. It did nobody any good to go spreading rumours without facts to back them.

And Nurse Dexter didn't have the facts. He was the one who had those, such as they were.

Now guilt came swirling down at him. Thick, stifling, deadly chilling wind-blown snow.

Why had he left old Robert Upward at Roanoke's mercy? He knew Roanoke was intending to make away with the old man as soon as suspicion was less likely to fall on him as a major beneficiary under the will. All right, Roanoke, greed pushed, had acted at what was really the earliest possible moment. But that was no excuse. He knew, all bar Courts proof, that the man had made away with four other old people for their money. And what had he just done? Out of sheer selfish curiosity he had allowed that bugger Sugden to make an appointment with him at a time Roanoke would be with his intended victim.

And he was a detective.

He was not only a detective. He was a detective with resources to devote to this single case that would have been the envy of his old force. And he had used those riches to no one's benefit.

He sat slumped on the *chaise-longue* where he had lain for so many afternoon hours listening to Roanoke's insensitively cheerful keep-on-the-boil conversation. From the speakers of his mock-CD player the sounds of Nurse Dexter laying out the body came quietly in. Stiletto reminders, if any were needed, of what he had allowed to happen.

At last he heard the door of the suite below being quietly closed. And locked.

No risk to be taken of disturbing the other wealthy patients of Astwood Manor. Death one 'little eccentricity' too many.

And then the old instinct reasserted itself. Slumped depression was heaved aside. A stale, sweat-soaked blanket.

There was work here for a detective. If Dr Hardew was going to sign a death certificate, as he undoubtedly was, then there would be no official inquiry into Robert Upward's demise. So what was needed was an unofficial inquiry. Carried out by someone who knew how to search.

Nurse Dexter had locked the suite's door. She must have taken the key away with her. Where would it be now? Her office for a certainty. And that shouldn't present too much of a difficulty.

One good long ring at the bell-push he had never yet used marked *Nurse*. Then out into the corridor. Crouch in the dark near the head of the stairs.

Here she comes. Tramping up wearily, poor bitch. Had a tough evening.

Back turned. Slip down the broad stairs. Keep to the sides of the treads. Old wood can creak like a foghorn.

Office tucked away at the back of the entrance hall. Listen a moment at the door. No sound. Risk it. Turn doorknob. Push. Unlocked, thank God. And empty.

And there on the little desk – cheap affair – bunch of room keys. Each one with a number stamped in its shank. What was Upward's? Think. Yes. Four. Tweak it off the ring.

Out. No sound from top of the stairs. Where to dodge now? Kitchen area. Should be no one there this late in the evening.

The big kitchen, lit only by the lights on the freezer cabinets, little red glints on plugged-in sockets. Wide working-table a dim outline. Smell of bacon. And something else. Cleaning liquid.

Wait.

When she finds no one in my room, what's she going to think?

Do? Decide I'm somewhere else? In the residents' drawing room? Heavily upholstered armchairs, *Country Life*, *Harpers & Queen*, *County Homes and Interiors* on low tables. Hopefully. With any luck too tired to want to go chasing someone she knows damn well is—

Here she comes. Treads of stairs creaking all right. Listen.

Yes, door of her office. In by now. Going to notice one missing key? Never.

Right.

Up one floor to Suite No 4, best in the place. Key. And in.

The search took almost three hours. All strictly in accordance with Detective School techniques, plus added experience. If he had been spinning a villain's pad he'd have found whatever evidence there was. If only a trace of gun oil. But here he didn't know what there was to find. Something to indicate how Roanoke had given Robert Upward whatever had ended his life before its time. Months before, even a year or more. Some clue to whatever poison had secured that shit his money.

Failure. Nothing.

Back at the door again where his circular sweep had begun, he forced himself not to go over the whole place once more. He had searched. He had not missed anything there to be found. And every minute he had been in the suite he had risked discovery.

Discovery would not have been much of a hassle. Just another 'little eccentricity' to be glossed over. But well to avoid it. Someone, Mrs Milton, the Major, might mention it to Roanoke if he came to collect his old friend's valuable furniture. After the business with the two flat-caps he distrusted coincidence.

Last look at the outline of that sheet-covered body on the bed. Last respects. But not the last jab of conscience. Not at all.

Creep downstairs again, look for a light under the door of the office. Nothing. Locked? No, thank God. Slip in. Have to risk the light for a moment, despite Nurse Dexter asleep on her camp-bed in the little room next door. Key bunch just where it had been. Slip No 4 on. Back up to bed.

Ah well, he thought, wearily stretching, conscious of his parched mouth, at least tomorrow I can say I'm cured. Leave this bloody place.

And what then? Roanoke had beaten him. Despite being just

174

one floor above the man's chosen victim, when the moment had come he had been unable to do anything. Powerless as a child. Marshall Wilcox's expensive apparatus as much use as a 'Young Doctor' outfit's stethoscope. The money spent on his suite and the comforts that went with it water down a drain. Dirty water.

Beaten. Defeated. Out-manoeuvred. Out-classed. By, damn it all, the less rich man.

Oh God. Get some shut-eye. Try to anyhow. See what the morning brings.

23

The morning, surprisingly, brought a development. Sylvester decided he would have to breakfast, like the spryer residents, in the dining-room. If he was to leave almost at once, he could hardly claim not to be well enough to go downstairs.

It was old Lady Grace who gave him the news. She was an unstoppable talker. Avoided ever since the first time she had caught him. Now the only one left at the communal table.

'Oh, Mr Silchester, have you seen in the paper? So interesting.'

What was this going to be? Surely not the Test series in Australia? But could be anything. So long as it was an excuse to jabber.

'Good morning, Lady Grace. But, no, I haven't seen any papers. I've only just come down.'

'It's about poor Mr Upward. Not quite a gentleman, but still a thoroughly nice person.'

Upward? But how could he be in the paper? Death'll be reported, naturally. All that money. But today? Well, yes, if someone on the staff here got on the phone sharpish. They'd have heard all right. First to know, probably. And quite likely guess it'd be worth a bob or two to them.

'What about Mr Upward, Lady Grace?'

'Well, you know, he went yesterday evening. Such a pity. He wasn't all that elderly. Not more than ten years older than I.'

'Oh, come, Lady Grace. Fifteen. Fifteen years, if a day.'

Old bag expected it. And if she didn't get it, she'd quite likely start talking about something else. She'd have realized he was interested.

'Well, there's an obituary in the *Telegraph*, quite short of course. After all, he wasn't a general. Or a bishop. Or even an ambassador. It was just because of him making so much money.'

'I must read it.'

'Ah, but that's not what I meant. What I meant was the news. On the front page.'

For a mad moment he thought there must be a story saying Upward had been murdered. Had Nurse Dexter . . .? Or Dr Hardew, after all . . . ? But it couldn't be.

'And what's that, Lady Grace?'

'Well, it's about what he's done with his money. I don't know how they find out such things. I'm sure I wouldn't like my private affairs to be all over the papers the moment I go to heaven.'

Colonial official's widow leaves all to cats' home. She should worry.

But he knew what Robert Upward had done with his money. Left it to Charles Maurice Roanoke. Who was going to do what he damn well liked with it.

'Yes, you see, almost all of it just goes to the nation. Well, I know that's very nice and all that. I expect it will mean we shan't have to pay so much income tax. Unless this beastly Government somehow uses it for something else. But all the same I do think one has a responsibility to see that one's money is put to the best use. Especially if one has no family, like poor Mr Upward. Such humble beginnings, you know.'

All to the nation? Or almost all? Old bag must have got it wrong. Probably the piece said all Upward's wealth was to have gone to the nation, and now was going to Charles Maurice Roanoke.

'Yes. I understood Mr Upward's origins were pretty obscure.'

Can I grab the paper from the old trot? Or just ask for a look-see? Oh, no, she'll say she needs it or something. Contrary old bitch. So what? Buzz off and find a copy for myself? Leave breakfast? But, damn it, I'm paying for it. And I want it. So sit the old bag out. Let her jabber on with whatever she takes it into her head to say.

'And then to leave just that one personal bequest. To that Roanoke person.'

Someone Charles Maurice has failed to work the charm on. Seen through him, have you? You're shrewder than I gave you credit for, even if you have misread your sodding paper.

Could try to make her look at the piece again. Get her to admit she got it all wrong. Never mind, she'd somehow make it out to be my fault.

177

'So he left something to Mr Roanoke? Does it say how much?'

'Oh, yes. And I think it's such a shame. I mean, money shouldn't be trusted to people like that. Who aren't one of us.'

Jesus, how can she do it? Bloody unblushingly. *Aren't one of us.* With me sitting here right beside her.

'Yes, I know what you mean.'

But that little piece of hypocrisy got the shrewd look it had deserved. No one who's not *one of us* to be allowed to claim the status, even by implication.

'Yes. Well, Mr Silchester, I ought to be going. One cannot linger at the table all morning. It's so unfair on the staff.'

Oh, double, treble rebuke. Doesn't know how to treat the servants. Very definitely not one of us.

'Yes, of course, Lady Grace.'

Telegraph firmly folded beneath scrawny arm.

Must have guessed I want a look. Well, ask once again. Nothing to lose.

'You didn't tell me how much it said Mr Upward left Mr Roanoke.'

'No. Well, it was fifty thousand pounds. Look, there it is.'

Paper unfolded, slapped on to the table – rebuke for asking twice – and there it was. Plain to see. . . . *to the nation, with one personal bequest of £50,000 to a Mr Charles Roanoke for him to use at his discretion for charitable purposes.*

So only fifty thousand for Charles Maurice. Well, well, well. Old Bob Upward not quite so taken in as all that. Fifty thousand. Enough for a certain number of emergency charitable pay-outs. But no fortune. Not these days. Less even than six or seven years ago Roanoke got from Mrs Bathurst.

Cunning old Bob Upward, too. He must have had some suspicions that Roanoke might not do with the money quite what he had said. So he'd allowed him to think he was going to get pretty well the whole lot, and in the meanwhile had changed his will to give him that nicely calculated amount. Old devil. And, yes, very likely he tipped the wink himself to someone he'd known on the financial pages of the *Telegraph*. Be why the paper had got its little page one scoop.

A thoroughly nice person, Lady Grace had said. And she was right, he had been thoroughly nice. Every word during those talks with Roanoke confirmed it. Always pleasant. Always courteous. Never sharp. Never waspish. Nice. Nice old Robert Upward, formerly nasty young Bob Upward. Transformed by all the lolly? Well, no. Almost certainly not. Deep down he hadn't gone soft under the influence of all the softness fat money brought. Been altered, though, eventually. By the gradual realisation that – what was it he'd said? – 'piling it up, piling it up' meant precious little in the end. And bully for him for seeing it. There were others who never had.

But, by Christ, this was going to mean Roanoke would be at it again. If not straight away, soon enough. Fifty thousand wasn't going to last him very long. Not at the rate he lived. And with debts to clear off already. Plus some obligation now to be seen to be making charity donations.

So, sooner or later another life in danger.

But this time, even if he had to hide under the fucking bed, he'd catch the sod.

But how? How? All very well, to blast out threats. But what more could he do than he had done with poor Robert Upward? And where had all his precautions got him there? Bloody nowhere.

He found he had slowly disposed of his breakfast without at all taking in what he had been eating. Waste of money. And what would Lady Grace have said? Unfair to the staff, keeping the girl waiting to clear the table. *Richesse oblige*. Except richesse had never felt itself much obliged, whatever noblesse might have done. Hard to see Gresham Gallitly, for instance, feeling obliged to think of his chauffeur's comfort, or that of that slinky secretary of his. And even Robert Upward had simply expected service in exchange for payment.

The same thought came back to him when, in the flat once more, he found a letter from Auntie Violet. Thanks for the next supply of port. Her curly old-fashioned handwriting. Spelling a bit rocky. *Rubey*.

No richesse there. But noblesse? Yes. Yes, by God.

He'd go and see her. Today. Bit of noblesse of his own. Could find the time now, too. No need to keep obbo on Roanoke for a week or two. Not till the shit had got his next target lined up.

'Didn't expect to see you, dear. Didn't you get my letter?'

'Yes, of course I did, Auntie. Very nice of you to write, too. And I certainly wouldn't have come chasing up here to complain if you hadn't.'

'No, dear, I know. I just thought you might of thought I was dead or something.'

'Dead? You? Not for many a year yet.'

'Oh, no, you're wrong there, me lad. I've not got so many years waiting for me. I know that. My bones tell me, even if that silly young doctor won't. But you don't want to hear about my troubles. What've you been doing with yourself? And with all that money?'

'Buying you a bit of port, Auntie. That's about all.'

'None of your clever answers, young man. I asked you what you've been doing 'cos I want to know. Now, have you been to see your mum?'

'No, Auntie.'

'Well, you go and see her as soon as you leave here. You got your duty, you know.'

Noblesse oblige.

'Yes, Auntie.'

'And don't think you can get away with it by any of your Yes, Aunties. You been up to something, haven't you? Otherwise you'd of come out with it.'

He felt a sudden desire to tell her everything. Who else could he have it all out in the open with? In the way major enquiries were tossed over in the force? This was hardly the Incident Room in the middle of a full-scale murder case, with the guv'nor updating events and anyone who had any thoughts eventually chipping in. But those days were gone. On his own now. All alone, and no one to share with. Not the problems. Not the successes, if there'd been any. Not the failures. And there'd been one of those all right.

OK, there was Jude. He could have talked it over with her. And she'd quite likely have something to contribute. More, probably, than Auntie Violet. Knowing her way around. But he couldn't confide in someone who might see as many as fifty different men a week, let alone the friends she had in that world of hers outside respectability. She'd mean to keep anything he said to herself, if he made her promise. But it wouldn't be fair on her.

'Listen, Auntie, if I tell you something, will you not pass any of it on? Not a word to anyone?'

'What you think? I been told a good many secrets in my time, and never let on about a single one. Besides, who've I got to tell, stuck away here with me legs?'

A raucous laugh.

'Old Marigold? I could have told her the lot, 'cos she wouldn't of heard a word. But she's dead now, poor old thing. Went just after Christmas. Think she waited for it. Not that there was anything under the tree for her, 'cept what I give her. Little bottle of eau-de-Cologne. And she never noticed that.'

He hadn't even realized the bed in the corner was empty. Too wrapped up in himself. Richesse not oblige.

He saw now the mattress was bare. Black-and-white ticking stripes, and lumpy by the look of it.

'God knows, I blame myself. I suppose old Bob Upward hadn't got all that long to go. But he had longer than bloody Roanoke gave him. And I won't ever forgive myself for letting that puffed-up pillock get away with it. Right under my nose.'

'Well, not exactly, dear. Not really under your nose, if what you told me's so. You said he must of done it while you were seeing that Superintendent Sugden. And, fair enough, you didn't ought to have gone to see him when you did.'

Strangely, blame handed down from Judge Auntie Violet seemed less harsh, more even-handed, than when he'd told himself he'd been so much at fault. He felt able to go on.

'Yes. But, well, it means I've still got to collar him. Somehow. And that's the trouble. How'm I going to do it, if I couldn't nail him when I was right there? When I was listening to every word that passed between them? When I searched that suite immediately afterwards? Even if I did miss the one moment he did whatever it is he does, and I'm not certain now I actually did that. I don't know what delay there is before that stuff of his works.'

'Well, you're the detective, me lad. You can't expect an old woman what's lived all her life in the place where she was born to give you the answer.'

'No, Auntie. I know. You're right, I am a detective. I ought to be able to find out what he's done. It's my job, never mind that I've left the force.'

'Yeah, well, it is your job, blinking millionaire or not. So you can't go on and on moaning. You got to get on with it, that's all.'

'OK, OK. But how am I to get on with it? Go back and start

181

keeping a watch on Mr Clever-clever Roanoke again? Yeah, well, and what if I do? Keep a watch on him for weeks and weeks to come, and then, OK, latch on to him one day buttering up some new rich softie? And then, if I'm lucky, follow him and find out where he's going to work his nasty racket again? OK. Get that gold-sprinkled idiot Marshall Wilcox to come in with his bugs, and sit there listening, once again, to everything that—'

Exasperation forcing a halt.

'Damn it, Auntie, I swore to myself when I heard Roanoke had been left so much less than he needed that I'd hide under the fu— that I'd hide under the bed next time and catch him. But I can't do that, can I? What more can I do than I've done already?'

'You could hide under the bed, you know.'

A swift lift-descent of disappointment.

Somehow he'd expected the old girl to come up with something. God knows, he'd no right to. Why should she, as she had said, an old woman who'd spent all her life in one tight environment, why should she be able to tell him, an experienced detective, years of service, how to do his job?

'I'm sorry, Auntie. I shouldn't have come if all I was going to do was bleed all over you.'

'I said you could hide under the bed.'

What was she going on about? Was she, despite her lively way, getting a touch senile?

'Well, I couldn't do that really, you know. Be a bit ridiculous, wouldn't it?'

Look of simple scorn in the wrinkle-set eyes.

'You could hide under my bed, lad. You trick that Roanoke into thinking I'm the sort of rich old fool he likes – and you've got the money to make me into one, I suppose – and then you could hide under my bed. Or near as damn it. And you'd find out what it is he does, wouldn't you?'

24

Christ, he was enjoying this. Spending and spending and spending. Bloody ridiculous amounts to pay for pieces of furniture. But being bought for a purpose. A good cause. Worth every penny if the result was Roanoke in the dock. If. If. If. But fun, too. No, exhilarating. That was the word. See now how Jude feels when she goes on one of her shopping sprees. I can buy anything: I can do anything.

£28,000. Mahogany breakfront bookcase. 'Superb example, sir, you're a lucky man, if I may say so.' And still got to find a dozen or so fancy bitzer to put behind those glass doors. But not to worry. The money's there.

£15,000. Walnut bureau with bun feet. Add a few thou, bun feet. Apparently.

£8,000. Louis XVI style bonheur-de-jour in satinwood. Neat little table. Do nicely for Auntie to write next year's Christmas cards on, if bloody Roanoke hasn't taken the bait. Rich old widow left with lots of high-priced antiques and wanting to sell. Hope he doesn't pounce, in a way. Because if he does I'll be risking her life. Her life. No getting past it.

£1,200. Only £1,200. Canterbury in rosewood. 'I'll be frank, it's not an elegant piece, but value, sir, value.' Well, Auntie can tuck her magazines into it, the way some bone-idle Archbishop of C did once, so he wouldn't have to get up off his arse to fetch himself what he wanted. Unless this 'antiques gallery' smoothie is telling me a tale.

£25,000. And something to sit in. Chair with shepherd's crook arms, hipped decoration at knee and ball-and-claw feet. 'I'd say 1720, sir, that or thereabouts.' OK, say it. Money's there. But what if he comes to look and won't or can't fork out? Or say he smells a rat? Well, then, he does. And Auntie's set up in a swanky

183

nest rest of her life. Good a way as any to dispose of large chunk of a million.

£9,000. Writing chair. 'We call them writing chairs, sir.' In walnut. About 1715. But bloody uncomfortable for an old lady to sit on, that square seat at an angle like that. Jut out between her legs. Still, not buying it for Auntie to sit on. Buying it for Roanoke to set his piggy eyes on and . . . But isn't this madness, an appalling, unnecessary, stupid risk? . . . And decide he's found an ideal victim.

£3,500. Regency *chaise-longue* in mahogany. Jesus, different covering but twin of the bloody thing I sprawled on with Marshall's box-of-tricks feeding me all those conversations. And those last god-awful minutes. Classier, this, I suppose. But not a lot.

£6,000. For the hallway. Bacon settle in elm. Circa, as they say – always – 1740.

£8,000. For the bedroom. Chest of drawers. 'Note the satinwood crossbanding, sir. Lovely work, lovely work.'

£1,400. Wash-stand, mahogany. Late Georgian. Do for a dressing table, but no more use as a wash-stand than that wreck of a one out at the Dringfield and Westmarch Dogs Refuge, clackety old typewriter on it. *The quick brown fox jumped over the lazy dog.* Got you, Mr Peter Maffin. Easy meat. But what about the man I'm after now? Sodding sight trickier.

Must have a few knick-knacks, too.

£700, knife-box with original fittings. No use to anybody, not even specially beautiful. But something to catch the eye of Charles Maurice Roanoke. Chuck in a few mirrors at anything between £4,000 and £7,000. And Bob's your uncle. Thank goodness, the flat's come with built-in kitchen, fitted carpets, curtains. All making it look well lived in. So only a quick visit to Jessop's for a nice comfy bed, couple of really big TVs, never mind the cost.

Deserves the best, Auntie Violet, obstinate old battle-axe. Upping and playing against a man like Roanoke. At her time of life. Damn silly thing to do. Damn dangerous, too, if it begins to come off. Am I wrong to have even let it go this far? She right that it's all I can do?

She was right. However much he hoped she would turn out to be wrong. He had kept telling himself that, in Nottingham going from one smart Derby Road antique shop to another, dressed up in his smart new suit. Looking the part. Rich git, as Mikey Cross had once said. Pouncing on anything that caught his eye as being what a game old lady whose dead husband had gone up in the world might possess. *Can't do anything else. Can't.* Repeated and repeated to himself as he had driven day after day to where it was safe to go on with his buying spree. Out of range of Roanoke's own activities. Last thing he wanted, to find himself looking over the back of a £10,000 eighteenth-century armchair at that man's fat gut, florid face, stony blue eyes. But he wished she was not right.

Finding the flat in the first place had involved complications galore. Somewhere with no busybody neighbour to tell Roanoke Mrs Lawrence had been in the place only three weeks. Somewhere outwardly pricey enough. Somewhere near enough to be likely for it to be Roanoke she would ask to look at her furniture, 'as I can't manage here much longer'.

Furniture in. Bit by bit so as not to attract attention. Plastic bag of dust from his own flat – plenty there – distributed artfully in neglected corners. Two chests of drawers, snapped up for £3 and £3.50 in a secondhand furniture shop in Alfreton Road over in Nottingham because odd bits of things had been left in them. Transferred to drawers of £28,000 breakfront bookcase, £15,000 bun-feet bureau.

Everything he could think of. Everything money could buy.

'This is the life, eh? Up in the morning, late's I like. Lovely sleep in that nice new bed. Get the old legs take me to the bathroom. All the hot water you could want, just turn on the tap. Whole place lovely and warm, and not a hand's turn to do about it. Big fridge full of anything I want for me breakfast. Then, come dinner time, pick up the phone, "That the Pizza Whizz? Send me a nice big one, with mushrooms." I do love a nice mushroom.'

'Glad you're happy, Auntie.'

God, was he turning Auntie Violet into a rich bitch? Glorying in it all?

'No, you're not. You're not glad I'm happy one bit. Think I can't tell when you put on that voice?'

'No, Auntie— Oh, well, yes. Yes, I suppose I was thinking you'd turned into . . . Well, into a Roanoke look-alike, if you must know.'

185

She laughed. Pleasure rolling out.

'Go on. I ain't changed. No more than what you have, with your million quid in the bank. No, me lad, when it comes down to it we're all what we are. Only difference being rich makes is you need a blinking lorry to carry away your wages end of the week.'

Was she right? Or did riches corrupt? Make you spend them in ways you wouldn't have done before? Make you feel you could do what you wanted regardless? Well, in her case that really didn't seem to apply. She wasn't glorying in the good things she now had in her possession in the way Roanoke, plainly, gloried in his Bentley, his big house, that boat down in Boston, the indoor pool he could show off to his pick-up girl friends. No, she was enjoying her good things for themselves. For the pure pleasure of them.

She was like – come to think of it – old Tomas Toth. Only he'd had to work and sell and sweat for all his money, probably cheat a bit, too, here and there. But when he'd got it he'd enjoyed it. What was it he'd said to Roanoke, that voice coming loud and clear over Marshall Wilcox's bug? *Enjoy. You want to enjoy.* Well, there are some who can be rich and simply accept it. Use the stuff for the good things it can bring. Loot the earth, and why not? And marvellous that the old boy is still there looting. From Fortnum and Mason, wherever. Escaped, by luck he never knew he'd had, from Roanoke's trap.

'Mrs Lawrence?'

Voice croaking through the entryphone. But recognizable. Hair at the back of the neck recognizing it. Roanoke. Roanoke arriving on cue.

'Answer, Auntie, answer.'

'All right, all right. Don't be in such a taking. He won't expect an old woman to go hopping over to talk into that thing as if she was a two-year-old.'

'No, you're right. Sorry. Truth is, I'm worried. But go on, answer him. Or he'll go away.'

'I'm going. But you give me an answer, never mind answering that. Why are you worried? Come on, out with it.'

'Oh, Auntie, if only I knew. Suppose it's half that he'll smell a rat somehow. And half that he won't, and get his claws into you.'

'Claws? Let him try, that's all. Hello? Hello? Can you hear me? Who's that?'

186

'Charles Roanoke, Mrs Lawrence. You were good enough to ring me up.'

'Oh, yes. Yes, I remember. You'd better come up then. Find your way, can you?'

'I don't think I shall have any trouble. Be with you in a minute.'

'So you pop yourself in your little hideyhole, me lad. And we'll see what we'll see.'

A big fitted cupboard at the end of the hallway. One of its walls shared by the drawing-room. Marshall Wilcox had supplied the pinpoint fish-eye lens, tiny microphone. He had installed both himself. Utmost care to make sure Roanoke wouldn't spot them wherever he might prowl.

Ring at flat door. Auntie Violet waddling to it. Pull cupboard door to. Good and thick, not easy to hear through. Just murmurs.

In the room now. Roanoke, fish-eye view.

Same florid, well-fed face. Same heavy frame softly ballooning the waistcoat as he unbuttoned his light tweed overcoat. Good suit, dark blue, fine narrow white stripe. In the thousand-quid bracket by the look of it. What they call bespoke.

The enemy.

'Lovely bacon settle you have in the hall there, Mrs Lawrence. Beautiful example. You know why they're known as bacon settles?'

'Gracious me, no. My old man used to buy all that sort of thing. Picked 'em up here and there. Over the years, you know. Never knew what to call 'em. Not the proper names.'

'Nevertheless, a very shrewd man, if I may say so. An eye for the best.'

'But you haven't said why it's a bacon whatsit. I never saw no bacon about it.'

The rich laugh. On the edge of patronizing. The very edge.

'Ah, you see, a settle like that would have been made for a farmhouse. The better-off sort of farmhouse. You sat on the bench part, and, in the cupboard behind, you stored your bacon for the winter. I don't know if you've ever noticed the holes at the top? Ventilation. Ventilation, not decoration. Things were made to use in those days. Marvellous.'

'Notice those holes? I should say I have. Dusted them often enough, haven't I?'

Good old Auntie Violet. Establish long ownership. Embellish

the trap. And prickle a bit. Give him something to fight against. Keep him too busy to sense any little errors.

'Ah, yes. A lady's eye. I often say it's you ladies who should be in my business. You'd spot the tiny things that make a difference. Take the feet of that bureau there, for instance. Beautiful piece, beautiful. But it's got what we call bun feet. Looking like a fat bun, see. Take away from the value, I'm afraid.'

Liar. Bloody liar. If what the chap told me last month is right, they do the bloody opposite.

'Well, all right then, what's it worth? I can't keep polishing and polishing, not at my time of life. What I want now's somewhere I won't have to look after a lot of furniture, but get a bit of looking after meself.'

'Ah, you've got no family? Or are they not in a position to have you with them? The granny flat, as they call it?'

'No, we didn't never have no children. More's the pity. So how much?'

Roguish smile on the sod's face.

'Ah, straight to the point. I see you're a businesswoman, Mrs Lawrence.'

'No, I ain't. I never been in business in me life.'

'Oh, no, no. I'm sure the late Mr Lawrence must have looked after you from the day you got married. As you, I'm sure, looked after him.'

Smarmy bugger.

'So how much? What's it worth me old bureau, buns or no buns? If I'm going into some nice retirement place somewhere, I got to have enough to pay the bills, long as I'm there to run 'em up.'

Clever old Auntie. Feed him the bait. Feed him the bait.

But, God knows, I'll be happy if he turns up his nose at it in the end. Because he's a bloody man-eating shark. And that's for sure.

'Well, if you really do have to dispose of it, I suppose I could give you two— No, three thousand pounds. I'll make it that.'

The sod. What did I pay for it, even though I probably paid through the nose? A solid fifteen thou, and I bet the bugger eventually sells it for more.

'Well, that's generous, Mr— Er—'

'Roanoke, Mrs Lawrence. Roanoke.'

Clever Auntie Violet again. Don't give away you've heard the sod's name from me a hundred times. Make a right good interrogator, Auntie Violet. Keeps her head, remembers the real score every minute of the time.

'But I'll have to think about it all the same, Mr Roanoke. Never does to go rushing into things. That's what Mr Lawrence used to say. Sleep on it. Never do anything that's going to cost you without you sleep on it. That was his way.'

He almost laughed aloud. Uncle Fred had been the very opposite of that. Always blundering into things that proved too much for him. Never stopping for one moment to calculate consequences. Poor all his life in good times and bad. And always ready to give anybody anything.

'And very good practice, too. Wish I always had your husband's sense. So, don't let me rush you. Think if you really have to part with it. And think about your other things, too.'

The sod broke off, looked round the room.

'That's a magnificent breakfront bookcase. I could give you quite a price for that. As much as twenty-five thousand even.'

Oh, yes. Scared now she'll get another price on the bureau, are you? Go to someone else? So, hint at a figure for the bookcase near enough its true value. Well, at least you're hooked, Charles Maurice.

Even if it is a shark we've got on our line.

'Well, goodbye then, Mrs Lawrence. And I'll be in touch in a day or two. When you've quite made up your mind. Oh, and by the way I might be able to recommend a retirement place. If you don't know of anywhere. But, remember, you won't be able to take very much with you, wherever you go.'

Last sweeping look at the goodies.

You can't take it with you. And that was the risk facing her now. No getting away from it. The bugger was hooked. He'd be back, and item by item he'd see himself getting all that fancy furniture out of her. At half or a quarter the price it had cost only weeks before. And offer her a retirement home of his choice. Somewhere he could then operate with maximum safety. Astwood Manor? Probably not. Taken too many risks there. But somewhere.

And then . . . The moment he reached his next stage Auntie Violet would be in danger. In danger of her life. The will in his

189

favour. He'd been bloody quick to find out what his chances were there. *Or are they not in a position to have you with them? The granny flat, as they call it?* All bloody concern. And behind the look of enquiring care, the shark smelling blood.

She must be made to drop it. Never mind that she'd managed the first moves so beautifully. He should never have let her make them. All right, it wasn't the crazy notion he'd thought it was. It had worked, goddammit. But it was dangerous. What lay at the end of it was bloody, bloody dangerous. He couldn't let her put herself into those shark jaws.

'But, damn it, Auntie, you're risking your life. Hasn't anything I've said about the man sunk in? He's killed five people. Murdered them. He's a totally callous murderer. He won't stop when it comes to you, you know.'

'If he's what you say he is, and I suppose you must be right – you ought to know – then he's got to be brought to justice. That's it, isn't it? Brought to justice.'

'Yes, Auntie. He has got to be. But there's no reason on earth why you should risk your life to do it.'

'Well, there is. There is one. I haven't got much life left to lose.'

'Nonsense, Auntie. Nonsense. You're as hale and hearty as ever you were.'

'No, I'm not. Don't you go telling me how I am or how I'm not. I said before: I haven't got much longer to go. I know. You can feel it when the time comes. And no jacked-up nephew, and no young doctor back at the alms-houses thinks she knows everything, is going to tell me different.'

'But all the same . . . Well, I can't let you go risking it. Listen, you didn't hear poor old Bob Upward in his last hour. It wasn't nice, I'm telling you. In fact, it was bloody horrible. Just only listening. He had convulsions. He was in pain. It was a bloody awful death.'

'Oh, yes, I know. You told me before. Or most of it. But that's not going to make no difference. If that man does succeed in doing whatever it is he does to me, well, I shall have a bit of pain before I go. But what's that? I've had pain enough in my time. I know what it's like.'

'But, no. No, no, no. I can't let him do that to you. I won't. And that's that.'

'So you'll let him do it to some other poor soul, will you? One what's not so prepared for him as what I am? One that hasn't volunteered? I didn't think that of you, Bill Sylvester.'

'Jesus, Auntie, you're a tough nut and no mistake.'

'It's a tough situation you got yourself in, me lad. But you're in it, and there's no way out. 'Cept just go on.'

'Yes, you're right. I suppose you're right. Oh God, what've I done?'

'You've got rich, me lad. That's what you've done. You got so rich you could do what you set out to do, and nothing to stop you. Now you're stuck with it. And so am I. Both of us are. Stuck with it.'

25

'In recognition of what he's been like a son to me. That's what the solicitor wrote.'

Sylvester at the other end of the line smiled. Then wished he hadn't.

'And you signed it, Auntie?'

If only the answer could be No.

'Course I did. Wouldn't be no point in it all if I didn't sign, would there? I signed. That nice Mrs Horrocks did the witnessing. Her and the maid. And it's all tied up neat as a new pin. Everything what I die possessed of to Charles Maurice Roanoke.'

Well, this was what he wanted, wasn't it? Was it? Had to be. Had to be, really. From the moment he'd decided he was going to get Roanoke. Come what may. Cost what it might.

He'd done all he could think of to push it on, too. Having Auntie put it into Roanoke's head she was ready and willing. *You're like the son I never had.* The suggested words had left his mouth bitter. A lemon sucked.

It had been worse hearing them said aloud. Crouched on a discarded garden chair, receiver clamped to his ear, in that rented tin garage two hundred yards from the Old School. Freezing cold. Flicks of snow in the air, even though it was March. *You're like the son what I never had, Charlie dear.* Trust Auntie Violet to improve on the original.

And it had been as clever, still at the flat, letting him see 'dear old Fred's will what he made', as she was clearing out the bun-feet bureau. Going a bit far perhaps having old Margolis, half a dozen forgery convictions, fabricate it. But worth what it had cost, not to give the least grounds for suspicion. All that list of securities. Margolis had made them really tempting. And what if the wheezy old villain hadn't believed it was just in aid of some elaborate joke.

How nearly it had all gone wrong, too.

Roanoke handing it to her to put in a drawer of the bonheur-du-jour she was to take to the Old School and saying 'Oh, I meant to tell you. I've got an unexpectedly busy day tomorrow. I shan't be able to come till Monday.'

Panic. Had the fellow spotted some mistake Margolis had made? Was he going to London, to the Wills Office, to check?

Then watching once more at his house until he set out. A long morning in the leaden cold of a sullen grey day. And losing him almost at once. Q-car incapable of keeping up with the Porsche that had replaced the tomato-red Bentley.

Back to the farmhouse. Fast as the wretched old car would go. Trespassing without hesitation. Running down the length of the big garden. Grass crisp with frost. Feet leaving tell-tale blobs of wetness behind him. Arthur Arkle there. Collecting kindling.

'Arthur. It's you. Thank God.'

'What you want, then?'

'Listen. I'm sorry. In a hurry. He's gone. In that bloody sports car. D'you know where? Is it to London?'

Long moment of consideration.

'Nah. Tell you where he's gone, old Rogue.'

'Where? Where?'

Glint of malice in the watery old eyes.

'Girl. Bitch. On heat. Told me. Boasted. Wanted me to know. "Just dropping into the town, old man. Lady that's got to be lunched, you know. Dare say I'll bring her back afterwards. Keep an eye on things, won't you?" '

Sharp mimicry. And relief. So that was all that 'unexpectedly busy day' had been about.

'Well, thanks. Weight off my mind, as a matter of fact. And thanks for what you've been doing. See you again in a day or two. Oh, I know. Something I'm always meaning to ask. What did he try once to give you fifty pounds for? You told me he had. What was it for?'

'I dunno. Took it into his head, s'pose. I come into his garage. Door left open. Wanted to ask could I have some of his apples. Going to waste. He was busy. Filling his fire-extinguisher, I dunno. Something or other. And then he—'

A sound from behind. A sort of shout. An inarticulate blast. He whirled round.

Roanoke. Roanoke there. Rage purpling the florid cheeks. Blue eyes alight in fury. From down behind the house the sound of his returning Porsche – something evidently forgotten – inaudible. Q-car carelessly left right outside. Black blob footsteps on the frosted grass leading in a straight line to where they were.

'You. What the hell do you think you're doing on my property?'

No answer possible.

'Now, just you listen to me, Mr Ex-Inspector Sylvester. Your former boss – Sugden – told me about you. Spying on me. Spying. God knows what it is you've got into your head. But let me tell you this. If I catch you anywhere near here once again, I'll see that you get jailed. And don't think I can't. Sugden told me where I stand, and, by God, I'll see you get every ounce of it. So, out. Now. Bugger off somewhere you can't make trouble, and spend all that money you won.'

And, tail between legs, he'd gone.

Beaten. But not defeated. One round to you, Roanoke. But plenty more to go.

'Listen, Auntie. It's for real now. Don't forget it. Don't forget it for one moment.'

'All right. Keep your hair on. He won't do nothing for a week or two yet. You told me how he goes about it.'

'I know. I know I did. But all the same keep your eyes peeled. You never know, he might change his technique. He was quicker off the mark with poor Bob Upward, don't forget. For God's sake never eat anything he's been near. Don't drink out of a glass he might have been able to put something in. Watch him all the time.'

'Oh, I will, dear. What I'm here for, ain't it? And you'll be listening. Stuck up in that garage you got. He's totting up quite a bill, ain't he, our Charles Maurice. Nearly as much as what I'm totting up here. You should see my first month's account.'

True enough. God knows how much he'd paid out in total. Marshall Wilcox alone must have had enough for half a dozen more bits of gold to stick on himself. Even his shaky business must have benefited.

'Money well spent, Auntie. On you. On Roanoke.'

'Well, that's as may be. But I wouldn't let you fork out all this much if it was only me, you know. I let you 'cos it's in a good cause. As you might say.'

'Yes, well, goodnight, Auntie. Sleep well.'

Telephone – only secure way of communicating – put down.

'So, how are you tonight, Auntie?'

'I'm very well, dear. Never better. Well, not since I had me legs and that. Saw the doctor today. Bit of a whizzer. In and out. But nice enough young man. Like him better than that girl in Nottingham.'

'But Auntie— Listen, I thought the doctor for the place was an older man. What was his name? Saw him while I was still in the force. Matheson. Yes. That was him. Struck me as having a head on his shoulders.'

'Oh, yes, dear. My young Dr Yeaman told me about him. Got ill. Was off sick for months. Only just back, and not doing very much. Dr Yeaman – he's brand-new, what they call a trainee – he's doing the visits here, and Dr What'shisname's keeping an eye on things.'

'But, Auntie . . .'

'Yes, dear?'

'Well, isn't this an extra danger? I mean, the doctor looking after you being straight out of medical school, probably doesn't know his arse from his aorta. I think Roanoke must have discovered what the situation was. Yes, I'm sure of it. That's why he suggested the Old School to you.'

'Well, I expect it was. Specially as there's only really fat Mrs Horrocks in charge. I mean, she's a nice old body, but she's not very good when it comes to thinking. That I will say.'

'Auntie, I don't like this. I don't like it one bit. We've walked into that man's trap. Listen, I think we ought to call it a day.'

'Don't be silly. We can't do nothing else than what we are. I thought I'd made you see that. And, besides, Dr Yeaman does know his whatsit from his thingamabob. I'm pretty sure of that.'

'Oh, I don't know. Listen, did you notice anything when he was there today?'

'My Charlie? You shouldn't be afraid to say his name, me lad. And, no, I didn't notice nothing. Just doing his polishing, he was.

You must of heard that noise, squirt, squirt, squirt, up in that garage of yours.'

'Yes, I did. All of it. But what about the polish? Did you smell anything when he was using his spray?'

'Course I did. Why he keeps the door open, isn't it? 'Cos of the smell. Flowery, but strong. Verbena, I think it's called. Don't much care for it, matter of fact. Funny, because I like most flower scents. What they put in stuff to keep the toilet sweet and that. But this is a bit much. Bit like old Charlie sometimes. Too much of a good thing. So I keep my mouth shut when he's going round with his old squirter, and blow out through me nose. You ain't heard me doing that, have you.'

He laughed. Couldn't help it.

'No, Auntie, you're very discreet, with your blowing out. But, listen, he does keep the door open when he's using that thing, doesn't he? Always? And you never feel funny at all after?'

'Oh, he makes a right fuss about the door. Has to be wide open. All the time. But you know that. You must of heard him on your little radio. And, no, I don't feel funny. Or not more than I've a right to. You'd feel funny, chatting away to a murderer. If he is.'

'Auntie, he is. He is. Don't you go getting any other ideas. Watch him, Auntie. Watch him every minute. He's a bloody dangerous man.'

'Well, if you say so, dear. And I'm sure you're right. Seeing as you were a detective all that time. But I must say when you talk to old Charlie, you'd never think it. He seems so nice. Really nice. Just a bit smarmy sometimes. But that's all.'

'Auntie, don't let yourself be fooled, for God's sake. I know he's got charm. I hear him laying it on. But, remember, it's done to keep you happy. And don't, for God's sake, let him begin to suspect anything. Make sure you never stop thinking of him as the son you never had.'

Down the line the noisy laugh he knew so well.

'We did that lovely, didn't we, me lad? The son what I never had. I could scarcely keep from laughing.'

'Well, that's right, Auntie. Keep cheerful. You are cheerful, aren't you?'

'Course I am. Why shouldn't I be? Snug as a bug in a rug here, aren't I? Lovely food, nice room, some nice people to talk to. Bit

196

posh. Used to having money, so they can't help it. But they soon forget it all when you get down to it.'

'Glad you're getting some enjoyment anyhow.'

'Oh, I am. I am. Haven't had such a good time for years. But what about you, me lad? You don't sound as if you're enjoying life.'

No flies on that old lady.

He sighed.

'Well, I'm not enjoying life. And that's the truth of it. How can I when I'm worrying all the time about what I've let you in for? Let alone having to be cooped up in the flat here, when I'm not sitting in that bloody freezing garage listening to you chatting away.'

'Well, you shouldn't stay cooped up. Why don't you get out a bit? Spend some of your money. You have got some left, I hope.'

'Oh, yes. You don't get through a million all that quickly, even paying out the way I've been. But I can't go out, whatever you say. If I meet him— Roanoke. If I bump into Roanoke somewhere in the town, he'll get bloody Sugden on to me. Causing a breach of the peace. I could end up in a cell. I really could.'

'Don't you do that, me lad. I need you. Wish I could see you sometimes, tell the truth.'

Poor old soul. Making her go through too much? But has to be done.

'You can't, Auntie. Not possibly. It'd wreck the whole thing if— If Roanoke got wind of me.'

'Oh, I know, dear. But it won't last all that long, you know. He's not as patient as he likes to think he is, Charlie Roanoke.'

He wasn't going to say anything to that.

'Well, goodnight, Auntie. Sweet dreams.'

'Bill Sylvester!'

Damn. Who—

He turned.

Sugden. Bloody, bloody Sugden. What was he doing here? Keeping obbo on the flat? No, never in a million years. Wouldn't stir his stumps. Not nowadays. Plenty of erks to do it for him.

But him. Of all people. In just the minute or two between coming out of the building and getting into the motor. Only Roanoke himself would've been worse. So what's he going to do?

Take me in with his own fair hands? He wouldn't dare. Not without having me bang to rights. I could make trouble. No one could call me a threat to the Queen's Peace here in my own street, going about my own affairs.

Or at least far as Suggers knows. How would he know I'm off to that bloody freezing tin garage, afternoon's chitter-chatter over the radio?

Now, box clever.

'Mr Sugden. Fancy meeting you.'

'Yes, Bill. Coincidence. I don't often come this way, but I'm off to the dentist. Thought I'd walk. Nowhere to park anywhere near where he is.'

'Oh, yes? Spot of toothache, have you?'

And I hope it's giving you gyp.

'No, no. Just a six-monthly check-up, you know.'

That figures. Careful sod. Not risking trouble with the molars. Not risking trouble with the Police Authority.

But what's he want? Damn it, it was him who called out to me. Might not even have seen him if he hadn't. Been away in the vehicle. Cutting it a little fine, as it is.

'Yes. Well, Bill, I have had it in mind to give you a bell, as a matter of fact.'

'Oh, yes?'

'Yes. There's been a development, you see. That matter you were investigating when you were – er – with us.'

What the hell? Development in the Roanoke business? What development, for Christ sake? Why can't the old bugger come straight out with what he's got to say? Must be on my way.

'A development? What's that?'

'Yes. Well, I'm not sure that I don't owe you an apology.'

Pause.

OK then, apologize. Apologize. And get on with it. Though what you can want to apologize for I can't think.

'Yes. Well, it seems – er – that fellow, Roanoke. Well, it could be he's not quite what he seems.'

You're telling me.

Well, well. So, what's made you change your mind? And made you come rumbling up saying *Sorry, nearly had you done for standing outside Mr Roanoke's sacred residence*?

Still, better make it easy for the poor sod. Or be here all afternoon.

'Yes, well, we all get it wrong about people every now and again. I've no hard feelings.'

'Very decent of you, Bill.'

Say goodbye? Push off? No. No, I'd just love to know why that elephant mind actually changed its direction.

'So, what is this development? If I may ask.'

'Yes. Well, bit awkward. Confidential, you might say.'

OK, you bugger. But I'm not going to let you off the hook. Not after the way you hauled me in for a talking-to.

'But what is it? In outline? I'm interested.'

'Yes. Well, suppose you have a right . . . It's this, actually. The Big White Chief had a call. From the Home Office.'

Christ, it's like hoicking a winkle out of its shell. Why did I begin this? I'll be here till next Christmas, this rate.

'Home Office, eh?' Prompt, prompt.

'Yes. It seems one of the vic— One of the people possibly involved, a lady who left some money to Roanoke, was the sister of a fellow called Gallitly. Don't know if you've heard of him?'

'Oh, yes. I know about Gresham Gallitly.'

'That's it. Gresham. Gresham Gallitly. Well, as far as I can gather, and this is strictly between us . . .'

'Yes, yes. Won't breathe a word.'

Get on, get on with it. Blast you.

'Well, this Gresham Gallitly apparently thought originally that all was above board about his sister's death. As it well may be, as it well may be.'

'Yes. All right. But?'

'Yes. Well, it seems a fellow Gallitly knew – another millionaire and all that – a chap who died recently, name of Upward, Robert Upward. Perhaps you saw something about him in the paper?'

'Yes, yes. I did. But how does he come into it?'

For God's sake, bloody Roanoke will be there in Auntie's room by now. Or nearly.

'Well, it seems he also left some money to— To our friend. In similar circumstances. And Gallitly took it into his head that this gave rise to suspicion.'

Another pause. Thoughts being marshalled. Someone knows he's got to go carefully here. But get – on – with – it.

'I don't say it is suspicious, mind. But, on the other hand, I don't say it may not be. However, Gresham Gallitly is, of course, on dining terms with some top Home Office brass. And— And, well, Bob's your uncle. Back on my plate.'

Needs some thinking about. But not now. God knows how late it is.

Quick goodbye. Word of thanks. Dash to the motor. Off. But don't go over the limit. Or not till the end of the street. Suggers well capable of booking me. Despite everything.

Risk leaving the motor outside. Don't think Roanoke knows it. Probably can't see from down there, anyhow. Even if he does look out from somewhere.

Doors open. Scraping the ground, as per usual. Push the bloody things. Be off their hinges soon.

Right. In. Switch on. Ah, voices.

You are a one, Charlie, and no mistake. Bet you didn't really do none of that.

Well, perhaps not every single bit. But I've had my day, you know. I've had my day.

And you ain't finished yet, I'll be bound.

I dare say not. I dare say there's a little bit of life in the old dog yet. But, talking of finishing, I think I must love you and leave you a little early today. Got one or two things to do.

What the hell . . . ? Leaving? Now? But he's been there less than twenty minutes. Surely.

One or two things to do? I bet I know what sort of thing. Thing in a skirt, I'll bet a shilling. If she ain't in trousers. And a sight too tight around the bum, too.

You could be right, old girl. You could just be right. So you won't grudge me popping off straight away, eh? I'll see you tomorrow all right. Don't you worry.

Sounds of departure. *Bye-bye then, be good.* Jokey reply. Door shutting.

What's he been doing? Variation in the pattern. Don't like it. Don't like it one tiny bit. Go down there? Yes. Definitely. Just wait till his ruddy Porsche goes roaring off.

*

'Auntie. Hello.'

'Here, what you doing here? You could of walked right into him.'

'No, no. I saw him off. Heard over the radio he was going early. I don't quite like that. Why I came.'

'Well, you heard what he was going for, didn't you? If you was listening all the time.'

'I heard what he said all right. But was it the truth? I don't see him passing up keeping you happy just for some girl he's got the hots for. Too careful, our Charles Maurice.'

'Oh, come on. No one's that calculating, not when there's a bit of free going. You know that.'

'All I know is that Roanoke's a bloody clever murderer.'

'Yes, but look at it ordinary. He's been coming almost every day. Regular as clockwork, arriving same time, going same time. He's got me nicely buttered up. Or he thinks he has. So it's perfectly safe, his point of view, go early for once. When he's got something to go early for.'

'Oh, I can see all that. But all the same it's a departure for him. And I don't trust that. Look, was there anything else different about what he did today? Anything at all?'

'Well, you was listening, wasn't you? You hear anything different?'

Confess? No, better not. It'd only worry her to think I was late getting to the bug. She'd start believing I'd be late again. When it mattered.

'No, I can't say that I heard anything much out of the ordinary.'

'Well, then. No, he was polishing, as per usual. You must of heard. Squirt, squirt, squirt. Went a bit mad with it. But I expect he was thinking of what he'd got lined up for himself.'

'Yes. Well, the room doesn't seem to smell of the stuff now. Didn't you say it was flowery?'

'No? Well, it don't seem to, do it? S'posed I got used to it. Though—'

'But, listen, Auntie, was there anything else out of the ordinary about today? Anything except this business of going early?'

'No. I keep telling you. All he did was polish me old bonjour-de-whatsit and then say he wants to go. That's the lot.'

'OK. Well, I suppose I'll leave it. But if there's anything you remember, or anything that goes wrong in any way, I'm there at the flat on the end of the phone, remember. And don't hesitate to call. Whatever it is.'

Don't actually have to stick indoors now, suppose. Not if Suggers is on the right side of the fence after all. For what good that'll do. But better stay by the phone. Keep Auntie happy, if nothing else. Owe her that. At the very least.

Though a smart half-hour with Jude'd be nice. Nothing like it, take your mind off things. Even if it doesn't do it for all that long.

And things on my mind. No getting past it. Just can't believe Roanoke would neglect keeping Auntie happy. Till enough time's passed between her making that will and— And what he plans for her. OK, he may be feeling fidgety waiting, and want to try bit of remedial sex. Good for the goose, good for the gander. But . . .

And if he is feeling fidgety . . . And Auntie thinks he may be, and she's a pretty shrewd lady. Then if he is, he could be jumping the gun. Now. Today.

Only there wasn't a damn sign that he had. Not a single damn sign.

Phone. Ringing and ringing.

Must have been dozing. Time? What's the time? Just gone eight.

'Hello? Hello?'

Someone retching. Sounds like.

'Hello? Who's there? Is that you, Auntie?'

'Yes. Me, dear. And— And I don't feel very well.'

Christ.

'Listen, Auntie, what's wrong? What d'you feel?'

'I feel sick, that's what. Sick as a dog. And— And I can't sort of see proper.'

'Auntie, listen, have you called for help?'

'Well, no. It's only just come over me. And I thought you said— Telephone. So— Oh God, I feel like I'm drunk.'

'Auntie, ring your bell. Get them to get the doctor. Hell, the old one, not that new kid. Quick, Auntie, quick. I'll be with you soon. I'm coming. I'm coming.'

26

Licence my roving hands to go
Before, behind, between, above, below.

'That all right, was it? You seemed ready enough for it.'

'More than all right, darling. Just what I wanted.'

He lay there beside her.

It had been all right. Good old Jude. Knows her onions. Done the trick, as he'd hoped it would. Blotted out everything. And it was still blotted out. But how long would that last?

'See they arrested that chap of yours. 'Spose it was the feller? One you once called a certain gentleman?'

'Yes. Yes, that's him all right. My certain gentleman. Roanoke, Charles Maurice. Charged with attempted murder.'

'That's him. But why, if he did all the murders you said, are they only charging him with attempted?'

'Couldn't dig up the evidence in the end, I imagine. Poor old Detective Chief Superintendent Sugden. Won't look too good on his record.'

'But they tried, did they? To prove he done those others as well?'

'Oh, I'm sure they did. Mind, I don't get to hear all that much. Not ex-Detective Inspector Bill Sylvester. But I happen to know in at least one of the cases a heck of a lot of pressure was brought to bear. And if they didn't come up with anything it wouldn't be for want of trying. No, Roanoke was a damn clever devil. No doubt about it.'

'But they got him for the attempted in the end, didn't they? Who was it he only attempted it on?'

He lay silent.

Am I going to tell her? Bring it all up again? When I've tried to push it out of my mind?

Well, haven't been too successful in that, have I? Might as well cough it all up. Go to confession, like the Catholics. Good for the soul. So they say. And a right nice Father Confessor here beside me.

'Matter of fact, it was an aunt of mine. Or not exactly aunt. But a cousin. Only I called her Auntie. Auntie Violet. Have done ever since I was a nipper.'

She sat up sharply. Propped herself on one elbow.

'Jesus, I didn't know that. I wouldn't have asked if I had. You know that.'

'Yes. Of course I do. But it doesn't matter. I'm glad you did, in fact. Can get it off my chest.'

'Well then, how come she, your auntie, whatever, was one of the ones that man did in, or tried to? I mean, was she rich? I thought you told me he only did it when they'd made a will in his favour.'

'No. No, she wasn't rich, Auntie Violet. Far from it. I just made her rich, temporarily. Though she is permanently now, as a matter of fact.'

'What you mean? How's that?'

A bitter smile.

'Because I've made over most of my million quid to her. What's left of it after I spent God knows how much trying to pin Roanoke's murders on him.'

'So that's what you finally done with it, is it? I wondered how you'd eventually come to terms with having all that.'

'Couldn't do anything else, could I? Considering it was my fault that man poisoned her. She's gaga, you know. The stuff affected her brain. There was nothing they could do about it. There's no antidote. Stuff called methyl bromide.'

'Poor old soul. But how come she didn't die? All the others did, didn't they? I mean, it was deadly, wasn't it?'

'Oh, yes, it was that all right. And Auntie Violet— Well, I think she may have even guessed. Or suspected. Or suspected just at the back of her mind. He used a spray-gun, you know. Pretended it was some special furniture polish he had. It was, in fact, until he came to the final dose. Some quite ordinary stuff, though he hyped it up with extra verbena essence. To give him an excuse, when he came, to have the door of the room open. Give him a sort of alibi. Couldn't be administering poison, not when anyone passing could see him. Then, when he thought it was safe, he'd load the spray instead with the methyl bromide. Took care not to inhale himself, and made off quicker than usual. Leaving them to die. Delayed action stuff, and almost odourless actually. Only Auntie Violet didn't like the smell of the perfume he put in the real polish. So she—'

Fighting back tears. Hadn't had to do that since he was ten.

'Damn it. Damn him. So Auntie Violet used to blow out through her nose when he was spraying. Asked me once if I could hear her over the bug I'd had fixed up. Did it every time, including the last. Saved her life. But she'd taken in some of the stuff, too, much to save her sanity.'

'God, I'm not sure that ain't worse than being finished off once and for all.'

'Well, yes, know what you mean. But she's happy actually. Just lies there. Laughs a bit every now and again. And she hasn't got much longer to go in any case. When they examined her they found that out. She knew it, too. Bloody heroine.'

She lay thinking.

'But where did he get it then, that stuff? You shouldn't be able to get something like that. A poison that's got no antidote nor nothing.'

'Drained it out of a fire-extinguisher. A bloody marine fire-extinguisher. Had it because he was into boats, and I suppose someone must have warned him at some time about the contents leaking. So he knew what he'd got hold of. I actually saw the thing the very first time I met the bastard. Had it stuck up on the wall of his garage. Bold as brass. Sodding cheek.'

'God, that's awful. I mean, could you have worked it out then, what he'd used the stuff in it for already? The methyl whatnot?'

'No. No, at least I'm not that responsible. It's very rare to get cases of poisoning with the stuff. Just accidental deaths, very occasionally. We'd have never known what he used, I'd say, only the doctor who came to Auntie Violet guessed. Bright young chap straight out of medical school. Had been reading up poisons. Thinking of going in for forensic medicine.'

'Well, at least you're off the hook over that then.'

'Well, I suppose I am. But I might have cottoned on later. Bloody Roanoke offered a fifty-quid note one day to an old fellow who sometimes hangs around his place, bloke called Arthur.

Arthur Arkle. And Arthur had mentioned it to me. He'd refused to take it because he hasn't any use for money. None at all. Thinks it does you harm. I suppose I was so struck by that at the time I didn't ask why Roanoke had tried to give him that much.'

'Know what he means about money, your feller. But can't help liking that sort of harm meself.'

'Yeah, don't you just. But I did get round much later to asking. And Arthur said he didn't know, but it was when he'd barged into Roanoke's garage and had seen him filling his fire-extinguisher. Actually emptying it, of course.'

'Jesus. So, if you'd thought about it then, you might've saved your old auntie. That what you're saying?'

'I might have done, yes. Just might have worked it out. Only at that very moment, just as old Arthur told me, Roanoke himself came crashing down on us. We were on his land, and technically I was trespassing. Well, he had a go at me, and all I could do was sheer off. It put the whole thing out of my mind.'

'Yeah. Well, I don't think you can blame yourself. Not for that.'

'No, not for that perhaps. And I did in the end put the investigating officer on to that extinguisher.'

'You can chalk that up then.'

'Suppose so. And I can chalk up a bit more, too. They bungled making the arrest, and the bugger took off in his fancy new Porsche. But I happened to hear straight away from a mate in the force, and I told them where he was almost certainly heading for. His boat. Kept over in Boston. One bell to the local nick, and they were waiting for him when he arrived.'

'Well then, you can say it was down to you that he was caught in the end, can't you?'

'Oh, yes. But it's what I'd been doing all along I can't get out of my mind. Damn it, I deliberately made poor Auntie Violet look like a rich old widow who hadn't a clue about anything, and then I put her in Roanoke's way. Put her in his way. Got her to ring him up, say she was going into a retirement place and wanted to sell her furniture.'

'Oh, Jesus. I mean, I knew you were dead set on getting Roanoke, not that I knew his name then. But I never realized you'd go that far.'

'Well, I did.'

'But what about her, your Auntie Violet? Was she really stupid like that? I mean, how come she agreed to do it? You didn't not tell her what sort of a person Roanoke was, did you?'

'No, no. What do you take me for? And Auntie Violet wasn't stupid. Far from it. She may not have been too good with writing letters, but she was a shrewd old lady all right.'

'So you told her all about Roanoke? And she agreed to do what she did?'

'Oh, yes. In the end she was the one who insisted on going on with it. I wanted to back out.'

'I see.'

Another silence. Lying there in her full nakedness. Thinking.

'Way I see it, it ain't your responsibility then. Not when all's said and done.'

'No? Nice of you. But I can't agree. I should have just bloody refused to go on with it, and stuck to that. I hadn't the right to do what I did. What she went along with even.'

More thought.

He looked at her. Felt no new stirring of desire.

'Yeah. It was your money that done it. Wasn't it? If you hadn't had it, you couldn't have used it the way you did.'

'Think you're right. And that's gone now, anyhow. Most of it in a trust for Auntie Violet. Chunk to the Police Benevolent Fund. Looked after my Dad when he'd been shot and had to retire.'

'Your Dad a copper too? What was he? Detective Inspector like you?'

'No. No, he never rose above constable. But he was a good copper for all that. Did his duty. Keeping the Queen's Peace. Or the King's. King's Peace when he began.'

'That why you went into the – the Police?'

'Yeah. Yes, it was.'

'So what you going to do now, then? Now you ain't a millionaire no more? You got to earn your living, you know. Got to collect up enough come and see old Jude every now and again.'

'What, you not going to let me have a freebie?'

'Never. Well, p'raps just occasionally. For old times' sake.'

'Yeah. Well, matter of fact I don't think I'll be around to take advantage. May be off to Australia. Try for a job there.'

'What as, then?'

'Oh, detective. If they'll have me. Couldn't be anything else, could I?'